In the S

of the Rock

In the Suavity of the Rock.

First published in Great Britain in 2024 by Splice,
54 George Street, Innerleithen EH44 6LJ.

Paperback Edition: ISBN 978-1-7384704-0-2
eBook Edition: ISBN 978-1-7384704-1-9

In the Suavity of the Rock

Greg Gerke

SPLICE

For Lily and Tess
and
in loving memory of
Tom Kelly

Coney Island

The blight overtook me in her first years, before my daughter's language came out. Twenty summers ago, Jane, Heather, and I went with Grandma, the in-laws, and other distant relatives to a family wedding in Ireland. Following festivities in the south, to enlist a former IRA member's presence, dozens from the party recouped to the north's northeast pocket in County Down, specifically to the village of Coney Island, which holds a small bay on the Irish Sea. Jane's aunt and uncle owned a house dating back to the 1300s, and for three or four nights they rented many of their neighbors' homes to house the travelers. We were given a lodging down the shore, in a modern six-bedroom behemoth near the Ardglass Golf Club. This steely million-British-pound structure had the air of a confab manor house built on tech money and already in decay, like an outdated spaceship aglow in ruination. It was a foreign architect's malformed idea of Richard Serra, a matrix of rooms and levels, wood and metal, with three steel wires fencing in a balcony over the largest living room. For no apparent reason, in the middle of the rear television room, a cracked circle of glass covered an ancient, retired well. A wall switch lit the bulbs built into the descending brick to reveal a pool of black water—poor cistern.

The staunch sea wind reverberated through the house, so that with the opening of the neo-French doors, seaside to the back deck, others would slam shut at horror-film volume. For the price of the view (at least they'd invited us to eat their food—jams, tablets of chocolate, a half-dozen boxes of expired taco shells) there were also four ovens and three stoves on the ground floor, with a washer and dryer that tripped the electricity three times in as many days. A relative of the owner had to be called to solve the conundrum of a huge electric box in a downstairs closet displaying a rainbow of wires and what looked to be many computing servers.

It was not an easy time. Heather fell sick with a high fever. Nights of multiple wakeups began after we'd been gifted a few months of solid ten-hour blocks of sleep. Also, because we stayed in the largest of the rented houses, it de facto became the socializing hub for the three dozen or so in the party, a number thinning out over the week. Downtime away from the bustle of relatives quickly became non-existent, and my plan to get in a few hours of work on my book during the less program-filled days came to forty minutes here and there. All right, but I couldn't be expected not to burrow into my time-honored tradition of passion-aggression; that is, since I felt like shit because I hadn't been writing, I would reflect my state onto others by mild chicanery: silly pap about noise edicts while Heather slept, and freak-outs about her safety when eating: She could choke on pieces of apple that big! Take the seeds out of the fucking watermelon!

And yet, I could sit on an overly frilly couch by the twenty-foot-high windows and look out on the Irish Sea, the strand filling and lessening by tide (leaving sea wrack and large egg-shaped stones in its wake), and also keep watch on the sky's light, ever-changing, with the blackened tops of Mourne Mountains visible to the south. Outside were picnic benches and chairs if I fancied some sea air—they were near the doghouse. The sad pooch had been left behind by the owners, though he wasn't to be let in the house, and he noodled about on the strand with his other canine friends when not stretched out on the cement—half-dead, half-depressed.

Rain came daily in glorious sheets and murky mists. We were fairly marooned on Coney Island because I didn't trust myself to drive on the left side of the road. We took only two journeys, driven first by the aunt and then by the uncle. Coney Island itself featured a forty-five-minute loop on an outcrop of land jutting into the sea, the actual Coney Island. The locals called it "going round the rocks," and we often made the constitutional during our daughter's afternoon nap as she lay frontally against my wife's chest in a carrier. Being bounced to begin the siesta, with additional hip swaying and jiggles, was the only way she would physically agree to sleep. Sometimes we went downshore in the other direction, toward the edge of the golf course and the myriad stones with dried or drying algae, finding a few golf balls for Heather to later squeeze and roll.

So I sat and sipped Barry's Gold Blend Tea with real Irish milk or drank one of the many Guinesses left over from the large parties while breathing in this fairytale landscape, this parcel of the rapturous shamrocked country cleaved into counties, its ground well-trod by the Celts in the Axial Age, when the first surviving philosophies sprung up all over Earth like a new bountiful but problematic species.

Not far away from Coney Island calm, the rageful Irish Sea pounded sheer cliffs, and among the hills above were ruins from centuries past. Maps showed we could connect to the backwoods trails from the local road, but we needed a ride to get there—

going all the way on a dangerous narrows with Heather would be exhausting and foolhardy. We were dropped up the roadway near Chapeltown, just past the more substantial village of Ardglass. Four in total. Eula, my wife's cousin, came along, as well. She lived in Amsterdam with her boyfriend—we'd stayed with her on our honeymoon. In her early thirties, she preferred the partying life. Once a phone sales wiz, she spoke vast amounts of words, mainly newly minted opinions and weatherworn anecdotes. I would have preferred just the little family. As we struck out down the winding lane toward the sea, my resistance remained and never left high alert.

The single lane we strolled was devoid of cars. Heather soon would need her morning nap, and until she nodded off an immense anxiety battle-axed any of my good cheer to a pulp. I leaked squashed sentiments, but remained distended and rotting while not being able to exit my finely furnished torture chamber. I walked, worming my hands around in the pockets of my smelly black Uniqlo pullover, as we passed new land, drawing in enlivening views under a sky slowly shifting, charcoal to blue. On both sides of the lane were large properties with some farming going on. Summer in Ireland still counted as summer, and the vegetation and fauna bloomed to bursting, the exquisite hedges overwhelming ageless stone walls, behind which dogs lazily barked on blacktop driveways or patches of grass. Bumblebees zoomed from yellow to purple wildflower, and the honeyed smells perked noses acclimated to exhaust, construction, dust, and urine sunbaked into the cinder-white sidewalks of a Brooklyn summer. I heard mainly non-mechanical sounds: the distant sea, birds, and insects—these muffled the stray truck or tractor. I could hold a meditative air for only seconds at a time.

Cousin Eula could sense my disillusion. And I could hear her distaste for me as she outlined the pattern of her problems with her quietly suffering boyfriend. She didn't have the coping skills of my wife, who put up with any parsimony owing to love and sacrifice—staking her future on a man who could overcome his demons for her and the child. What to do? Confrontation had always frightened me. I crabwalked around a coming clash, familiarizing myself with every bit of the surrounding landscape before the voices forced me to act.

There were many people in the world like Cousin Eula, cavalcading through life by giving a public play-by-play, and I loved them for that. Differentiation is—well, really, I mean to pronounce an old-time porn channel's mantra: *Variety is the spice of life*. Opposites attract—a few of my friends were such announcers, though I wouldn't have been married to one of them. And? How would the melancholic poet make nice? The loaded panegyric falsifies. "Melancholic" summed me up as succinctly as "cold" when it's fifteen Fahrenheit. The world needs reminders, examples, severe beings who get more and more lampooned because their eyes are not googly with delight about how great everything supposedly is.

Years before, in the dusk of childhood, my agita had been seeded. Concealing my unprincipled rejection of the nearest people only redoubled the pain—I had to unleash. I did so to my closest childhood friend when I was ten, eleven years old. We would be together until I decided—enough. I didn't want to be around him anymore, my cup had been filled. A sleepover had been planned, but at around eight that evening I called my mother and announced I wanted to be picked up. *It didn't feel right* was what I told myself. He was two years younger, and devastated.

When I arrived home he called me on the phone, with aid from his mother, and could barely put a sentence together, weeping loudly, blearily. Why did you leave? Come back and play. I remained severe. Weeks would pass. Then, owing to the friendship of our mothers, I'd see him again, press in close, and, some months on, repeat the isolating act. *It didn't feel right*—this was my truth. The world was already rent, jagged. My sensations demanded this newly efficient torsion. I had to persevere.

Farmland went only so far, and this was not a tourist-festooned piece of earth. We didn't exactly know if we could get to the sea. The online map seemed to say yes, but out in the country, thankfully, there was no internet. After almost an hour, hiking signs pointed seaward and we went downhill between overgrown hedges, through wildflowers, berry bushes, cattails, thistles, the drone of bees. An aboveground tunnel—a three-hundred-meter bower with a true canopy. I walked with my arms up and lips shut, to shield against getting swatted or stung or having a cob-web stick to my face. After five minutes, the vegetation receded, and the sunned coast glimmered with the deep bass of the Irish Sea's tides scalloping sandstone and shale bedrock just below. Anchored in the distance, the Isle of Man. We headed south, up and down ground retaining its patchwork of drumlins, kames, and kettles formed some ten thousand years ago, while passing an obligatory Catholic cross and devotional station etched in the vegetation. Cool and warm winds mixed, and we each nutted about, in awe of the sightlines.

In taking a measure of that moment, I took a measure of my wife and sleeping daughter. The strange colors and curious odors in this vector of time I would often revisit to cross out, defang, dismember, making it ghastly so I couldn't pretend to miss it after I lost them both: but of course I did. The scent of berry bushes choked; the bees I had always feared became more menacing. The Irish light was replaced by the harsh Midwest light in the core of summer, my bodyfat asking to be added to with more junkfood to escape the heat.

The mountebanks of memory. Every moment grows more spidery, there is more moss to drag. This is aging. We begin in a fog and then accumulate, develop recall, learn our lessons, change the tune, change the city, change the partner, bounce a check, bury a friend, find love again, then take in the sunset with a smidgen more intensity before saying goodbye. A chambered part of myself began to contend that we live in the moment so that we may re-experience those moments many times later on—thereby not living in the moment. Impressionism is a flimsy kind of word for a painter's style, but if branding a retroflexed way of seeing it goes further. Impressions do not eternally exist, they must arrive. One's recall and reliving may be crisp, the recapture succulent—but one has to forget memories when too many, and have patience to wait until they come again, since they are stored in the body, safely turned to blood.

On the bluffs of the Irish coast we saw a distant church, centuries old. It was probably a few miles away and, with unseen twists and turns, maybe even more. Aside from some back-and-forth about hiking too far out of the way, making it hell to get back (I wouldn't budge on this), Cousin Eula and I held our tongues and endured each other. The Ardtole Church, the one we'd started at and left for later, would be back in our direction of home, then on to Ardglass along the narrow highway. Maybe we could call a relative to give us a ride from there.

We reversed course and Cousin Eula resumed talk of what her

future with her boyfriend held. In retracing, I again stood before the Isle of Man. The sun, near its apex, cast a high arc light on the blurring-blue water up close, the gray-green far away. I lost the thread. Colors strengthened and mixed, erasing hard reality. The magnetism of Ireland enforced itself and asked the writer to extinguish something so that a broken precept could be married, so no camera obscura could drag the afterimage through the tidewrack of the mind.

I once met a man, a cool customer, an intellectual force, who related to me how most times he preferred napping to socialization, even with his few close friends. It was enough to be by himself, while reading, writing, or thinking. He did not need to feed on people to fuel his creation. I could regret such a severe outlook, though I'd also sometimes judge it noble, if vaguely psychotic. It's a fusty Nietzschean paradigm, one I've slovenly practiced—it might even be a state many serious writers have to find, with allowances. The act of separating, maybe destabilizing, concealing my destructive path: for years the urge to separate haunted me, but I had no recourse to true creativity, until the attempts became bolder and loftier. My love of film, and a need to make one of my own, was curtailed when I accepted I didn't work so well with other people. The words of Bergman's characters could inflict pain and, translated, they poked me to take up the pen and produce ripostes or at least approximations to outline the small bitter world of Milwaukee, though the rough hours of work occurred on the coasts. My sentences weren't alive, the language inside stilted and bulky like chunks of hard, overturned soil awaiting water. My storylines weren't compelling to anyone over thirty-five. Preternaturally shy, I had to learn people, go at them, even if I flailed. I had to see how they lived, what they did all day, their toils, breakdowns, loves.

My life followed the kaleidoscopic path—different sections of living rising into focus at different times. Intuition and, to a lesser extent, dreams have guided more than live advice, though books pointed the way as well—those quotable potables I'd reenfranchised like a man who has no place in the world and continually parrots wise phrases to stave off bringing himself to order. Did my melancholy transfer so tidily to worry? Did my uncouthness sharpen itself enough to carve a deep anxiety, a suavity in every rock I see? I feared the death of my daughter or wife more than I feared my own. I feared no real reconciliation.

Greener Days

In Ireland I was a tourist again. There had been a time when I wasn't. Young and wanting to fuck, I'd swapped my country for the continent and ended up in Heidelberg, a medium-size college town full of U.S. Army bases—the center of that army in Europe. Touristy, too—it retained its old-world beauty because the Allies hadn't bombed the old town since they planned on living there after they won the war. A river ran through it—on one side, the Altstadt, terminating in the sixteenth century castle, a quarter-ruined by the constant French and German grappling over the sandy loam beneath; on the other, showy views of that piece of history from cosmetic foothills giving way to densely forested slopes of beeches, oaks, and firs. Upon leaving, I'd stay on a farm in the south of France for six months, toiling away, kamikazily in concert with the earth. An opportunity.

Physical labor—after I dropped out of film school, a few years earlier, I'd lived on an organic farm in Northern California. There's a poetry to the body's movements in hard work. The muscles cook for solid hours since the mind can't quite fixate, but instead meanders from dirt pile to dust pile, flower to flower, in strange glades. The effort to become obsessive is too much in light of the arms buckling, shoulders wrenching, and thighs quaking from spearing and heaving out shovelfuls of dirt and pitchforking free knotty, earth-aged weeds. Dust and dirt cake the face, lips, and nostrils, but fresh farm air keeps the breath firm. Someone knew somebody who'd had to drop out in France. I wouldn't get paid, but farmers didn't farm for the money. Seasonal worker? I didn't care about a title, just a new life. I'd needed to erase the failure of so many things, not just the failure to create. I needed to quiet my head. Something screwy had begun going on up there.

I could still be alone for vast tracts of time, playing into my own stupor, as I had in childhood, but being out of the country, away from touch and trying to keep to the proud strictures of the new language, I began to tighten. Riding my rickety old French grandpa bike through the deep green hills at the edge of the Odenwald, an unimpressive mountain range, or walking over the river to the ancient hedges and vineyards on the other side and glowering at the ruined Schloß didn't steady me anymore.

My European experience in Germany had been a benighted one, but at least I knew you went to Europe to become a writer, not a filmmaker. I wasn't naive enough to think it could still be Paris in the twenties or Prague in the nineties. Berlin didn't want me. I did glom on to Hamburg, leasing for a discount, but the friend who was supposed to be in Milan for three months came back very early, heartbroken and nightly whinnying. He wanted me to watch bad movies with him. I had to change my life from watching to making and told him how I needed to get back to copying out pages of *Gatsby* because I was learning a new trade. He bitched and said hardly anyone would be reading novels in fifteen years and he was right.

I corralled a hovel in a suburban shithole near Heidelberg. My neighbor worked at a computer company, and he set me up proof-reading translations of their manuals. The next week I fell in love with Ruth, pronounced Hrut. Red hair, really vermillion. A graduate student with glasses so close to the color of glass they seemed frameless, two lenses magically suspended. She often wore black to damper her abundance of chest. One of that breed of Germans who patterned their English with a British pronunciation—she adored London and all its paraphernalia, the Tate and its paintings, the truer Soho, fish and chips, faces weighing their envy. She disdained America but liked me—for a time. Three seasons, not consecutive. We broke up in July and came around with December's holiday chill, following the course of most relationships between people our age. The only reason she let me in the door was my middling talent for writing and "Your pelt," she said, while petting my massed chest hair as we read verse naked. "And your resemblance to Ted Hughes," she added tartly. She moused around with a sort of official yet unofficial writing group to which friends of the enrolled showed up sporadically and gave critiques, while violently defending DeLillo from disrespect, then disappeared, though those who attended the university did earn credit. The instructor, if he could be called that, was a Londoner—a great anamorphic schnoz, his dominant feature. Sometimes he had students to his office and gave them middle-shelf sherry. I knew of no improprieties. Several classes were held in beer halls or gardens, the bar food dripping German grease. Everyone seemed so happy the few times I went along. I was treated with the utmost kindness, an effervescence rivaling what my closest stateside friends held in their arsenal. There was none of the horseshit of men showing off to cajole women into sleeping with them. Yes, a host of ribbing, foisted through English-style snark—given the leader—with people preying on another's tics, weaknesses, and phobias. A similar show in any writing class, but the undercurrent was warm enough—the core clan of seventeen or eighteen felt comfortable and spit in the face of competition, with no vandalizing intentions, though surely this was easy to do when enjoying liquor or beer during class time.

Ruth knew another woman there: Sonja, a temperamental blonde with a holy subduing voice husking, in short time, only after me. Ruth said nothing about her—they were different women. Sonja resembled one of those hydrocephalic figures in Cranach the Elder. From her eyebrows down (dainty nose, slit of a mouth) her face appeared scrunched, but that high, intimidating forehead went on and on, the heavy cranium behind a bowling ball, ready to dissemble for my inches. A psychologist, she breathed high art and enunciated both of her fluent languages deftly, her nickered consonants continually cracking the air. Her last boyfriend, who'd turned dopey, had just been dropped and, threatening suicide, got himself admitted to the hospital she worked at. When able to roam, he knew which angle of his unit's glassy see-through stairwell to stand at to see her go to or from her office, three floors below.

Her pursuit of me was all too obvious. Ruth didn't want me to come to the class anymore. There were only two more to go. She said she wouldn't want me to hear and silently judge her latest story about a dying grandmother. Then only one session remained, to be held at an exquisite old university-owned house just off the Neckar River, near the old town, by the Schloß. A celebratory evening. Many insisted I come and read something. Even a poem. And I did have a poem. Something unfailingly naïve and chichi, with one good metaphor in its seventy lines. After fifty people stormed through a crate of wine, we relaxed in the large second-floor drawing room, where priceless lamps hummed their jaundiced light, color-coordinating with the June sky's pink hues. Most inappropriately, I read something about driving in Montana, a poem overloaded with ennui. Silence reigned when I finished, and before anyone could say anything, Sonja issued a fart loud and large enough to shake the creaky wooden floor. I couldn't believe it. I also tried to believe that no-one but me noticed—a fantasy despoiled by dozens of people holding their faces in their hands. The teacher delivered his edict: Epic, lad, epic. People exploded, and all the swirling faux melancholia of the poem evaporated. I had to hand it to Sonja and even said so later, opening myself to be swatted down again with some sassy suggestive remark. But no—she was too soused, too sad, and in the gloaming of turning twenty-eight while emotionally albatrossed to a douchebag who wouldn't let go of her. Instead, the retort came later that night in bed, from Ruth. I dinked about statically and spooned her after we finished. She remained still. Then: Unhand me, sir. Words said seriously enough for a child to translate them as "fuck off." Maybe just a drink-infused, late-night irruption? I slept peacefulish. But it was the warning shot, followed by a "Let's take some time off" the next morning.

The summer passed. I began to hate computers and not just their manuals. In October, Ruth turned friendly. We read *Mrs Dalloway* together. Then the holidays were bitter. January: more suffocating. You know yourself, she said, I detest Americans.

I thought "disdain."

Now you'll have something to write about. Oh, do you need Sonja's number?

For the next six weeks, I couldn't write a sentence. I took to the hills across the Neckar and the famous Philosophenweg, where august luminaries from the oldest university in Germany were said to walk among the trees and find their deep thoughts. The paths had since become a requirement for tourist groups. Long weeks of mindless trudging in the jewel of the Rhine Rift Valley, its earth filled with sea-sediment and under loads of leaves that never seemed to disappear, even in summer. Damp days, each one gray and severe. Unending chills. The coldest winter, in one of the warmer parts of Germany, for thirty years. I had a sweater and two jackets and was still cold. Magnesium, my mother would have warned. Eat some fucking beef, a crass California friend would have shouted. Eating wasn't a favored activity, but neither was starving. Something had broken, though I didn't know it. When you're not yet thirty you don't tend to feel too keenly, that's why most of our derring-do occurs before then. What was I doing in Europe? Pretending? Possibly. I'd stopped all contact with everyone there and back home. I stopped reading. I developed many infections.

Each day, just after seven in the morning, I would cross the river from the old town and again zig and zag though the network of winding paths, coursing over the Schlangenweg and up through terraced vineyards to wander on a concentration of well-maintained trails. I circled and reconnoitered before rising to and eventually locating the lookout towers, the Celtic remains, the Thingstätte—an amphitheater built by the Nazis—climbing and gazing, waiting for breath to escape my nostrils and mouth and let me know I was alive. I used what extra money I had to buy new boots and by day ten they stank, years aged. I carried a thermos of hot water and a bag of carrots to get me through to lunch, often tea and a day-old dessert.

Glacial-blooded after four hours of breathing dampness, I would sit in one of two cafés for that bittersweet break. More often, I returned to one in the old town, by the Church of the Holy Spirit, where I'd taken Ruth to see the Bach Cello Suites performed and fell asleep midway through number two's allemande. I stationed myself by the steamed-up windows, cradling a pot of peppermint. They had the *Frankfurter Allgemeine Zeitung* and the *International Herald Tribune*; I stuck with the *Zeitung*, reading only enough to get an idea of the darting language with the verbs caboosing the sentence. Then I'd pore over the numbers on the financial page, primarily the DAX. I noted that the stock of the computer company I'd worked for had risen considerably after my departure. I'd quit my job the day of the breakup; I left because I thought I should go back to school, even in Germany, to better myself. What if one day I was to be married, even in a kind of gauche way, clipped onto Ruth like a pendant, because I fully believed we'd get back together like all lust-drenched couples eventually accomplish? Thoughts like this crossed my mind, and I would hold on to them for unaccountable minutes until I realized I had left my body during the questioning and any more queries I had didn't matter until the tracing-paper of my consciousness fit over my body again, and the soul came to life.

I usually sat in the café for two hours, perked as the beans, watching the passersby on the brick street in Altstadt, which did not allow cars or even trams. I followed people, urbanites, whom I was shocked to see messing with their phones. A texting craze had taken over Europe because the telecom companies charged so much, even for local calls: so texting began as a cost-effective measure and not because people didn't want to talk. I peered down the street, my eyes made sick again by storefronts for designer shoes, clothes, handbags—there a bar, there a Turkish restaurant. Behind these was the red-brown brick of taller university buildings and, half a click south, where I could see, the psychiatric hospital, where Sonja's ex had once pitted himself against her. She had called me after Ruth's departure. We flung about for some weeks. While I was dressed in puce lingerie (hers) she had me read her Sir Alfred Noyes' 'The Highwayman,' lingam unrestricted. She taught me about wine, we argued about Rilke. Rumor went she'd returned to the douchebag.

One late night, I ended up in an old university building at three in the morning with two strangers I'd drunk and danced with. The man was a member of the fraternity house there, a truly exclusive society stretching back to Napoleonic times; the woman, an American, traipsed along, delighted she could smoke in such an atmosphere. He showed us up a grand staircase. It's all cherrywood, he said brightly, fondling her ear. The halls were laid out with long thin carpets and portraits of elders, fusspots with cut-glass assholes, along with annually staged photographs of the assembled members going back to the invention of the art. While I made eyes at the history, rooms where Hölderlin and maybe Hannah Arendt had once stubbed a toe, they made them at each other. I soon left them to fucking.

The other café was across the river on the southern crest of the Odenwald. After bumbling around the evergreen forest until almost noon, I would arrive at the moment of my only drama for the day. Would I cross back through the wald, then scamper over the newer tram, bike, car, and pedestrian bridge, or else one of the two two-hundred-year-old ones downstream and visit my regular café, or would I stay in Neuenheim and enter a curious building I'd come across, the American University at Heidelberg, and stomp up the marbled stairs to the unwindowed, fluorescent-lit café inside, a place always struggling to attract any clientele other than university personnel? The nondescript café had no periodicals or newspapers except a university newsletter, but it had Americans. Much better-dressed, coiffed, and cut than I was, they sat in their seats while turning the pages of course books and loose-leaf notebooks, pastel highlighters in their soft hands. I pretended Deutschness and it worked, though I had many conversations in my head with those I watched. Attempting not to fantasize about seducing women, I concentrated my daydreams on forging friendships, finding someone to commune with about art. And for many, many minutes, I wouldn't touch my tea and would dream falsity into my life, akin to talking to life-size cardboard cutouts in a basement, away from discriminating views.

Depending on the weather, maybe on less biting February or March afternoons, I would veer off to the Thingstätte in the deeper recesses of the Odenwald. I did this to commune with history, to try to feel something unimaginable and to stretch my humble mind—a touristy principle, but I had no camera, took no notes, sketched or painted no pictures. An abandoned egg-shaped amphitheater in the middle of the woods, it had been completed by the government in 1935—Goebbels spoke at the dedication. These sites, multidisciplinary outdoor theaters, were part of the Thingspiel movement, a craze in the early 1930s, but their popularity dwindled just as this one opened. After the Allies won the war, the U.S. Army held jazz concerts there. It was a solemn, well-kept place, and one entered at its high point because it was built into a cleft of forest: one descended from the last brick rows to the stage area, all in a wonderful, horrible symmetry, and when turning around one would look up to the exact point of arrival. I tried to understand the foolish glue of history through ruins often restored to some semblance of heyday reality. There was nothing there for me, but I kept visiting, and each time there was even less. I shouldn't have returned, but I'd long convinced it was myself the perfect place to shelter my plague for an hour.

I never asked for loneliness. It came to me prepackaged, the flip side of melancholy, boring easily through me. The French opportunity didn't register as a decision to go to a farm and endure large stretches of complete solitude—it was the natural next step. If despair steered my destiny, then I would celebrate it. I'd prepared for my course of deprivations—months with only a few understanding people around would be a snap.

A few days before the journey, I dropped a fraction of my catatonic act as if to murmur, Yes, I have such a deep need to open up, to talk anecdote, to utter useless syllogisms, but also to say to someone, no matter sex, "I've never fully revealed myself to my parents." The yearning stayed alive in me as a medium flame through my preparations, as if at any second the simmer would shoot high and burn all to a crisp, but as soon as I boarded the tram to the Hauptbahnhof, a frozen quality descended. I had to steel myself for a life in France, no matter how long.

A different life required a different me and real country living demanded something I'd never been. These feelings grew out of imagination—what they were in reality made little sense except as an ebullience, tinged with fear, and then demoted to hot sweat running out of my pits in rills. Perhaps I'd realigned myself in an undercover fashion during the final conscriptions in those days of preparing. I certainly wasn't ready to die.

Through some back channel that got in touch with an official channel and its prim diction, a message came from the U.S. Consulate in Frankfurt. After not hearing anything for more than two months, my mother had contacted the State Department, and on letterhead depicting the open-winged bald eagle, I was asked in plain language to please call her as soon as possible. I logged into e-mail holding the hundreds of unread messages and typed a brief note.

Would I start reading again in France? Weekends, aside from some small duties, I would have free. I quickly made two piles, choosing a few novels I'd already read and a book on writing poetry that a friend had sent. Something to cheer me on if the mood hit. I'd grown up with a reverence for books even before I could read. Some mighty ones were around my eyeline in a bookcase my father had constructed—impotent were the words, but behind glass doors with a small push-button handle, the spines, hard and soft, with no formal arrangement, and then: the covers. The thick *Brothers Karamazov*, small-fonted to save paper, but with the menace of a large, black, typically stout Russian torso. Like a dolmen—no features, no dress, just blackness. The softcover of Thornton Wilder's *Our Town*, with a man in a bent fedora and a side-mouth cigarette on the cover: the famed stage-manager, though he seemed out of film noir and the book had been reissued like this in the seventies—no, there was no cigarette, that would be my father's two-packs-a-day habit. I began to seriously acquire books in my twenties—my friend Arthur and I would empty our backpacks and bike to a variety of St. Vincent de Pauls and Salvation Armies in our college town of Eugene, Oregon to find outdated Norton anthologies, pocket paperbacks of Hemingway and Flannery O'Connor. The poetry sections, even if so marked, were always sparse and henpecked. We were both on a course of studying verse, and neither of us thought the pop star

Jewel, whose lone book always seemed in stock, a force to compare with Marvell or Elizabeth Bishop. Arthur adored Rilke, as many twentysomethings do, and found an old translation of *The Notebooks of Malte Laurids Brigge*. He's not known for that, I said, making fun of the ridiculous invented Dutch name, but my friend persisted, swatting down my shitheel vibe. I looked for that childhood Dostoyevsky, but came away with a moldy, pocket-sized *Crime and Punishment*. Where were my books? Would I ever return to continue building the library I had begun? They were then in Oakland, and I hoped no-one was rummaging through them during a drunken party.

I couldn't contrive much else for my existence. Living in Germany had been intriguing but not a full-blown challenge. You make friends, build a routine, go to places you like, as in any city. Now I'd have a farm with farmland—nowhere to escape. Everywhere you go, you find yourself. I needed crisp mountain air to fill those endless, awing expanses of rock, trees, soil. Only something that alive could cut through my placidity.

I brought only a small selection of clothes. On the many-acred land there would be a washing machine, but no hot water. I took nothing electronic. I didn't expect to find anything there except maybe a radio, and I was nearly correct.

A parade of trains on a cheap ticket, first to Mannheim, then Offenberg, Strasbourg, Lyon. I came into chilly Grenoble around three in the morning. I'd have to wait until five-thirty for the next train that would lead to Volonne. The station was mostly deserted on a March weekday. I fell asleep in that antiseptic space, hugging my pack on a metal bench while watching two young Chinese women in neon snowsuits pace the floor below the main hallway's big board of upcoming trains. My stray passages of sleep were emblematic of nothing but my own hairpin style of living.

The Hautes-Alpes train was white as snow, nothing like the flaking rusty red or serge blue of many in the SNCF fleet. Not sleeker, but more boxy, narrower to make it through the geologic fractures and folds—the tunnels made by dynamiting millions of years of gneiss and rhyolite. The alpine terrain went by in a blur, then flashes. Clods of snow pressed down on gigantic evergreen branches; in the blindingly white vistas, sparkles merged into one long band by glare and refraction. I still couldn't read. I either looked outside or at my hands, soft and barren of work scars except from a few youthful blunders with a Swiss Army knife and a can of tuna. We passed through the jagged Alps and then slowly descended into the orogeny known as the Massif Central, where I switched trains before finally arriving in Volonne, where André, the farm owner, would pick me up. There were no buses from there into the tangled, broken earth of his property, twenty kilometers away. The farm rested on some plateau, near the town of Châteauneuf-Val-Saint-Donat, though to walk from the farm to the centre-ville, with its two bars, three brasseries, a post office, a tabac, and one café would take nearly an hour. Fine by me. Space would heal all, I nincompooply bet.

I deboarded at Volonne around two. Bruise-colored sky. Maybe snow and, at least, sleet approaching. Volonne—a small, mean town. Cobwebs in windows, the shutters and curtains slightly jiggling after someone checked you out. Men smoking with no pleasure. Anchored atop my pack, I waited while locals eyed me bitterly before reordering themselves to their drudgery. An ashen dog loped by, his nose stiffly pointed to the ground before he gave me a cursory look and then disappeared around the corner in the direction of the tracks. I grew foggy from loneliness.

Slivers of water needled my cheeks alive. I slowly noticed that I'd been waiting forty minutes. I'd told André the time of the train, a mode of transport so exact on the continent. I paced. Nothing. I gathered what euros I had and called his house, speaking hackneyed French to a woman who must have been his wife. I couldn't get her to understand what I was saying—I barely understood what I said when I enunciated it, given how I translated every phrase or injunction into English before speaking. André is not here, I said to her. Yes, but he's not here, she replied. No, but he is there, don't you see him? We both said this, though I used a wrong syntax. A bearded man in a big van? she said. No, he's not here, I said. Another woman came on, younger-voiced with a spattering of English: the children's nanny, I later learned. She said, André just called me. He's at the station waiting for you. We went around a few more times. But I'm at the train station here, in Volonne. Volonne? There was a pause. Why are you there? The directions said to come here, I emailed him about it. Volonne is the closest station to Châteauneuf-Val-Saint-Donat. Châteauneuf-Val-Saint-Donat, she repeated. Was there a French variant of *Who's on First?* There is another Châteauneuf, she said. The farm was at another Châteauneuf, Châteauneuf-les-Orgeus, about thirty-five kilometers away, but with no transit services. Could I hitchhike to their town? You need to get on D4085, and then she named a matrix of other numbers I tried to copy down.

I'd tackled my share of hitchhiking. Luckily I had shaved that morning; also my journey wasn't too long. By a short ride I made it to the main highway, then waited. Cars came as often as they did in *North by Northwest*'s crop-duster scene—and they didn't stop. A light snow began to fall. Why this ordeal? What if I turned back? Shuttle back to Deutschland? But nowhere to go. Fuck a Ruth or a Sonja for a few weeks before the inevitable push and pull and claustrophobia, while orgasm came to be less mistaken for love? Return to a garbled country running on faux-patriotic mode with flags, ribbons around the trees, and the hysteric signs in diner windows?

I'd waited longer than an hour sometimes. Like in Nice, when I eventually took the train. In Mount Shasta, too. But someone came. Something always happened, I would get to where I needed to be—think positive. It was over an hour. A white minivan pulled up. A mother and her two young children. In her thirties, with a discriminating cast to her brow, she didn't hesitate to invite me in. A farmer as well, or connected to a farm, I believed. I sat on the floor in back, facing the children in their special seats; shotgun was filled with boxes of vegetables, cartons of jars with something recently canned. The girl and the boy were surprised at first, but then they regarded me innocuously, almost as if this happened a few times a week. Maybe Volonne appeared mean, but in the rural life, with its country manners less denigrating, the codes were quite different—the number of buckles or buttons is irrelevant, there is the crop, the weather, and the invaders, those damned wild boars.

In a quietude that began as suspect and then became comfortable, we drove about forty-five minutes, near to the regional line with the Hautes-Alpes, until I was let out around La Peyrouse. We'd left the area of snow many clicks before and had come down in elevation a few hundred feet to what I wrongly assumed was the maximum for a fully-operating farm, a little over nine-hundred meters. Châteauneuf-les-Orgeus, or the line of its limits, was still around fifteen kilometers away. It had to be near four o'clock, though I had no watch. A narrow back road, completely empty then, would lead me to the main town, leaving one last jaunt to the farm. It yielded one passing car in the next hour. The slanting sun began to poke out as I walked past modest houses holding small plots of vegetables. A slow-moving creek bordered the road, meandering near and then running away while I kept passing installations displaying a dog and sometimes two or three, who stood or sat, never on a lead, just behind the property line, giving me a few obligatory hard looks before letting their day get back to normal. Six or seven miles would probably take around eighty minutes if I went at top speed without running—impossible with the immense backpack. I began counting in French. As I neared two hundred, my mind began to detach from how pained my feet and shoulders felt with twentysome pounds pressing down. I asked one of the few people I saw, an old woman in a sundress, who swept her driveway, how far Châteauneuf-les-Orgeus was. Cinq kilometers. Merci.

When I arrived, I saw the two bars and the closed post office. I had the address of the farm. It would be another ten-minute car ride, but I'd hitch on a more traveled road. Another woman, younger, picked me up. I showed her the address, which brought out her teeth.

About a minute into the drive, André appeared. He came from the opposite direction. He slowed his van and let up the clutch. Eustache! he yelled. He knew my driver from the small town they all lived in, another ten kilometers past the farm. I think you have a hitchhiker I should take. He sported a large beard on the order of van Gogh's famous postman portrait, with an appropriately aquiline French nose. The Châteauneuf mix-up was no big deal, we were already friends.

We drove uphill into earth having suffered relatively recent geologic upheaval—the sepia-toned fractures and extrusion left gargantuan boulders resting near the valley's stream, then at its highest yearly mark—yet not that high. You could walk parts of the riverbed, even in March. The landscape's bareness (the few structures were well-hidden from the road) gave it an uncanny resemblance to that of the *Land of the Lost* TV show, something I'd watched with great enthusiasm for its kitschy representation of prehistoric times.

The road had three long, looping switchbacks before the entrance to the completely organic farm André and his wife had purchased a decade before. We arrived at the golden hour. Variegated sunlight cast across a peaceful land already growing cold from mountain currents. Threshing mistral winds from the north could have dramatic effects on temperatures. The van weaved and veered, climbing in elevation through the forests at the property's edge. Two horses, Ulysses and Pénélope, neighed from a distant field. We rose a little more and pulled up to a structure half-buried in a grassy hill, a combination toolshed and granary. An upper floor grew out of the grass enveloping the lower. André gave me a quick tour in the fading light. The kitchen, just north of the structure, was connected to the bathrooms and showers. Deserted caravans were spaced out on the land, each outfitted with bedding and a medley of items: flashlights, tools, lures, line, and other fishing equipment, old books and maps—the kingdom of a seventies private eye, à la Jim Rockford. There I was welcome to stay, sleep, reside, make a temporary home. In any of them. André introduced me to the greenhouse and the small barn holding hay. He gestured proudly to the large planting fields downhill. They were bare, the ground just coming out of its deep freeze. Yet soon, maybe that week, we would start planting after a horse-drawn till cut the rows, mixing the uprooted soil with "fume"—cow shit—from a load to be delivered the next day.

I followed André to the upper floor of the granary. Tall and gaunt, he carried hard-country muscles owing to a supremely healthy diet and many farm hours. He wore a rastacap, keeping his voluminous, meter-long red hair spiraled up inside. A serious being, though he carried a side-pocket smile. Once, while I battled an illness, he told me, I am not afraid of sick people—in fact, I want to be near them, to hug them, to give them my healing energy. This no-nonsense approach ("hippie-dippy" if stateside) was coupled with his theories indebted to Rudolf Steiner and his biodynamic farming methods, which include refusing to use mechanical tools (work by hand produces better, heartier vegetables) and planting at the best times according to the zodiac, depending on the particular seed to be sown. Coming from a permaculture internship in California, which stressed the sacredness of soil and plant, I must have been destined to appear at this man's farm. He had a feminine side, especially in his lilting, coruscating English-language voice, even though in French or German (one parent from each country) a deep timbre harnessed pique to his sentences—the older brother I would have preferred, the buddy I would have wanted to watch out for me: to watch me cry under the stars and hold me, semi-tight. But I saw him really angry only twice in eight months. He mainly walked an enlightened path—not much bothered him—and, not surprisingly, he had a holy practice. That structure atop the granary wasn't necessarily for workers: it was a Sikh temple. The address of the farm had been printed in books and on the fledgling internet as a place that any Sikh could come and visit, any time, and be given refuge and food. The space, all varnished wood floors with hardly any furniture (shoes to be left at the door), seemed recently built. A sound system with two large speakers had been placed on a shelving unit, as well as a CD player and four discs—the extent of the electronic entertainment farmwide, except for a transistor radio, culling two English-language stations, the BBC and the Armed Forces Network in the evening. The farm's one phone was in the mice-infested kitchen, though limited to receiving calls. Even if someone had a cellphone, and André didn't, reception would be nil in these graduatingly high, off-the-grid elevations.

During those cold early nights, I planned to sleep in the closest caravan, which was also the newest, though it had been manufactured in the late eighties. Still, the bitter evening winds often made me start chopping wood just before dusk. The temple had a fireplace in the middle of the room, pipe to the ceiling—the only heating on the property. I would load it up for the night around eight-thirty, and although it died down after a few hours, it would continue emitting warmth through the large lava stones until at least two. I needed every impress of that heat. I slept in multiple layers of sweaters and long johns with a wool blanket over a down sleeping bag and I could still feel cold.

My days on the farm began. Mornings were chilly, but if the sun was out, by one o'clock it would get so hot with that high-elevation corona sitting on one's shoulders we often took an extended break—any relaxing after lunch easily turned to siesta. And from June into September, the clear months, which baked for almost half the day, there would be two to three hours of downtime to preserve the body's energy. We plowed, then shoveled in the fume, but delicately. We waited. Then we planted the first seeds of the year: carrots. Mindless enough, it passed the time so effectively, I was barely conscious of needing to get to a certain hour on the clock. It helped to be not getting paid.

During those first weeks, only one worker accompanied André and me on the land. Originally from Dijon, Elise lived in André's small village and worked with his wife, a schoolteacher, a few days a week, but also spent three or four days at the farm. A little older than I was, she never started conversations with me, but she and André could get into an avalanche of French, mainly about special tinctures and her experimental ways of dieting to combat serious internal-health concerns. I couldn't detect any imbalance in her calm, erect posture, a stoic spitting image of Falconetti's Jeanne d'Arc immortalized in Dreyer's film. When I did approach, I told her not to make allowances for my thin knowledge of the language—I had to learn. If pressed, she would speak of her relationship to the farm, the soil, and her relishing of the exceptional nutritional value of the vegetables we planted as if they were close friends, as if she could feel vicariously the light and dark moments in their lives, even as they imparted their vitamins after eating. Luckily, she treated me like a necessary agent in this wellbeing.

Along with two novels and the poetry-writing book, I'd brought a wilderness-survival guide with information on building shelters and fires, types of knots, animal tracks, and edibles to consume when starving. The farm had plenty of pine trees. A sentence grabbed about pine-needle tea—that it had more vitamin C than freshly squeezed orange juice. One day I pulled some needles off a branch, before dicing, boiling, and letting the concoction steep. It tasted awful. I dumped it and turned to the pages about knots, in time learning the lariat loop, the sheep-shank, and the stevedore knot. I gave myself some credit before I hung my head in disgust—at what, I did not know.

In the mountains, there you pee freely. For the first month, I spent almost every night alone. The still sporadic weather wasn't inviting to many others. And André's wife and two children wouldn't start staying out there until after school ended in June, usually packing into that newer caravan. Then I'd need to move. André expected more seasonal help to arrive at the end of April, the beginning of May. The summer would be a different story, complete with a few yoga and meditation workshops that helped pay back the bank loan on the land. I planned to be away for a few of those weeks—somewhere. I couldn't see more than two days ahead in my life.

To remember those first nights alone—and my body does. I had never been so physically separate from other human beings. The nearest neighbor was a true shepherd who lived about fifteen minutes southeast of our boundary, so extensive was his property. There was less to do during many of those first weekends, given how André often stayed home, and if I were killed on a Friday night, no-one would have found my body for almost three days. On the farm in California, I had slept in a tent on the edge of a meadow, but thirty other people lived a tenth of a mile away. At Châteauneuf-les-Orgeus, for three-quarters of the day, it was only me and the two horses down the hill, to whom I doled out hay twice daily. As I adjusted to the farming (and a twenty-seven-year-old can absorb a host of strain) my body demanded more sleep. Eventually I would begin to get a good nine hours a night in the temple. No alarm clocks and no TV to fall asleep to. And, though exhausted, I might still wake up a few times—primarily to pee, because a body fighting cold will get higher blood pressure, setting the kidneys to produce more fluid as a correction, but also because of the powerful wind, rattling the incorrectly hung wooden front doors and sometimes knocking free an already loose roof thatch. Noises revitalized my fears. I yearned for the time when others would be nearby, so I could easily dismiss thoughts of any evening marauder. I based this on a harpooned logic that groups of persons rarely get attacked. Until then I remained in a green state, still half-clinging to the catatonic spell from Germany. The shift from there to here had not worked. I'd done it all wrong. You don't go from the loneliness of not being able to speak to anyone around you to a pure aloneness, almost solitary confinement. During the week, André might be around for an hour or two, but then he'd be gone, covering the other corners of his life. Elise remained standoffish, like most of her countrywomen. She had no call to worry about me advancing on her. If I even unconsciously hinted at the chance, all would collapse and be infinitely worse. But I didn't need another affair—so why not embrace solitude? Because, very slowly, I was going mad.

The process of cracking up cobbles together its own active ingredients and patterns its own drug. My head had ceased to see reality, and now things were in fish-eye shapes. I began to squeeze my eyes shut many times a day for a number of seconds each time. Even though I could see only certain parts of my body at once, I didn't want to see what I'd become. I'd fooled myself for a while, but on April first, to my distress, I had to admit I couldn't fool anyone else. So I admitted defeat. I kept thinking that getting this out of the way now, this falling apart, before more people arrived, was the best thing—almost as if I had planned it that well. I continued to fool myself, just in a different way. And then it was April third. I would only create more impervious chimeras so that when they proved insuperable, I could send myself into shock over their supposed strength.

I could tell André nothing. He viewed me as dedicated, but he often had to repeat the orders, my list of tasks. I couldn't keep more than one in my mind at a time. The ammonia and hydrogen-sulfide smells violated me and putrefied, though I had no claims against them. Soon these rotting, distended nitrate-rich air leaks transformed into a Paradiso of sorts. Not a happy-cakes farm lover, I recognized the land's important purpose and would not knowingly compromise anything. To do so I would have to rein my madness in. Near Elise, I more often froze up and tried not to clasp my eyes when I thought she might be looking at me (though why would she?), holding them for long blocks of many minutes without a crisp blink because I couldn't know if she'd turn and judge my intentions toward the soil. My eyes—their jellies grew cold from keeping them open in the chilly winds. Either way, I appeared insane. What a relief to finally disappear from her on breaks and at lunch, wrenching my eyes closed until the force of the lids' grip heated them into semi-hot coals. And during those closures emerged the afterimage of my mother, but in her youth, when I was five or six. A prime time of innocence, when doing something bad or having someone be not nice to me, namely my older brother, seemed like the end of the world. One day, I hurt the thing I'd grown to love: books. Our local library had been laid out in a unique semicircle, with the heavily windowed inside rim looking out onto a small courtyard of tough shrubs and a birdbath filled with boisterous chickadees.

Inside, right up front by the checkout, book carousels were loaded with paperbacks. While my mother checked out, I studied these carousels, with all the glitz and embossed covers of those paperbacks written by hacks, romance authors, people with the audacity to use an alias. On impulse, I grabbed the metal tine of an empty holder and, as if it were a campy game-show device, gave it a tart whirl, so that many of the books on its half-dozen levels flew off in seconds. Led out to the exit, I cried and begged for the time when I had not done what I just did. But no, my mother pulled me by the hand, out into the weak morning light, below cloud-banked Milwaukee County, cold air further shriveling me before I was loaded into the car, my ongoing tantrum silent to the outer world. It was the first pure embarrassment. People looked at me, though I believe the way they saw me changed after I started bawling about the act's wrongness. They went from empathetic to non-empathetic because of my noise. They misunderstood my needs, as so many do with the people closest to them. Signals were getting mixed and desiccated, with what was perceived so far afield from what truly was. I needed their pity when I started crying, not before, when I wasn't—when I was just an innocent. But any pity vanished after my attendant "scene." They would have almost respected me more as the little bastard who pulls off his mischief and laughs, though they'd still sue to see a parent belt me before the ushering out. My mother was only a minor player here—she could have done anything or nothing. It was the crowd. They had found out. I had compromised myself and would never forget, and I would have to go forward with this knowledge—living my whole life lying to myself that it didn't matter, only to then feel this iron pain at three thousand feet in France for nearly the first time. From the mountain you see the mountain.

Wasn't it too early to be tormented by these episodes? If I couldn't manage now, why would I stir myself up with the contusions of a life I deemed forgettable? It was plainly most important just to ask the questions and leave the answers for another era, if I could reach it. Maybe I'd only get to ask the questions. Maybe, at least, I'd have asked the questions. Some people don't.

Weekends could be worse, and the weekend was coming. I thought on weekends I would use my two wide-open days to learn French and write more, continuing a novella I'd abandoned in Germany. I kept writing novellas—obviously I didn't have a novel in me. At eight in the morning, I usually cut up a semi-hard baguette (there would be no fresh delivery from André) and press the fetid brie into its pockmarked dough. Then I would have one chunk with butter and marmalade or raspberry preserves while drinking black tea and listening to the supposedly nocturnal mice scurrying behind the oven, expecting more crumbs to have appeared since dawn because they heard me clumsily reciting the French words for certain kitchen utensils.

I looked out the glass doors of the kitchen to a side view of the temple, behind it a few bleak, tawny ziggurats like a theatrical rim of fractures and formations in the distance. I wanted to be mystified by the grandeur in a decay still beautifying, but I shut my eyes by leaving them open in wronghearted desire. Shouldn't I have found imagination in the midden just outside the door? After a few weeks of day-to-day work, an internal program of eating quickly so as to move on to the fields and the first tasks of the day took hold. Now nothing held me. I chided myself, tried to relax and abjure the need for any eye-squeezes. This would be an open day, a pleasure day. I slowly made circles with the large cup of viscous tea, the browny liquid glimmering as if it were sludge. Camus' *L'Étranger*, Gallimard edition, rested on the table; I had also brought along a French/English dictionary. *L'Étranger*—central, but easy. I wanted to start dreaming in French. That was where the real strides would be. It happened sometimes, but much later. I studied the sludge, jangling that bottomless cup as if it were a lasso, a yo-yo. This was to avoid hard work, but, more especially, writing itself. Nowhere to go, no-one to see. The death knell.

To cope during the first weekends, I would mess around like this for an hour: read awhile, write down some definitions, then pull out pages printed in Heidelberg and a bundle of notes housed in a ripped blue folder, before reordering the two sets, the second descending from newest to oldest, though it was already in order. I'd sit back and stack the two piles on the long wooden kitchen table in front of me—the only thing on the property that resembled a desk—only to gaze out of the glass doors to that side view, the risen earth gathering more light, remaining stable with no human involvement, unlike me. Then I'd think about making more tea, my latest cup lukewarm in under two minutes. I'd decide against it. I'd glance at the latest notes: "She is half in love with herself, half in love with the idea of herself" and similar naïve tripe, until I made a bet that I wouldn't start a new sentence until I heard the jiggerings of a mouse, though then it was ten in the morning. And I'd wait... two minutes, five minutes—were they really asleep? A tap behind me, hands and feet scampering through the oven—no. I'd begin with an indefinite article and a noun, the time-honored pufferbelly and coal car of written communication, and I would freeze. Again, eyes up and out the window at the same distant gaunt rocks of earth. With pique disguised as haste, I initially, mistakenly, called them "zircons" and thought about that hard, scaly word, "zircon"—where did it come from? I couldn't find out. I assumed it was Persian or Assyrian, like "ziggurat," but I had no true dictionary. I required lexical history. Games like this would go on for fifteen, twenty minutes, until I'd rouse myself with thoughts of lunch—more baguettes and cheese, carrots and apples from last autumn. I'd already lost some fat, gained some muscle. But after lunch, then what? I'd usually take a hike up the trails that led out of the farm at so many junctures like the arteries of a heart. The trails sometimes passed through other private property, but eventually led to public lands with more unmarked trails going high into a wild upland. Yet on this Saturday, when I approached a full madness, I thought I'd need to do something unique before something I couldn't control would do it for me.

From the table I could also see the long, snaking driveway, at least to the beginnings of the primarily evergreen forest, about a kilometer away. It wasn't uncommon for unannounced cars to motor up the dirt road. It had already happened a few times, and André reminded me it would probably happen again, especially as people searched for the elusive dirt road to deliver them to those untended trails in the upper reaches (Sikhs would eventually come in the warmer months and stay in the temple). Some would get lost and question me, and I would have a hell of a time explaining where to go when I barely knew the area, the layout, the language. I kept locked on that road disappearing in the pine woods beyond. Being too vulnerable, I let fantasy claim me.

Juliette Binoche was making a film nearby. With Louis Malle—no, he was dead. With someone—William Friedkin. Some silly spy film. She had a day off and went driving for some reason—

she liked to get away, lose herself. An expensive vehicle, a film crew car—a Range Rover, given the year. I stand at the table and strain my neck to see the black Rover shooting over the gravel roads. I clamor outside. The car rolls to a stop. She rises with dark, bug-eye sunglasses. I am tall, she is not. She smiles at that. Her English makes everything easier. Yes, I am a caretaker. I'll be here all year. How long is your shoot for? Really—only a few more days. Juliette, have you ever had an affinity for the Sikh religion? Well, it is the world's youngest religion—

The temple doesn't make an impression on her, maybe because it's not a temple. This is where I chop wood, let me take you to where we are planting carrots. Look at these rows. I've nearly made them all. Elise was sick the past few days. You're tired? Well, there's a caravan right over there. I've just changed the sheets. You can have a nice nap. It's very quiet here. Very cozy there. Cold? Plenty of blankets. Oh, that kind of cold. Well, I, um... I haven't shaved for a few days—don't hold that against me.

Hours on, I woke up in that caravan. Emission had occurred. Through the slatted window I could see the temple and the kitchen just beyond. Someone sat at the table. Since the person was writing furiously, I immediately knew it wasn't me. No bother. People were free to come and go. André didn't have many rules—as long as they were working. I studied the shelter of the caravan, still smelling Juliette. She had had to be back at the set for a night shoot.

Outside, the weather had shifted. With a warm rush of wind came the cold rains, spawn of the small mountains. I didn't know the hour—it could have been three or six, given the clouds. After chopping wood, I changed into a slicker I'd found in another caravan, and walked uphill to the pipes connected to the filtration system, which reverse-osmosed the uphill runoff. There had been some problems with a valve, and André wanted me to check it once a day on the weekends. After this, I continued higher up to the public lands, and in a little under an hour I sat in a field of spry wildflowers with a grand easterly vista—beyond it, low clouds where the Alps would be, and below, foothills blurred by mist and pockets of sundowning light. Wisps of my breath preceded my intention to live in what I saw. Above the jagged line of those new coppery hills, the ziggurats below melted away, becoming dissimilar scenery a few thousand feet beyond. Then two low-flying fighter jets passed soundlessly in the direction of the Mediterranean. I waited for the reverberation, but none came. Soon the rain stopped, though the sky darkened. I backtracked. Near a copse of pines were three deer. Their eyes were almond-shaped, unlike any other deer I'd seen. The rain briefly started, then ceased. The deer moved on.

A few years before, following my land internship, I'd spent a month living on Mount Shasta. A woman I'd met had a retreat center there, and she invited me for a few weeks. Jokey and smiling when away, at home she seriously guarded her time and her riches. My main hours were spent digging out gnarly manzanita roots with a pickax to lengthen a walking trail—all this sweat for sleeping in a tent. I'd brought one of my own, though there were empty cabins. Sometimes I'd be thrown off by coyotes yipping through the night or the approach of a snorting boar or mountain lion—even bears were not uncommon—yet she kept suggesting I'd be happier in my tent, while never ruling out my staying in those mostly unlet "writer cabins," as they were billed. If you truly wanted to be in one, she'd said with a queer exhale—since there was a comfortable desk and a chair inside. She knew I was "in the process of" trying to become a writer, whatever that crapulous lingo I used then meant. From the first, I never returned any sexual tension or innuendo—she had thirty years on me—though I smiled to reassure, and maybe that was enough. She had already whisked me onto her turf and could show me off to her various visitors, new-age gurus and musicians, and her friends in the city, while coquettishly mooning to me, as if I were her sister, about the Lotharioized men (often named David or Dravindra) dressed in pirate shirts with abundant chest hair and too many rings on their fingers—skeptically eyeing my naissance but knowing my sexual predatory powers were hampered by youth and Midwestern fish-out-of-water faux coyness, not just lickerish leanings toward books. At night, I dutifully read Henry Miller with a chaser of masturbating to mental images of the few women I'd gone to bed with.

These memories were with me on the plateau in France, not because of Mount Shasta or the woman, but because of Castle Crags State Park just down the road from the mountain and what I did there and what I planned to do on the high rock of the Massif Centrale. Castle Crags and that region in France have a mild geological resemblance, but more so, with their remoteness, a shared feeling of freedom, an abandonment emboldened by my captivity on land very near them. Naked in California, I had run around the last significant flatland before the main crags, in what was my first full view of them nestled together like a pack of giant grungy demons. They are mostly hidden from view on the way up and on I-5, which borders the park on one side. Large stalactite shapes, the crags are granite bodies formed by intrusion underground and are now shown sun by glaciation having ripped off the surrounding rock, leaving them to sell postcards. I snapped out my scrunched penis only when fairly sure no-one was nearby, and in France, leaving my boots on, I did the same. More aware of my hippie stylings the second time, I tried to locate the primalness of our arcane past, until I realized this to be the first time I'd shed everything and trampled around without the yelling and woo-wooing indicative of some Hollywood story of growing up and overcoming what many would be embarrassed to call adversity. Now I carried greater weight, avoirdupois, beginning with the ability to call out my scuzzy ways of avoidance. I ran and then quietly stopped, falling out of measure. Around me were the shale shelves and a few lonely boulders—trickles of remaining rain ran down the slope, off the branches, through the vegetation, falling toward the filtration system to become water I'd soon be drinking.

The day wouldn't end. An hour later a pale wine light clung to the picture before me. I'd gone far into the highlands, clothed, and I came back down half-naked on our neighbor's property. I waved to the shepherd, who I made out standing at an angle from me. He pointed to where I wanted to go. I waved again and then went there. On that jaunt, pitch dark fell like a cloak. Nearly at the steps of the kitchen, I noticed the door open. Some of my papers had blown out. The light I turned on revealed a dozen mice in various poses until a second later they vanished. I would be searching for papers across the property for the next week.

The rain began again. I loaded the fireplace and went to bed, curious about how the next day might proceed.

Sunday—bright with spring sun. I wasn't necessarily better, but I was alive. It began the same as the previous day: at the table. I made a list of the missing pages that in my laziness I hadn't paginated. Forty-seven from the manuscript I had, with eight still missing. I kept examining them. More than half were crinkled with water damage. Then I flipped through my pristine note pile to see doodles and faux inspiration before pressing the pages together and using my arm as a rolling pin to straighten. I dipped a shred of stale, rock-hard baguette in olive oil to soften it, delicately topping it with two leaves of fresh basil. When I finished eating, I picked up the stack, mussed its order by rechecking a note I thought might unlock something, and then went to straighten it again. I ate more. I slipped the papers back into the folder. I opened the browning maps of the area. The rest of the day would be for hiking.

The days lengthened. If I'd counted on improvement in my body's fitness, the results were in. I not only felt strong, I was strong. The same twenty-pound sack of last year's potatoes I'd struggled with when loading it into someone's car in March now felt a third lighter. To test, I carried two at once, the bottom halves leaning against each breastplate and shoulder. Not too bad. Four weeks.

One day, Elise made a comment about my arms. That felt good. The wave of attention went right through me, and luckily the baggy junkie blue jeans hid the hard-on. There would be nothing. And I didn't want it, though I wanted to elope with her sentence, even if a slippage. She pined after her childhood love in Dijon, but he had turned out to be a phony. Years on and she wouldn't give up—all this came from André, who liked to talk. My listenership cemented our trust. I'd been people's sounding board before. In Ireland I'd been an easy mark in pubs, and old men would corner me, stretching their Franz Hals faces to laugh the drunken laugh of forgetfulness, though all they offered was their past and how good everything had once been. I could never be grateful enough that Elise hadn't confided in me about her history. We did speak more about the language when working together, and she threw me French to help, even though with the labor in front of me I could be vexed to offer the proper conjugation, the words most fitting my feelings.

Sometime in those weeks, I'd stopped wondering when the other people would arrive and accepted the time as it was. I almost liked being the sole caretaker at night and on the weekends. It called up the film I'd centered on most in my early life, *The Shining*. I wouldn't say I was completely comfortable, but I was content. There were barely any mirrors on the property, just two, in the good close caravan and in a far one, by the shepherd's property. If I came near either, I was very conscious not to look. It would only move things in a direction I'd been wanting to avoid. Sometimes the German catatonic spell reared, but I tweaked it and its strength diminished to single occasional vestiges, which might pack into five minutes here or there after a long day's work.

My weekend routine changed. Because almost everything shut down on Sundays, around ten in the morning on Saturday, I walked to the main road and hitched the seven miles to Châteauneuf-les-Orgues. My tall figure in those dirty jeans and a green Eugene Celebration T-shirt—the raggedy, torn, and holey one I wore during the week—marked me as the outsider, a Brit, or an American if they knew their minor US cities.

The hub of the commune's population of under a thousand was the circular centre-ville, with a few ruins from the consecration time of the area's most notable landmark, thirty kilometers away: Notre-Dame de Lure, an abbey from the twelfth century.

Within the centre-ville's traditional round layout was a main square, though traffic circled it in an oval. In the square's mostly vacant middle, a farmers' market took place every few days, though André kept to selling in larger cities—Carpentras, Orange, maybe Sisteron—to make the travel time worthwhile. To appear ordinary and not just linger, I would buy a few carrots and some lettuce—the first of the season, some offshoot but upgrade of Boston lettuce. It was so buttery-tasting, I blotted olive oil on it only once from my small vial. I sat on a public bench in the square, munching these vegetables and what was left of my Friday morning baguette for lunch. I'd never say anything beyond the order and a *merci*, and would then sit, eating slowly for almost an hour, a book open for show on my lap. If I wore sunglasses, I'd be more suspicious-looking. Yet people left me alone. Some seemed to know what I was doing there and that I worked all week just to have this.

Even if I couldn't articulate it then, a strange apprehension kept following me around: I wouldn't be very surprised if someone did kill me. They wouldn't have a good reason—I was often quiet and respectful—but they wouldn't need one. Because if they decided to end my life, what could I do about it? Maybe it wouldn't have to do with my quietude—they couldn't read into that so well. Maybe I'd come to take their wife or daughter into my arms and make them crazy. Yes, America had ruined me, and I would ruin them. My only antecedent to this living was my few years in small-town USA. But the more ill-at-ease cliques there worked in sham-minded superstitious torpors, with gossip sloppy and pitiful whether deserved or not, and whatever the ideas, being reconciled to truth was very low on the list. Even when I was visiting the community called 'The Farm' in Tennessee, all the people other than my lover were always surly, mistrustful, and moving away. Well, I did have a sign pinned to me: *Stay the fuck back.*

Baguette-, carrot-, and lettuce-infused, I filled my water bottle at a public spigot and hustled over to the D113 to hitch a ride to the abbey up the grade. Cast in the higher hills like so many prominent structures of lost times, it was heavily shaded by a stand of large beeches, possibly planted around the time the abbey had been designated a pilgrimage site in the 1700s. Inside, a dour atmosphere: a narrow chamber with two rows of pews facing two long windows, and a couple of statues, some candles. No sound. No spectacle. Get on your knees or get out. My meanderings around this eight-hundred-year-old structure became ritual enough for some weeks. Behind the abbey were large patches of grass where one could escape the onslaught of tourists' cameras at the front framing the stark line of the bell, the oculus, and the front doors, one on top of another and between trees, to preserve a harmonious pose for posterity. In the back, I sat zazen or lounged otherwise, a millimeter of denim separating the earth from my oily skin (often next to a garden full of lavender, domain of the caretaker). The abbey's hindquarters had a few rectangular additions mounted over time, and walls of white rock, with a roof made of small stone tablets assembled in fish-scale patterns, extending to cover each new station. Beyond it were denser beech forests, on ground gradually ascending, almost by steps, and sometimes I would take up a covert position on a small rise with an arching view of the abbey's back side. I listened in on the sound bites of visitor language, most of which I could understand—when we are confronted with beauty, words are at their most un-unique and quickly crest and drown away, ashamed at their frivolity. C'est beau. No shit.

In my European journeys I'd often ended up at old churches—a touristic commonplace. Once I took a cheap slow train out of Lisbon, to get to the not-quite-famous Templar church in Tomar, installing myself at a primitive campsite, though they sold grilled cod, so I could be one of a couple of dozen people on that day to visit this lesser-known but guide-marked site. I wanted to be near a history so far removed from the fanfare, it would make my pilgrimages worse than futile—all my longing would be eased, and, I hoped, with it, my need to exist. What would I do with those experiences? Become the lovelorn guy who takes excruciatingly exquisite black-and-white pictures of ancient cathedrals? Upload my hobby to the internet for all to see, even offering prints for sale? For bragging rights? I never had a camera with me on these quests, but I could still switch to this mythical man in spirit. Perhaps I had already done so? Having grown up on technology and celebrity worship, I could never drop the omnibus of our collective egos, dry-drunking my way through the last hours of the twentieth century. Those traveling days had already grown sepia-toned. Days of looking and exploring, mostly tight-lipped. Watching the people around me, afraid of them and yearning for them. Soldiering on in front of the dusty, bitter-scented tapestries in the Palais des Papes in Avignon, wishing I could say to someone, *What do you see? Pretty goddamned interesting wouldn't you say, if you could speak my tongue?* These unhappy fantasias of comparison must be how experience infuses feelings with some deeper, apocryphal sense of worth—a subjugation few would call better off than the deliberate squandering of life. Youth is not wasted on the young, because that green consciousness doesn't recognize regret, it doesn't greedily page through past time with the growing mold of the middle years.

There I sat, my sit bones going weak, but not jellied enough for me to upbraid myself to stretch. I had to keep fixed in faux penance, looking at that rear view of the abbey with its crusty entablature. No dome, no gaudy views. White and nothing else. Quiet, powerful, and apart. Not like the most famous church of my youth. It jutted up beaconlike after we were coasting down a decline of I-94 in a southerly direction, just after the downtown's Marquette interchange, with its nexus of major freeways twisting and spiraling in a debasement of what the French can do with concrete—rounded with a bouquet of a yeasty flatulence from the many breweries nearby. Around the Basilica of Saint Josaphat (though we said "Josapfat" instead of "fit") lay the sprawl of South Milwaukee, with the steeples of smaller churches marking the landscape every few miles or so—while beneath and undetectable were the famous bars and beer halls of an area heavily populated by the working class. The basilica was constructed in 1900 in the Polish-cathedral style as a church aimed at Milwaukee's growing population of Polish Catholics, who were just behind the Germans in immigration at the time. We spoke of the basilica in hushed tones because there was nothing else like it in our crestfallen city. Trips from our house to this district, only two miles away, were infrequent, though a great-aunt lived nearby. And one tends to ignore what one's town is known for—I passed the basilica in a city bus every morning and afternoon for four high school years, but it never stood out, because I was at the beginning of that great phase known as "I hate most everything now that I'm old enough." One couldn't see its splendor from the restricted view of a bus seat anyway. The Pope declared the basilica a pilgrimage site in 1929. It's still there, full of some kind of dybbuk power. Presently, the online reviews of the basilica are positive: "Amazing church with amazing liturgy," and "You just feel the presence of God." The algorithms even tell you that on Mondays around two p.m., the church is "usually not busy."

When I was taking in the confluence of the thatched sloping roofs of the abbey, memories of Saint Josaphat's assaulted, though the basilica's model, St. Peter's in Rome, had been three hundred years away when Notre-Dame de Lure was built. Was it strange how I had to go across the Earth to find that my roots and my butt-of-many-jokes birth city mattered more than I thought? I took in those ordinary roofs and compared them to the basilica's dome not by necessarily remembering the latter, but by conjuring my family—at the time I might have been introduced to the basilica, say the early years, when my memories begin to track month to month, instead of episodically until age five. And when I studied the abbey's bare backside, over the course of those Saturdays, the oscillating temperature of the spring winds sometimes pushing me to put on or remove my brown fleece, I remembered, more keenly, blunting my mind to pull the needle through the thread and behold the peeling granite cheeks of my father or the high, piercing tone of my mother's exhortations for me to do something around the house. It happened in a rush. I became further from my parents while not being old enough to see that these people were more a part of me than my limbs. In communing with that relic of Europe's bloody religious history, I foolishly cast myself as apart from—not better than—and in concord with the duplicitous Jim Morrison bullshit ("I never talked to my father again") that is as widespread as it is dispassionate—a false badge of honor—good only for an insert of dialogue in a screenplay. I was thinking a new chapter of my life was beginning. It wasn't, I still wasted time, even if it was only the weekend, abounding in fruitless searchings, restoring out to seed memories, and gardening sparely among the eclipsing lights inherent in sun-drenched youth. And as usual when someone plunges about too much in the shallows of the mind, finding no way to the depths, I did what so many do—I hurried away to have a drink.

Bar Mirceau was one of the two establishments I found. More rightly a saloon, it suited more of my needs. In the first pages of *Crime and Punishment*, a sad one in Saint Petersburg is described. At basement level, it is a quiet, dank place of menace: "Unbearably stale, the atmosphere... so thoroughly soaked with alcohol..." I spit on the idea of the American sports bar with multiple TVs blaring, feeding our robotic impulses eye-candy to ignore the living. In France, people sat and drank, some talked. I required the forced anonymity of silence or shell-shocking improvisation. I figured that in these small French towns, the watering holes I would find might resemble my preferred—a place fostering an enormous man who tugged at his megabeard, an older woman who'd put on too much face glowering at everything with a heartbeat, and the other provincials who smelled like piss or cat piss, along with the meanest drunks imaginable. At Bar Mirceau I scored my fantasy, and from that dream I made more daydreams. The space: not too big, but wide enough for me to disappear in a corner. On the walls, small old landscapes, a marooned schooner on a beach, something green, gray, and slurging, like a Courbet but nowhere nearly as fine. Here or there a cobweb in the underseat of the bentwood chairs. The bar had a long mirror, flashing me back to Manet's *Bar at the Folies-Bergère*, something I'd once thought fructified the sanctity of French culture—no, new doubts darkly swarmed. Even if made at roughly the same time, Dostoyevsky's Saint Petersburg bar might not have such a grand mirror, but beyond this I would never sit at the bar, only at an open table. A sweating, barrel-chested barkeep with a full scalp of impeccably kept silver hair nudged his eyebrows up in expectation. I would order in an oarlocked manner, in a cotton-mouthed accent, having to repeat my request for a simple beer until the fourth Saturday. To my mind, with that first pour, he went from disinterested to more grandfatherly, though his eyes scoured the grill under the taps, toggling between accepting his life and blaming customers for it.

Over the course of those first weeks I equivocated, too, stoking the combustibility of a very old and ugly feeling: being unwanted. Did the barkeep really contain his shifting countenance, or had I created it? I bowed, I walked to my table, I drank. These concerns didn't struggle to leave me. But time moved them back on my shore, because I didn't want to plumb that sickening question of my pusillanimity. Then I'd turn and see him in a presumptive light, bending forward over the bar, the white towel on his shoulder expertly folded, doing one of those puzzles in the paper. He was just a worker, and he had made his life his own. A wife, a kid or two—and no-one was happy at work. Nothing special, just a guy. Then, slowly, a gauze would plainly overtake his features because of the one determined to make a better nest on mine. I couldn't get to the core of him, and I'd never know someone who would help me to. I'd need to figure it out alone, and by my second beer I'd abandoned such hope, preferring a quagmire. I didn't know it all amounted to finding out about my lonely self. Who else could make my life come to truth?

Sitting at the small short table that the tops of my thighs would lift up if straightened, I decided to drop the poseur spell I displayed at the square and the abbey. I took out a lined notebook and a pen to muse, to dabble. A free-spirited aunt who'd lived in France told me that once I was armed with my writerly paraphernalia, people would leave me alone—they'd know I was just another American in love with van Gogh's myth, searching for inspiration. I had nothing to write—everything I thought up I immediately judged as puerile, merely coping. I'd have to talk to someone, but if I had the notebook and kept writing down misremembered phrases from Shakespeare, no-one would touch me. At that age, in that bar, I couldn't clearly see the face I made to those around me, despite the mirror, which I had to avoid—and I did so by superimposing the Manet painting where I would be if reflected. If I switched from a frown to a half-frown, I didn't know how long I'd been frozen in the former. But I wasn't there to be seen, only to see. I supposed people would know that. And I didn't want to get drunk, I didn't want to make myself fall to or find a woman of the night, some sloe- or doe-eyed beauty to save me. So nearly everything about my attendance in this quiet, unswept bar came out to an improbability; something tarnished, without honor or accreditation, worse than using an exercise tape to exercise—potlatched, a ruse only a nutty American would come up with, led by his own unhinged assertions of reality. What I did might attract a few women who dug the Orpheus vibe, probably because they'd been raised on whiny eighties British pop, but the people I would want to care about me would never envy those month-long, sparks-before-courting fuckscapades.

At that time, early evening, unaccompanied men much older would walk in purposefully. After a day of Saturday work, they stood at the bar because they were there only for a brief time before they had to get back to their unalterable lives. They took no more than a minute with their liquor—a complete about-face from the tendency of my countrymen to hunker down as if in a den and imbibe continuously, deepening their depression, celebrating their swamp. The European stands, coarsely but meditatively. When you encounter one, you might think how arch and fastidious, feeling yourself being silently put in your place. No. To stand is the best approach to their problems. Once, aboard a four-hour train from Toulouse to Marseille, I witnessed a man, well-attired with no combover to his thinning hair, take a stance at the window side as we left the depot. Leaning into the breeze, he smoked and skirted his attention across the passing landscape for every minute of the journey. Although it was irksome at the time, I now recast this incident as a thing of beauty—his endurance, his willingness to absorb the latest injustices dealt to him, called up those heavy, heaving gladiatorial bones of the Gauls, some meters under that speeding train.

The men in Bar Mirceau weren't slapping the bar or asking the barkeep to make them happy in any backhanded manner. They drank and left. Or drank two, then three, then left. Unknowingly, I believe, I'd chosen a "men's" bar. Though I never came in on any other day of the week, I'd peek, when with André on an errand, to see the same barkeep or a different man, with a similar body, along with mostly checkered male ensembles. Women were just scarce, or they didn't exist as public drinkers for ten or twenty miles. Yes, the odd couple would come in and delight in two glasses of wine, but a woman as a type of life-size-piñata center of attention, as in American bars—no, not there, though I didn't dwell on this then, a few months into my skimpy tenure.

One late afternoon, sitting with my first beer at a different table than my usual, I noticed a man straddling a stool in mixed attention. I'd not seen him before. He appeared local, yet his face didn't. His face lacked the French-male features—what they were I couldn't fully describe, certainly not the swelled aquiline nose of the region. And then a word floated up to me like a long, slithering piece of help: *Minnesota.* I hardly ever saw him in the bar again, but when I met him months later, in André's village at the harvest celebration called Bénichon, he said, Michigan, with a shy smile. A Midwesterner who'd met a Frenchwoman in the Peace Corps, then got married, had children, and here he was. He told me why he left—the hypocrisies, the bestial manners—but didn't push me to stay gone, too. I was able to recognize the breadth of his character and respect him for it.

I stayed at Bar Mirceau for no more than three hours, but to sit for even one was morose. If my buddies could see me now—that phrase flitted around my brainpan until I became so hot, I decided to never think in such a fashion again. That false breast-beat—it equaled a fishing for envy. I should have been ascertaining my outward makeup, but I chose the past. Dostoyevsky kept creeping back to me then, shifting me to my late teens. I fondly recalled coming home from supper one summer night to continue reading *Crime and Punishment,* to sit in my childhood living room and inhale the words in the gray light of an endless June evening as I turned the small, brittle, almost moldy pages of that pocket paperback—it was the original from my father's bookcase. I thought Dostoyevsky would appreciate my reading his work in probably the same unelectrified evensong many scenes took place in, the same light he wrote it in, and in the summer setting of the novel itself. Wouldn't he like it more if I wrote about it? Write about reading when young?—but I couldn't pivot into even a consideration of that question. Some of us need to remember our lives over a course of years before there is material. And if I thought like this then, I wouldn't have done the age-appropriate work—the watching and listening, losing oneself on the road to the slaughterhouse. Those un-American days, hours—they made me, and sitting at the foot of Notre-Dame de Lure or in the bar counted as the first spate of events I remembered with a yen toward living in them at some future hour.

I did not celebrate the harvest then, but maybe a decade later. A few times a month I would recall that matrix—not a specific scene in the novel, just the act of reading, but as if I had read the events of Dostoyevsky as I lived them in small-town France. In Brooklyn, I cultivated this way of being and came alive with the lived art passing through my consciousness, a kaleidoscope I slowly turned to absorb all the translated words describing not Raskolnikov, but me—and I would wish to share this memory in vivid language with my wife, my life. But if I ever had recourse to tell, later at dinner, after it had bubbled up in the afternoon while writing, I would summarily dismiss it, feeling it campy and overwrought. I may have been protecting myself from not getting the response I wanted or perhaps keeping it concealed as part of my secret world that no-one would ever know, because it hadn't been catalogued on paper or on computer or in email. Do you enjoy being enigmatic? my wife said at some bend in our relationship, but I waved it away—just then coming upon what the main character should do next in my latest novel, destined to be diluted by a hack editor. I had intercalated that time with my year in Châteauneuf-Les-Orgeus like tightly bound pages jammed into great sheaves, like cards shuffled by a beginner trying to make the deck look pretty.

The first significant visitors of the season were a family of four from the German-speaking part of Switzerland. Passing through the country, with some tangential connection to André, they stayed for four nights and did no work, because the mother nursed a baby and the three-year-old boy occupied the wide-eyed father, a man with an uneven haircut and a thin beard growing only in zigzags. I thought some company might be a nice diversion, but the boy cried constantly, even if he didn't hurt himself. The days grew long, and André pretended the disturbance wasn't happening, while Elise unaccountably took the rest of the week off.

Near the barn, away from mother and baby, I saw the father slap the sullen boy to the ground. He couldn't know I had a vantage from up the hill. After waiting some seconds, he picked the boy up and wildly jiggled him, before hugging tight. This episode made me believe I understood something syllogistically, but I comprehended nothing. We see much, but seeing is not enough. One realization keeps us nourished until a better one comes along. We can't know too much about life when young, and we won't remain so fixed in that perspective anyway. How to imagine being older?

After the family left, I recounted the incident to André. His silence sent me into a horripilated trance. No assurances, no explanations. I had erred, I was being impolite. Nothing more was mentioned.

The first workers to join Elise, André, and me in the fields were a young couple from Brussels who brought a four-month-old puppy with them. They were transients and would eat out of garbage cans wherever they landed, but when desperate, they had a source. Someone's mother or father would wire funds. All this came to me during the weeks of their residence, a period when they melded with and sometimes nearly stood for the types I had known in Oregon and California. The girl: bug-eyed with greasy hair and no bra. She stared at men too long and liked to call out Spirit and lead morning yoga before work. The man, gaunt from wandering, wore a kind of young communist outfit, a beige military shirt with epaulets—up top were glasses and a messy Vandyke. He had a miniature mandolin strapped to his back each day until André instructed him to please leave it at their caravan until lunchtime—he should not be weeding with it on.

The puppy kept getting in the way, and then it would go off and get lost, and they'd go searching for an hour. Though André had free-range thoughts about almost anything, he requested they keep the brown bundle on a leash.

When André wasn't there—a few hours, usually in the middle of the day—the couple would start to fall away from the work, finding a way into their personal mischief. The woman would initially disappear, and then after about ten minutes, the man would set out to find her. They carried an intricate store of young-relationship problems, going hot and cold many times over the long days full of nothing but sun, wind, and scents. I didn't want to know, but how could I not? The young man confided. She doesn't want me to love her all the time. She says it's too much. Just do it lightly, I need freedom, she says. I've tried everything. Too lightly is too much. Ignore her, and then is not enough. I strained to respond. This described all my entanglements, from one side or the other.

We were in the shade of the granary, just after lunch, squatting, bundling old onions. I could smell my unwashed crotch, which I'd only get to with a cold shower before supper. That dream the night before. It wasn't Ruth or the Belgian girl, or even La Binoche—it wasn't human. I'd be laughed off the continent if I took to proselytizing the experience in spiritual terms—yes, ether had a role, and maybe a certain succubus could almost round out the picture. I laughed off my improprieties in favor of wanting to comfort this man beside me, this version of my once beating heart. I said, Look, and made the second and third digits of my two hands into legs, facing each other, poised on the dirt below them. I said, A woman I knew some years ago showed me this—a history of nearly all romantic relationships. The right hand's fingers walked closer to the left's, but slowly. Soon the left's retreated a few finger steps. The right's bore in and the left's retreated more. The right's rushed in and the left's rushed out, backing far away. The right's stopped, waited—then retreated, stopped, then went back more. Soon the left's came forward, slowly, then paused. Then they closed fast to catch up with the right's, and soon they were fingers to fingers. A pause, a deliberation. Then the left's started retreating again. The prior motions repeated. I smiled a frown and examined him—his glasses were fallen on the ridge of his protuberant nose, with four small spikes of hair growing from the nub. He pulled in his lips. I like it, he said. Like it.

Yeah, do you see it? I said.

See? *Oui, bien sûr*. I see. I need to show to her, and he stood quickly.

Wait, I said, maybe just wait on that.

Why?

I don't know. Maybe on a good day? A day when you are happier together.

Non, man. She take it now or never.

The jape went on. Elise barely said anything. She even seemed upset with me, as if I caused the couple to continue. I knew this wasn't so, but only in retrospect. The puppy wasn't cute anymore. The couple needed to exit. Though Elise wasn't required to be there, André called a meeting, making it plain the work, the land, had to come first. And certainly the morning yoga sessions had to come to an end—I'd abandoned them days before, when they started dragging into morning chores—or else occur during the break in the afternoon or at night. The girl began bickering with André in French. The puppy kept yelping. The young man, who had begun to wear the mandolin again, started strumming. I joined Elise to tend to the rows of lettuce and pull off some romaine leaves. I guess it's hard to find good workers, I said to her in French. She nasally hissed out some air in the vain Francophone way. It's the same everywhere—I'm sure you're wise enough to understand this, she said, in perfect English. Unsettling, these words snapped me out of my torpor, making me think I was being shadowed constantly, watched and censured for my laziness in relation to others, and that my inability to reach out and be intimate, but not sexually, was really at issue. I had a gift for taking things out of context and worming them into a biography dependent on its future's being immediately fulfilled. I carried this thorn for a while, but she never activated her English in such a rearguard manner again. It left like a flock of migratory birds at change of season and never found its way back.

Time passed. The couple had long left, though the man returned alone a few weeks later, looking for a book he'd forgotten. He had lunch with us but said little. After, as he walked back down the drive to the main road, I saw him stop, squat, and cry into his hands. By the time I decided to proceed and care for him, he had risen and left.

Others came and went. In June, André's family would begin to stay a few nights a week, and when school ended, they'd be here much more.

The energy would be changing. A few workshops would be starting soon: in organic gardening, yoga, and qigong. My sanctuary to cease, it would be like a small village. I would be visiting the south in a month or so—but where? Only the tourists went south in summer—and the title of tourist still belonged to me. I'd gotten through two months, and I'd made peace with the longueurs. I wanted to believe that everybody tried to destroy any equilibrium achieved. Some days I was young enough to believe so. That stain remained. I didn't know what to do so I continued to live with it. Everybody else did.

One Friday, just before the summer-ending mark of six-thirty, André approached with wide strides as I knelt between rows of vines, pockmarked leaves, squash, and slimy neon afterbirth. Because I'd been weeding and clearing all week, my pants were caked with days' worth of grime. There would be guests tonight, he alerted. Can you come help me clean up the temple?

The first Sikh visitors of the season were about two hours away. Three extremely large white vans of young Sikhs from London had crossed the Channel, had driven through the entire country, and were now climbing the southern elevations. They were headed for the Mediterranean coast. But they weren't going to make it—they needed a stopover. Somehow, sixty people were going to sleep in the temple.

They arrived just after nine in a chilling dusk. I counted sixty-two, a few more women than men. They were about my age, beautifully vibrant people who'd been in those air-conditioned vans much too long. I didn't think they fully understood what it was they were in for. Many asked after the showers, and I pointed to them, but had to add that there would be only cold water. The women thought I was joking. Then I showed them the scant quarters, not separated by sex. André had assembled a stand of towels with three large bars of soap. I offered to boil water for the visitors. Recoiling, but saved by their youth, they talked their way into accepting the situation.

A jolly bunch. Everyone seemed to know each other from top to bottom—the eccentricities, foibles, what they needed to forgive in others and what they loved. It wasn't necessarily like college, but that was the only experience I could align it with. The tight fittingness and support of the group: something I'd eschewed, but forever desired. Perhaps that's why it gave me immense joy to bring people into contact, to introduce different friends and smush them together on the basis of commonalities, an act only making their embarrassed smiles more ungainly.

The frenzy of sixty-two souls, plus two. Beauty left, beauty right—front and center in their nut-brown faces, for they all had blood dawning on the Indian subcontinent. A parade of sound, that spritz of affective English, the voice in the souls. They overfilled the space. I suddenly couldn't see my failings so easily—and it scared me. Every time they laughed, or goofed off, or teased, I knew I needed the sunfire of separation to keep me boiling in my murky miasmas. While they became more settled, pulling linens and belongings into the temple, I went off to a higher ridge. The stars were beyond bright in a sky with a trace of purply charcoal. In retreat, I regained some agita, as well as appreciating the group's formation and unfoldings, its improbable aura protecting me from dangerous forces. It was André, me—and them. If someone came for me, I could easily swim back to the group—they'd hold me if I cried loud enough.

When I returned some forty minutes later, a plan of action had been set in motion. A dozen women were packed in the kitchen, making dinner, stretching out flour to construct bhatoora, small fried breads, for everyone. André continued preparation at the temple, where there would be what I could only call revels: singing, a meal, and then, much later, at two in the morning, or so I thought, sleep as the only way to curtail celebration.

I couldn't fall asleep for a while. The beautiful women in designer jeans, the creamy dark-calico faces, arms, and ankles; the perspective of sixty-two people sleeping head-to-foot in a space I'd once claimed for myself. So I did covet. My childhood tower rose again. Those slippery embattlements against my lost friends, against many, were proud to be erect again. The crenellations had to be refined. So much raced in me, whether good or bad I couldn't say, but I spun, literally. A vertigo of sorts. Even on my stomach, I kept feeling on end or turning end over end, forsaken in space.

I wanted to be over there with them, but I didn't have a place, a real enough reason. I had been shown the pearly spiritual way of life. Call it dharma, as they would have, or Tao, or Christ-consciousness—it all comes to the same thing. That only briefly engaged me. They had the group, but beyond, they had one another, sociability keeping them proper and bounteous. Loneliness has the power to kill. My worst night of sleep in years.

Up at seven I already saw a few early risers, all yawning men, walking the grounds, filing in and out of the kitchen with cups of tea. The poor mice—so many more crumbs but so many more people. André had also awakened. He greeted me, wondering why I hadn't come to the feast, to the singing. It was hard to break my schedule.

I refilled my water bottle in the kitchen and made my kind of tea, grabbing a few leftover but still tasty bhatoora. I offered the pot to those who straggled inside. Two women arrived, and we came to talking. They weren't shy, and asked after me in a way I could only recognize years later as featherweight flirting—a bashful signaling, by which the knowing gives a lengthy look at the hunted, chagrined at how the pursued can't be so fruitfully developed to grasp what they think obvious. We stepped outside, into the sun. The taller, very attractive woman had that crisp, street-smart London accent like the voice of English literature itself—Lear by way of Brontë, Shelley, and Woolf's vocals. Hoda, her name. She commented favorably on my ruined wardrobe. The whites of her eyes, turned out of the sun, were like miscolored magnets. The group planned to find the beaches with spiking-hot sand, probably Nice—to swim in the blue, blue waters. More of the visitors assembled, and the energy expanded in clusters and nodes rather than in one big gale. Waves of bizarre origin came over me—I wasn't conscious of my facial mechanizing. Where would they stay in Nice? Haut Soleil, a Riviera hotel, and probably a few others. Why didn't I come along with them? Comical, but a notion delivered only when the mood was right. I sloughed it off, laughing girlishly, quietly cherishing the invitation. Wouldn't it be something? Sixty-two Sikhs—and me. Everyone wants stories, but even more so anecdotes. What could it mean beyond, in my future? Sitting at a dinner party and sharing the tale of trotting on the beach with all of them, arms hugging in a Rockettes line. Photos later mailed to the farm, kept for years in a shoebox to prove it and disfigure the memory with each glance. Recounting that high number of people again and again—all tied to an outrageous punch line: who was the one who couldn't take her eyes off you? My wife sidelonging—the glance that says, My once wild hubby.

I had no great investment in André's farm, though I'd already agreed to keep working until the middle of July and then travel. But the chorus requesting I accompany grew from two to four, four to seven, and soon they were showing me the open rear seat in the one all-women's van (couples and men shared the other two). Suddenly a sound of supersonic nature exploded overhead, and they looked toward the noise, which lagged far behind the originators—two low-flying fighter planes, which had fired on the afterburners and shot onward to the Alps. Since I'd been through this a few times, I knew enough to crane my head in the opposite way to get the least glimpse before disappearance. Everyone celebrated for a minute, then they went back to trying to persuade me.

It would have been like me to do such a thing then, abruptly duck out on some large venture. For years, I'd avoided college, or I couldn't find the right job and settled for couches rather than paying my way through hate. I'd been frozen, unable to see past the stones I'd tried to move to teach myself value, but, more so, understand how impetuous fortune is mythical. Nothing was going to just fall into my lap, and if it ever did, I'd be so busy with other machinations, I wouldn't conceive of it as sprung from my own districts. Like the invitation to Nice. I didn't ask for it, but it arrived so naturally, I'm sure Hoda's friend, who first suggested it, didn't debate its implications but just uttered the words as they flashed before the last of the tongue lashings. This freshet of suggestion, which I swore to be the desire of all sixty-two of them, I would hold onto—taking it with me for a while. I knew how to live off broth, and this was a cornucopia.

My declination was finally accepted. Before leaving, Hoda gave me a solid hug and her address—postcards were still in vogue. The first van started to drive off, and they wanted to stay close to one another on the highway. Hoda raced into the last van and waved through the window. André and I stood there watching the departure. For thirteen hours the farm had become another world—it all ended suddenly. He would go home and get some sleep. I would walk about not completely sure I'd done right by not going. I did want to be in their bubble, their womb. I wanted to keep laughing, though it's possible I'd have been deceived. Best behaviors would step aside, they would see me for who I was. Maybe. I still knew how to keep aloof without knowing how I did so, putting off guilt for another decade.

Midday on June sixteenth, the corona of the sun at its apex quintupled, setting fire to my core. I wasn't ready for all those hidebound days of Germany to be blanched out of me. Reading about the awful Mediterranean sun in Camus didn't help. The first of the workshops started and the property filled. In my off-hours, I was invited to attend any of them for free, since many would be held over weekends—diverse Far East-based classes I could ground myself in. But no. And not a result of the old teenybopper urge—to make myself appear special—but in a shiny new victimy faux-martyr way: the more maturing epitome of caring what others think of you. This had been inherited from my betters and their hot/cold burnishings—the endgame being to foist projections back on those they viewed as their oppressors. The object of such a game is to draw attention and, one hopes, pity, to one's self—a practice I had employed when in wily congress with my boyhood friend all those years ago, though I had no idea. Yet, strike three again on the farm—no-one cared that I didn't join in.

Some Saturdays I still did a town run, and two I spent with Scarlet, a young woman from the Bay Area, showing off the abbey until I dropped the tour-director act and just let her explore. She'd only promised to work on the farm for a few days, but stayed two weeks. Scarlet came from a family of professors and rightly abhorred academia—traveling in lieu of going to college. Diminutive, she wore John Lennon glasses, had long, straight amber hair and an olive complexion signaling her half-Italian heritage. She spoke less than I did, and so, at first, I toiled to make our shared space comfortable, but soon I picked up the cues. She also accompanied me on those long Sunday hikes: ten, twelve, maybe fifteen miles. Foolishly, we'd set out at midday and had to endure the endless uphill switchbacks in the worst heat; reenergized, we returned in a cooling dusk. The young often do things ass-backward. Obeying an unarticulated though agreed-upon rule, we barely spoke in those first grueling stages of the hike. She could trust me, and though I'd never left a diary opened to my most carnal secrets, she understood I wouldn't try to bed her. Animals base their lives on the intimacies of scent, and we are no different if we care to prop instinct up to its rightful position. We'd even hug each other goodnight sometimes. It made no matter. I don't know what exactly we shared on those hikes, but we must have come at the world in a similar way. I never saw her again.

André's wife, Françoise, was a bony woman who wore stretched tops to easily and lackadaisically breastfeed the one-year-old girl who toddled after her. With her widely set eyes and greasy, unwieldy dark hair, she resembled the seventies Patti Smith. We didn't talk much. When Elise came, they were often together—unsurprisingly, since Elise worked with her at the school some days. The other children, a six-year-old boy and a three-year-old girl, flocked to Elise when their mother was busy with the baby.

Françoise seemed to take me for a dependable worker—the rock of the season. Sometimes a shy smile escaped her, but no more. She'd been on the farm long enough not to be taken aback by anything. And I would have thought she'd been raised in the countryside, but no—the sixteenth arrondissement, a father still high up at the bank. Every day some other bubble of mine was burst.

I played ball, as in throwing or catching a rubber ball or kicking a soccer ball, with the boy a few times. But it became rote quickly. We couldn't talk about anything. He had a harelip and, facewise, more resembled his mother. A strange patch of brilliant white hair grew on the back of his head. I didn't ask. One of us would miss a catch, and the ball rolled into some high weeds or tumbled down the drive, and the other, usually me, would put his hands up and say, *D'accord,* signaling an end. We'd both go our separate ways.

The sun continued to broil me inside out. I wanted to sleep the whole day and think at night. If I had to toil, I sought to do so in the shade of towering vegetation. The skyscraping corn, like a silent army of seven-footers, reminded me how words were meaningless here—maybe forever. I heard Bach in those excruciatingly long sunsets and the gravelly vocals of Beckett's narrators. I should have hoped to be in love. Three weeks since the night of the Sikhs. The high-altitude heat brought out clusters of scents, and slightly honeyed huffs from wildflowers like cowslips, marguerites, and several varieties of orchises. Almost overnight, the garlic stalks shot up two feet above the ground. Just when I began to realize how grateful I was to the land and how invested I might be—I felt an urge to get away. The blazing sun didn't serve me. The nights were comfortably cool, but the days were interminable. Heat overcame all the caravans. Only one, the worst, was available then, and stifling; I choked on the high-pitched smell of old fabrics boiling up their dust whenever I entered for a nap. So I pitched a tent on an upper ridge, under a stand of pines. It faced the shepherd's property, which was cut from ours by a long-dead rill, now just a narrow channel for the high-desert miniature tumbleweeds to descend. Warm winds in the shade were better than anything else I could find—besides, the main buildings were full of workshop attendees, André's family, and the half-dozen other workers on the property.

My body continued its metamorphosis. I was so fit I felt I could model from the neck down. I had to punch three new holes in my belt to fit preposterously puffy jeans onto my dwindling hips and ass. André finally offered to give me a pair of baggy dress slacks he never wore for the days I went to town. Maybe the change helped with my low-grade anxiety. I didn't get rock-tired like in the first two months, when I had no trouble falling asleep in any location. Something else had been born—sometimes I couldn't feel my feet on the ground. Especially in the afternoon, I couldn't dispel these surges of energy wanting to push me on, into another dimension. Yet farm work didn't drain them. There was no outlet.

My naps in the stultifying heat were of a different order, full of feverish chimeras and sheepish oracles. I moved a wet washcloth around on my naked body, occasionally dipping it in a bowl. I felt as far away from writing as I'd ever been. No literary thought I carried belied any hint of profundity. Not that I even had anything important to say. From the start, my way down the writing road progressed in piths and gists and with sloppy attentions—I hoped, someday, the muse would unfold. I didn't think getting down on my knees and begging would help, though it had been suggested. I hadn't read for weeks, though I'd only be re-reading what I'd already read in English, the ghost of Camus's *L'Étranger*, or again cracking John Berger's leftist *G.*, running over the sections I'd once made an undulating line around the second time I'd read it in California. I made selflove infrequently, which I counted as a modest, though bittersweet success. Those uncindered urges pointed to the bacchanalian, but they weren't of Bacchus in themselves. More floreal and vegetal, I was just like what I had worked so closely with for three months—a reproductive energy, though bereft of a vessel.

Once folded, I liked to center the washcloth over my eyes, because of a nerve disorder that made the vision in my left break into two, the top separating to the right and the bottom to the left. I wished to heal this more than anything, since I wasn't going to start taking anti-seizure medications to cut it down. Lying there, I tried to empty my mind and push healing waves from my core to my vizard. For many minutes I'd be decked out, slab-like, with a teeter-tottering consciousness that soon switched to off. After, I'd awaken comforted with the washcloth half-stuffed in my mouth or clutched in my hand, because I had flipped onto my belly, pressing onto the damp Therm-a-Rest to get close to cool ground. My shorts were stained wet. Discharged, but owing nothing.

Around this time a Dutchwoman who attended a yoga workshop began to silently signal that she wished to get to know me better, or at least my body. Tall, veiny, athletic, but non-practicing; puissant; alluring, but not assured; thirty-five at least, but not forty. I'd never admit to a "type" or needing a woman who looked like my previous ardent desire, and yet my lot had been determined. I'd noticed her at the Saturday lunch of cold lentils and salad—I must have done more than I thought suitable. She walked up to the tent on one of those blindingly bright afternoons when heat levels all living things. She complimented me on the faraway shelter she'd followed me to. Yes, we could both scream into the rift of the valley, no-one would hear, except the sheep and the shepherd.

When she joined me in the narrow tent, there wasn't much room. We sat facing each other, and when we bent forward to avoid the top's hot lining, our crossed knees almost touched. I offered the washcloth, dipped and wrung anew, and pressed it against her neck, covering her left collarbone's cranberry mole. She lifted a little, swiveled swiftly, her cocoa-colored hair brushing my resting hand. Her eyes were closed, her cheek at my mouth. I want to feel you, she said, with the abrupt resonance of a ballpeen hammer striking steel next to my ear.

She was a woman you'd have to get in line for and would still be waiting to greet on your deathbed. But this would be more about the remoteness of the place than about me. What we did was clunky, until it turned almost splendid, before shorting out. I kept smelling her lunchtime apple in her mouth, licking her two giant front teeth, throttling up in thinking I waxed the two tall plates of her superstructure, touching something so untouchable, like a Vermeer or the Shroud of Turin, commoners would be happy to meet me. I want to travel with you, I told her. Want to see you in all seasons, want everyone to see I have the most beautiful woman in the world next to me. I'd tried to be as direct with some women back in the States. It worked about half the time, probably an acceptable rate. Maybe I was getting good at this. We made love less queasily and fell asleep sweat-wet and too hot to be conscious.

We awoke during the same minute. We might have had little to speak of, but everyone has parents. I said something about missing time with my father. He liked cars and building things, watching TV at night to immolate any memory of his workaday labors until the alarm went off at dawn. He wasn't going to read the *Ulysses* I gave him as a birthday present. Not *Dubliners* either. Our closest, greatest moment? At ten years, I found him staring at the blearing summer dawn in the kitchen of a friend's country house. Drinking coffee, waiting to go home. Anxious, out of sorts, souring. It was myself I saw, and she understood exactly, if not morosely, what I meant—my first maturities blatantly shared in a bid for more sexlove. Her long fingers bolted to my cranium, and she mothered me with heavy caresses, before all the flowers in our hearts became ice flowers. There and then I did think she was my destiny, the fuse linking time to myth, pulling us through an ordinary afternoon.

Some sleep, some more holding still and listening to the earth, our breath. The distant bells of the sheep, the winding wind, the sweet grasses with a tincture of our malodorousness and that of the horses. Heartbeats, stomach gurglings. We had to spoon to fit comfortably. Aren't you missing yoga? I said. I used no cross-patch tone.

I've done enough. Too much.

A red ant bit my leg, and I tried to clear the rest of them out of the tent—a segment of the zipper had failed.

I need to be here, she blankly stated. Not with you, really so. But you are wonderful. Here, in this country, country setting. Vestiges of Dutch rushed off those syllables like raindrops from windows by hot forced air.

I didn't recognize she was telling me a story until several half-formed sentences in. Sometimes I had to help her find the words, but it seemed she should utter them in her language, that their offertory was more for her than for me. She'd had a son at a young age. The father flit in and out of their lives, but her parents supported them—then she had to move back home. They lived cityside, in Amsterdam, near its largest park, the Vondelpark. After being under her parents' thumb for a year, she broke out and met a man who could keep his scoundrel side hidden, and she quickly advanced into his house. He professed to act as father, and they went to adding another child. Infertile: though he would not accept the doctor's finding. They broke apart after two years. She returned to her parents' house, enduring the tempestuousness, the leaning-in on, the corrections. One May day, mother and child were playing hide-and-go-seek near a copse around one of the park's ponds. The boy, Lucien, went off to hide. She closed her eyes as promised, not for more than ten seconds, nine counts. He went towards where she knew he'd go, the large oak she'd always impressed upon him, but he wasn't there. Hours on, an ambulance had to take her away into lockdown. There were clues, legitimate sightings, but nothing came of them. She'd gone back and forth, slowly and diurnally—some years no hope, some years nothing but. If it had happened in the current year, she told me, with more and more cameras around... Her parents lied when they said they'd forgiven her. Nothing would ever roll it back. For a few years, blackness—little satisfied. Then yoga and meditation. You can't imagine what it is to lose your life and keep living, she said. Lucien would be twenty now. And I thought to tell her, Yes, your overriding sheen of sadness is more than palpable. But I didn't tell her, and if I died then I would have left out the most mortgageable part: how her sadness had an aspect of my mother's clamorings, only without the anger. Still, I didn't know if Dutchwomen really had the impacted fury of Americans.

I'd held her throughout the retelling, feeling alive in her history, though her story would seemingly have no bearing on my life, and we wouldn't pursue one another. It wasn't time for me to grow with this knowledge, but I would many years later. When she left the next morning, I thought of how we can be a witness and listen. In the future I would have something to offer as I tried to cheer all the sad people I attracted.

In my holt, when we were coming out of reverie, tears long crusted, our minds jouncing about as if adjusting to being out of g-force speeds and her face reassembling after the shattering, I remembered the thermos of lemonade André's wife had made and given me that morning. I'd stored it in my sack and tossed the sack on the ground outside the tent, in a push to get inside. Luckily, it had remained in the shade. Would you like some cool lemonade? It will refresh you. The ants had swarmed the bag, panicking over the cool thermos, though they could insert themselves no further. As I was whisking them off, another bit my finger.

She drank. I hoped the moment wouldn't end. To go on comforting her made the sex as ludicrous as it was necessary. Sadness has followed me my whole life—the line of my existence. Wouldn't it be more honest to say I carry it like two invisible iron maidens? No. Destiny is what you invoke when the night will be otherwise lonely.

A week later, the incoming call I expected arrived. A close cousin had had her second child, another girl, the night before. I told the crew, and we worked with some euphoria for about twenty minutes as we rubbed clumps of mud off garlic, but soon settled back into our agenda. The caller, my brother Clayton, hadn't asked too much about the farm, but he rarely betrayed his timeless self-obsession.

The hottest part of the summer dawned, and I had to begin planning my weeks away. The sixty-two Sikhs had sent a postcard from Nice. Unsigned. I examined the handwriting, wondering if Hoda had penned those leaning *l*s and *b*s and *f*s, creations like sailboats taking the wind. For my trip, the town of Nice, with its pink adobes and partying atmosphere, nude beaches and chic shops, wouldn't be of interest. There was Aix-en-Provence, full of boutiquey toutes les choses, tourist dollars, and the mountain Cézanne painted again and again. Or maybe Arles, where van Gogh lived the most celebrated years of his life. But also Nîmes, with its heavy Roman influence. Like Arles, it had its own amphitheater and other ruins. The whole curving cookie-cutter coast seemed holy to me and history showed through the land once settled by the Gauls, then the Romans, then the Visigoths, overloading and bloodletting upon this serried earth—a hard and broken but fruitful land carrying the scars of all those civilizations in its extensive plateaus and vineyard-lined slopes, its slightly centipede-like ranges. I had swept through all these towns before, a few years back, during a summer in Europe, staying in hostels and campsites. In Aix, I had stumbled into the company of a famous writer—Paul Malix. I'd used the experience there with him to write my first novella among many. I had trouble with the title, so I branded it with the gauche *Day of the Poet,* which probably gave away too much of the story—of what little there was. A young American poet in Aix loses his manuscript and must go and retrieve it from a mystery man in a small art museum late at night after closing. The mystery man offers him a choice: he can have the manuscript or save a small Cézanne painting (taken from the wall—no alarms) because the mystery man will otherwise soon destroy it with a knife. I thought I was on to something grand by tackling such a storied dilemma, but I can't even remember what the poet chose.

Malix was an expat who had a well-regarded novel at twenty-nine, but in the thirty-five years since then had put out nothing except a book of essays called *The Mysteries of Fulcanelli's Cathedrals,* a tome mainly dismissed as "out of touch" and "thoroughly sexist." He rose up to me at the aforementioned art museum—it was Musée Granet—quite by accident, but maybe that was Malix's manner. A cascade of white hair struck my eyes, and though he wasn't tall, he appeared imperious, surviving on nuance and celerity. Craggy old body, but the voice carried a modulated squeak. He had a razor edge to his relating, drawing in and distancing at the same time. You were the object of his obsession, but you were also the thing that kept him from getting his work done. He hated his mother and started off the essay book with two long pieces about this intensity, how it clogged and enervated. He could have been said to be getting even in the writing, although she was long dead, as were most of those who dared celebrate her. Nothing to gain, but he risked his reputation as a young genius for something Diogenesian and sullen to the core, joining the already swelling ranks of the embittered. Success would never be the same. He'd taken the money and bought a place in the more bucolic part of town, then married or lived with a Frenchwoman, and that was the end of the trail. As for the roughnecks who still adored the first book's streamlined prose, almost folksy Salingeresque—no matter the overburdened diastole and systole of discursive sentences in the much-smeared second book—they knew where to find him and they made their pilgrimages, only to be received frostily. And why not? They all wanted help in some way. Make a phone call or send a letter. It sickened him. He preferred people who didn't know him at all, like me. That way neither side held any cards. Perhaps that was why he opened the door, by a very forward approach, though for weeks I was sure some yet-to-be-realized thread lurked. But no—and I hadn't yet read *Death in Venice*. Even if I had, I would still have devoted myself to the cause with his name. I needed to see the world. I craved impressions. I had to chase all opportunities.

I went to dinner at his house. Malix was alone by this time; his wife or lover had left him. I wasn't exactly sure what he did to keep active besides visiting the museum, walking the chalky streets of the downtown. Was he in retirement from love? I wouldn't have known what that was, I wouldn't have recognized any mean omens of it.

There was a preparatory drawing by Cézanne that he owned and of which he snorted, There are many Cézannes around. He spoke in aphorisms, though he would have called them aperçus, with a brittle East Coast inflection, tossing off the English diphthong nestled diffidently. He said he didn't want to complain too much, but he always did. He didn't talk much about literature or books, but about movies, which I knew a thing or two more about. When writers get together, movies are all that matter—Kubrick, Cassavetes, Godard. No-one gives a shit about the latest great American novel, not even if one of them wrote it. Malix did eventually lecture me on writing, all of his advice wrongheaded, except this: Read your Shakespeare! After a few hours of talk, and just after the day servant left, he crossed his glazed eyes and said, What I'd give to look like you. You could probably have any woman in the world—and a lot of the men. If I had what you have... Ha—I wouldn't be any happier, just mad about what else I didn't possess.

I thought this to be a good endpoint, consistent with his harrumph-ending style, but no, there was more: This will strike you as you age. Everything you thought when you were young—your own suppositions, not the facts—all of it will turn out to be deeply wrong. You will be sitting quietly, and suddenly it will attack you—and it will attack you, I can see it. You think too much. His tongue waxed his teeth for two interminable seconds. I don't mean now. Now you are adventuring, but later. When this stuff usually comes out. The thinking too much doesn't go away. And this recognition will not be too good. You'll need someone then. Friends will go only so far—they'll be busy with their own families and dramas. Stock up on who you think will go barren.

Presumably his muse had filed for divorce.

He wanted me to write to him and I did, even sending something by John Berger, more his age-mate, who lived a little over two hundred miles in away in Mieussy. But he never mentioned it in responses. A few more letters over a year, then nothing. I thought he might be dead. I checked the internet right before I left Germany; I even called his London publishers. A milquetoast told me if Paul Malix died, he'd have heard, for these are the great dramas of the book world. I forgot all about this and then returned to it in the days when I had to make a decision: would I go back to Aix for my holiday?

It wasn't him in *Day of the Poet*. In fact, I'd made the character more dastardly. I'd taken an execrable vow never to us real people for my work, basing them only on the literary or film characters I knew. I really did this. And for the mystery man there was the nihilist Svidrigaïlov in *Crime and Punishment*—though, of course, he was Malix as well. I'd never tell Malix about the novella anyway. It was for a class. No-one would ever publish it, nor would I want them to. On the new journey, I didn't want to talk about writing anymore anyway; I only looked for something to do with my time, and finding someone familiar seemed a good use of lonely hours.

I took some local trains to Aix, shabby SNCF's with the battered engine car pulling the smelly, sticky-floored cars behind it. Aix was lush with tourists and locals who regretted remaining during the cramped weeks of summer. I had nowhere to stay and so went immediately to Malix's. A year earlier, I'd luckily transcribed the address from my important persons' address book to the internet. A down-on-his-calling writer told me of his fascination with the forgotten man. Pursuant to good cheer, I sent him the address, after I'd drunkenly revealed that I'd met Malix. I never knew what came of it—not even a "thank you" for the address.

Aix, the first time, had stuck out for experiences. When I took a local bus to the youth hostel from the train station, I found a driver who bore an uncanny resemblance to Bruno Ganz. After letting teenage girls on for the price of a cheek kiss, he celebrated my giving him a one-hundred franc note for a six-franc fare with exhortations in a nasally Southern dialect I could barely parse—though he might have said "Jackpot" because he had to scrounge in his change tub to deliver me fortysome coins. I possibly took the same bus I needed to get to the hostel when I'd returned, because Malix's house was up in the hills overlooking the centre-ville. I also desired to see if the same bus driver worked. But no, the character sitting high on the jump seat was an even more plain-faced, heaving, and frowning man—obliterating my guiding notion of the South of France as this bevy of people high on life.

When I came to the address, a black gate barred my entry. I couldn't remember it being there before, and soon after my buzz a middle-aged woman appeared and told me of Monsieur Malix's relocation to Arles—about an hour east.

With a light pack on, I took the bus out a little farther, to the nearest highway. An art history professor in a red French sports car picked me up. She drove the equivalent of a hundred miles an hour while explaining Gauguin and his propensity to rape, so we arrived in Arles ahead of schedule. The mood of the town was much like that of Aix. The old men in berets and antique shirts and blazers, no matter the heat, were still playing bocce and still communicating in a kind of underhand I was no nearer to decoding—wild gestures and facial contortions—though I began to suspect no secret codes applied; they were just reacting to the game.

Because it was late afternoon, I thought I'd go to Malix's in the morning and strolled the urine-scented streets of centre-ville, only then realizing I'd need a place to sleep, and this time I had no tent. There were plenty of hotels with their narrow entrances leading to three floors of high-ceilinged rooms—an antiquated sign often hanging out in front. Could I afford that?

My father hid money from my mother, just as she did from him. All their fights led back to the question of legal tender. So enmeshed, when out of high school I revolted and began to base little of my life on the dollar. I spent small sums and worked part-time for minimum wage, so I would never have to lose too much of my writing time.

I had a one hundred dollars worth of francs with me. I figured the rate at a hostel couldn't have gone up that much, but I'd grown out of that bashful, ebullient stage of travel—I had no net, I needed at some point to make money or I would die. Also, I didn't really know what I was going to do with Malix. What burning imprecation did I have to share? That I had written about him, in a veiled way? But that was surely too trite for him to see. That I was, in fact, not a writer after all?

I kept winding around Arles in that still high summer light and then headed toward the ochre walkways along the river, where a sloped gray-brick embankment leads to the oily Rhône. Soon I found a small post with a rectangular placard, the size of half a page of newspaper: a van Gogh river scene more than one hundred years old. These posts, I didn't know how many—a dozen or so—were still there, scattered around town. In Germany, the previous summer, I'd read a newish biography of the painter. I grabbed it from a free box in the halls of a university. Orange cover, holding one of the lesser-known self-portraits. The world's choicest artist. Hadn't I come to Arles the first time because of van Gogh, the hysteria over all that raised paint? Hadn't I seen a few of his in Chicago and gone gaga? And didn't Kurosawa's *Dreams* have a short episode with him, and didn't I go searching for that drawbridge, then reconstructed over water in the film—the real painting morphing into the filmic scene as it had been in 1889?

On a bench by the stone wall lining the river, I ripped a significant hole in the pleated slacks from André on a loose bolt. That set me down to my one pair of outrageously large work jeans, which retained a few weeks' dirt on them. I had no clue about the French for "safety pin," and I didn't have underwear on. There were no obstructions on Quai Marx Donary—I couldn't change anywhere. Public restrooms in small-town France were notoriously hard to find. I kept trying to think of a proper metaphor for my predicament. Nothing glimmered. I couldn't pay ten or fifteen dollars for a meal when I'd already planned to put out for a decent hotel; besides I'd already purchased my baguette, brie, tomato paste, three carrots, and a cylindrical packet of cream-filled cookies at a supermarché—I couldn't waste its limited supply of gooey. I wandered inland to find a hotel, since a giant hole in the form of a gaping feed bag exposed half of my right thigh. I tried to hold it up calmly, but with my strides it kept tearing even more. The characters I wrote also had bumbling moments like this, and in fact *Day of the Poet* featured something very similar: the poet's case or book bag containing his manuscript gets thrown over a large gate enclosing the front yard of a rich-seeming house, as so many in Aix appear, by a random woman the poet meets at a café. There they share an attraction, they talk, and then she grabs his sack and runs some blocks before tossing it over. The poet climbs the gate and falls. Deep cuts, clothing is torn. He gets the bag, but the manuscript has vanished. Nothing like that ever happened to me, though in the months before composing, I'd read a story in John Fowles' collection *The Ebony Tower* where an intruder burns a writer's manuscript (the only copy) for no good reason, maybe just because he is young and the writer is old, uppity, secure, accomplished. Because I wrote by hand and transcribed later, I was keenly aware that if I lost something before typing it, I would be given to instant hyperventilation. I didn't know then that losing one of those black unlined sketchbooks—with hundreds of pages of bad writing—might have been the best thing for me, might have made me a better writer.

I burrowed through the twisted involutions of the French centre-ville, maze upon circle. I didn't know many months were required to master this squiggly grid. Past large gray and umber official buildings I larded, then wound around corners expecting small only to get big. Long ropy streets of four-story apartment buildings, streetlamps with black fleur-de-lis coverings every fifteen paces. Under the sun's strong pinnacle, I went past clothing shops and an antiquarian bookstore, seeking some kind of life (a room to let) and sometimes glimpsing bits of the nearly two-thousand-year-old amphitheater, until I reached an opening with ten spaces for cars and a red sign: Hôtel La Muette.

I entered with my bag awkwardly covering the hole, and though the staff seemed to not so slyly check my banknotes for authenticity, the key was soon mine. The hotel had originated as a manor house from the time of Chaucer. Unsurprising, but a selling point. I wondered how the hell they had constructed the plumbing and kept the structure intact, but of course they just rebuilt it all—people would often pay more to think they were living in history. The small, impersonal room suited me fine. The only thing out of place was the bathroom and the over-the-topness of its bright pastel mid-eighties coloring. There was a small desk with a beige puffy-seated chair and a violently bad picture of flowers over the bed. The one window looked out on more buildings—the lengthening shadows of the approaching dusk crawled their brick. I showered and then rubbed the thin hotel soap into the grimy jeans and hung them out the window. I walked about in a towel and saw myself in the room's long mirror, taking in my full body for the first time in months.

The baguette with squished tomato paste on the brie tasted exquisite. I lay on the bed, quietly content, with a slight wish to have a beer on such a sweaty day.

What did I think I was doing with my life? Why did I hanker after seeing this man? I had stopped writing. I believe I had also stopped thinking, because I didn't ask myself these questions then. Like slowing a whirlpool, I kept calming and calming, and then I was asleep.

I went downstairs for my morning baguette in jeans half-damp, since I'd forgotten to turn them over and they cooled unevenly in the night winds. A young couple shared a table a few away from mine—they spoke English with Canadian features. Their hands not holding baguettes held onto each other. The amphitheater would open soon, and they wanted to be first in line. I'd gone there a few years back. During one of those endless summer days, I met a guy from North Carolina on the street. Blond and lean, he irradiated contumely, but he'd made his life his own and was a true expat. He saw into my situation and I tried not to smile. He lived on the outskirts and worked on a fishing boat, propelling me to think I could do the same. He kept poking a finger into his mouth. A tooth was loose; he'd considered a bottle of brandy and pliers. We went to a Bizet musical at night in the amphitheater for around five dollars. A live horse came galloping in. Cross-eyed, the guy stared at my ear, muttering, Beats the shit out of the Oscars, right?

These memories safely buoyed me. Malix might have brought me here, but my purpose might not have anything to do with him. I'd often gone on instinct during these travels. I could look for myself or the version of myself I had left behind.

Later that day I was confounded. He was in a nursing home. He'd had a stroke and couldn't speak. He could scribble things, but the attendants didn't want these actions to go on too long. Detailed questions were impossible. I hadn't expected to be the one to do the talking. Jaundiced and morose, he bit down hard on a coppery biscuit. Without the shrill voice, he still carried an assumptive air, and maybe that impelled me on. I told him I would probably never be a writer. Maybe I lacked discipline. I continued to do a half-assed job at things. Yes, I worked at André's farm, but I would leave in a few months. And then?

He wrote, *The middle of the story is just as important.*

I could agree, but I also stoked up my anger and began ranting.

Why was I even in Arles? Every mediocre artist came there to get inspired. I was just on a lower rung. I'm too young, I began to say, but left out my even lower opinions of myself. I need a tent—it's the only way I can stay here. I have to go back to the campsite, it's way the fuck out of town—I'll need a bus. I've done this before—I'm just repeating myself. Burning my energy to save a buck.

Malix massaged his heavy eyebrows—those masterpieces of manipulation were like old wire brushes. Then he made a peace symbol at me and wrote down an address, followed by "two weeks"—mouthed by him. I understood enough to know Malix didn't want me around to bother him.

He had a friend at that address. An old house. A woman gave me the key and pointed me up the peeling stairs to a room in the attic. Essentially the same setup as the hotel room, though the bathroom was down a flight, shared by two small floors of boarders. One room to another, the design remained the same. A bed, a desk, a chair: the main components of van Gogh's bedroom, except for his paintings on the wall.

Among my short-lived fascinations, there remains a flirty affair with the Gnostic Gospels, including explanatory books by Elaine Pagels and others. I wrote down their once spurious aphoristic sayings, coveting their patented jolts of wisdom, yet still burned to be motivated by the words. Nuggets from suppressed scripture joined those storied literary ones, especially one from the Gospel of Thomas: *Open your eyes and see what is before your face.* This directive had often haunted human knowledge well before its presentation in our century; it was filtered down over time, in various guises—mainly poetical. The act of seeing became central to the triumvirate of Flaubert, Cézanne, and Rilke—sources

I kept swimming near to and then retreating, the latter especially. I'd sat on the grassy banks of the Neckar in Germany reading the *Duino Elegies* and trying to get it, to see, to find, when really the process encompassed the growth of imagination—a gestation which may cause disease and hypertrophy of fantasy. I pressed the German through my vocal cords, living as close as I could to the original utterance. I desired the original sound to leave the tang I sought. And if it didn't? I could remain anonymous by the river with only minor self-admonishments. Or leave. And I did. I wished to know German better and went to the Volkshochschule to learn it, but I came no closer. I returned to the embankments. I opened my eyes and watched the water. Waited. I closed them. I opened. Water. Close. Water.

Water.

I hoped for an aftermath of nascent meaning, forgoing the urge to recapture the old feelings with a false nostalgia, disdaining the old American rah-rah of groupthink for something more my own, something solid and still but staunchly alive—a bowl from the Ming Dynasty. How would I take advantage?

I didn't believe in vortexes or leylines, though they'd been explained to me countless times on the West Coast. Obviously the light in the South of France, and in Arles in particular, had such a quasi-magical quality, two of the most important Western painters used it to illume the pictures in their head before the hands pressed line and color to the canvas. Something—not necessarily spectral—had to be all around me. Seeing might be translatable into words, and sitting at a small table in a café near the street, waiting on an Orangina, I opened a book of W.S. Merwin poems to fill the space, reliant on his images to filigree my graying hours: "I have been cruel to a fat pigeon/ Because he would not fly/ All he wanted was to live like a friendly old man." Too much time had been cafés, drinks, jazz and classical music, watching people and fantasizing—forking myself into lives I imagined so much more special. This continued well into my thirties until something snapped and, inexplicably, I had everything I wanted. If I didn't have it inside of me, then I knew where to get it—fantasias finally unappealing.

There, slurring those Merwin words back through a sieve of restitution—I couldn't know satiety. I kept an eye out for Mr. North Carolina. Where had he gone? Not, What had he come to? With Malix's gift I had currency to order another drink, something more sumptuous, a café au lait. Waiting for it to cool, I had an idea independent of Merwin's ontology or my past, things I gladly, falsely merged. I had no pen and quickly called the waiter, getting to use my favorite-sounding French construction for asking—*Puis-je avoir votre stylo*: May I utilize your pen? Despising something I reminded him of, he handed it over. So armed, I scribbled what I had to say inside the Merwin paperback.

I wrote some fable called 'My Journey.' It involved a donkey. Wrought by lifeworrying, it might not have been as profound as I at first thought—and it was meaningless. Still, it came from a very tender, malleable crux, one I didn't know resided in me. I would transfer it to paper, but never fully read, even when old and drunk. It was the only notable item I wrote in those two weeks—and it kept as a souvenir. I tried to give the waiter the pen back, but he insisted I take it. I licked the nib.

I continued moving towards some phantom end in those two weeks, which might have been the dead zone I needed to not hurry through. The land under Arles, which had been laid into the earth on both sides of a great river connected to a port, half bordered by a very large protected natural preserve of wetlands running to the Mediterranean, held steadfast. The rage of Malix's spirit, though I would never hear his voice give words to it again, guided me with a scurvy New York accent, webs of paint-heavy blood girding its authority. I don't think most epiphanies arrive the way they are reputed to, "placed" in our life story so as to be conveniently recapitulated in anecdote. Epiphanies can have a long durée—days, weeks. They begin unnoticeably, in the belly of our hesitations, in the spoor of distractedness, and continue so, waiting for the private self to go public with *Yes, I am doing something in a much different way. I might have learned something, but I'm unsure what it is. It might be only me, but I need to put it in an order for others to see.* In this field, the epiphany is still proceeding, because it can't be separated from the action of living—there isn't a "No, I get it," and then change. Change has already come, and one sees that the natural direction has uncontrollably grown a reef.

If epiphanies in life are misapplied, literature's understanding that a human being's life is long and that a story remains short is overdrawn. In fiction, epiphanies are easy to understand. A change in thinking is something teenagers can catch out in fiction—it's plain what is happening. Unsurprisingly, Joyce and *The Great Gatsby* marked me early on. Even in high school, many scenes in *A Portrait of the Artist as a Young Man* annealed some notions about what constituted a dutiful existence. As I re-read it, I gained more panache, inserting myself (a lapsing Catholic) again and again into Stephen Dedalus. I would talk about him with people who knew him, yet at some level I was also speaking of my own concerns and convictions. Art can jugger like that—it pries into our everydays and wrenches out the ego's mocking snarl in favor of pure soul. The major epiphany in the book—

that of Stephen realizing his desire to be a writer—unfolds at Dollymount Strand, where he sees a girl wading and knows he must express such beauty in words. This entranced, and I carried it very much in mind. I decided to read the scene out loud to my mother the first time I came home after moving away. Clayton had come in for Christmas, so it was the three of us—a few years after the divorce. On the night I arrived, we went to an Irish restaurant, and, so influenced by a nature girl I had met in Oregon, I pulled out my own personal set of chopsticks to eat a salad. I could accept the quizzical scrutiny, but when I insisted on reading the epiphany scene later at home, the words disappeared into a well. What could my family say anyway? I wanted them to feel just a fraction of what transpired inside me when pronouncing "To live, to err, to fall, to triumph, to recreate life out of life!" Silence. Would this be their reaction to my creations too? Years on, I discovered how writing for their approval, or for one's pigeonholed lover, only ambushed the creator who needed acceptance from strangers instead.

I kept asking all the questions my age demanded during those two weeks, especially the lark of whether to leave and return to the farm's easier exile. The farm could wait—I shouldn't be disenchanted because some of the excitement had bled out of it, and after a few more days of freedom I didn't miss it. I didn't miss anything. Everything remained in front of me during those hot hours in the small city. I returned to places I had visited years before and remade them, leaving them more charged. The proverbial gauntlet—back to the amphitheater, Les Alyscamps, the van Gogh sites. All the time, trying to barricade myself against the power of the tourists, their greed for the best sightlines. Other velleities lurked behind those vortexes, other stranger powers only I could see, because they refracted off the real objects and back to me, as I then drilled a laser into their unreal hearts.

I sat in public parks eating my cheese-and-tomato paste baguettes, watching the old men's rictuses respond to the velocities of those bocce balls. What slow-cooked could be applied only months on, as the epiphany that wasn't.

When I was in Les Alyscamps atop some cold stone, a blaze of sun crossed onto my thigh. I moved my squeezed hand left to right across my forehead before carefully pulling it away and gazing at the pool of sweat in the top of the fist. No epiphany, only science. Arles had been a favorite city of Constantine; he built baths there. One sees this information everywhere, repeated like something plagiarized but in translation. The coliseum predated the one in Rome by seven years. The Barbegal aqueduct was "the greatest known concentration of mechanical power in the ancient world." Now its rubble, overgrown with shrubs, looked like old half-vanished settler houses in the western US. I had to get away.

As I had done years before, I took a long walk out of town into the demarcated farmers' fields, crosshatched by a system of canals, to find the drawbridge van Gogh painted in 1889. Sweat spread down my back, dampening my light pack. The azure sky heralded a day like the one that had greeted van Gogh.

One can now purchase *The Langlois Bridge at Arles with Women Washing* on cotton canvas, billed as "an affordable alternative to original art," for $143.00 plus shipping. In the original, women stand on canal banks full of river weeds and dip clothes into the water. In Kurosawa's *Dreams*, a tourist/sojourner walks into the painting (then in Holland) and speaks to one of the washerwomen on the canal bank, before finding van Gogh in a farmer's field, painting crows above the bounty of cornstalks. I thought I sat near something constructed one hundred years older than the image of it already heightened by acid-trip coloring. No: steep beige brick walls had replaced the soiled bank to keep people from thinking of going in. Like many such objects of public fascination, the real drawbridge had been upgraded from a reinforced concrete bridge forty years after being painted, and was then destroyed by the Germans. Soon enough, the Arles Tourist Board paid for a reconstruction, renaming it Pont Van-Gogh. I found out about all the inner workings and history only many years later. When I traveled, I didn't access the internet. I'd get a map of the city at the Tourism Office and that was all. Yet I twice sat there eating my lunch believing this to be the same bridge van Gogh had seen, even if repainted in the intervening century. Perhaps this is the very crux of tourism—the insertion of oneself into a part of history, with photographic proof never interesting to anyone not in the picture. And, on the first occasion, ten minutes after I arrived, two busfuls of Japanese tourists pulled up. Even if those people, happy and breathtaken, knew what I didn't, they still took pictures like it was history, though every single thing depicted in the painting was now gone—except the bedrock, which one can't make out anyway. The painting held the most value, but it was now protected in an institution.

On my second visit, after my first night at Malix's gift, by some means of inscape, I refocused my mind on the painting's washerwomen because before me another busful of tourists had landed and began to take hundreds of pictures. Same nationality, better cameras. Both times, I sat in a parking area, on some rubble and young grass, devouring my carrots, but only during the second occurrence did I inch my way through to what was buried within the specified drawbridge, unaccountably unchanged—the woman of my time—art so often being not about the subject, but about the viewer's interpretation of the subject.

My mother routinely gathered our family's soiled clothes in the damp basement—a four-person pile overcoming the bounds of a laundry basket, set under the laundry chute on the first floor. Behind the bathroom door, this convenience fascinated me throughout childhood, because I would often get on my knees to open the door (the size of the family road atlas) and yell to hear an echo in the darkness below. My mother did multiple loads of wash and then, in comfortable weather—every few years even a Saturday in March could hit sixty—she strung a wash-line between three trees in our backyard: a cherry, an oak, and a maple on two twin plots of grass, cut by the sidewalk from the cement of our parking spaces to the steps leading to the back door. One spring, the cherry tree had to be removed because of disease. Then two large hooks were screwed into and anchored high on both sides of the back-porch face, affording more line, as one strung from hook to oak and to maple, ending with a long diagonal line from the maple back across the sidewalk to the far hook. Because of the inevitable sag when wet clothing noosed by clothespins is hung upside down, six- or seven-foot green poles that had a declivity in the middle of one pointy end were used to prop up the line with one midway between oak and maple and two between maple and hook. These poles had been shoddily painted years before because their jungle-green paint constantly flaked off after being stored outside under the house, revealing splintering wood underneath. If strong enough winds gusted, the weight of wash could jangle the line, and the poles would give way, since many times we returned to clothes half-crumpled into the grass or on the pavement.

In most of my younger years I did not help with this work, but instead watched from the porch above or from across the alley, about seventy paces away, in my paternal grandparents' backyard, where my father grew up in the 1940s and where, retracing those diagonal paces, he would buy a house, a three-bedroom bungalow, the one I then gazed at. Upstairs and out of sight, Clayton furiously read the *Lord of the Rings* series to be able to remind me that he had read the whole thing at eleven, while I, in the third grade, was still at a third-grade reading level.

I am there in my grandparents' yard, just before they'll have a garage built on their back lot to obscure the view to our house. Their neighbors will follow suit a year or two later, making it next to impossible to see across the street from the yard without going to the back gate at the foot of the property. I watch my mother prop up the lines with those wooden poles before dilatorily hanging the laundry—she's smoking. I see the house where I pass most of my days, but I am secretly, or so I think, in the magical realm of my grandparents' property, which is much more mysterious because of its full history and the lived-inness of a house smaller than ours, though it oversaw four full childhoods throughout World War II. I can go to this place anytime I want because my grandmother is pretty much always inside. Health problems keep her marooned in the living room on a small blue-and-white flowery sofa in front of a large Sony TV. As their youngest grandchild until shortly after my grandfather's death, I could count on getting spoiled. On entering the pre-War two-story, I would be given or ask for a few fig bars from a tin kept in the pantry, something our household never bought. The fig bars were packed in two sturdy lines, tight like piano keys in a package with red lettering, since sometimes I saw my grandfather unload them from a shopping trip, puncturing the cellophane to fit them into an oval tin, though some grudgingly stuck together until pried apart and a few bleached crumbs from the top broke off. The soft bite into and taste of a fresh or pretty near fresh fig bar became one of my primordial pleasures; when a bar was old, hard, and crusty, it was a letdown—it hurt. But my grandparents kept up on their fig bars, so those moments were rare. The pungent house smells can never leave me: the keen sweet stench of the fig bars, the heady steam of the dumpling soups my grandmother made, the heaping tart chunks of Borkum Riff pipe tobacco my grandfather used—it was the kind of old-person cocktail made when two people were home most of the day, the main ingredients consisting of borax soup, the trail of food recently cooked or being prepared, and the bodies and their clothes, laundered with plain pure detergent leagues different from the fruity ones to follow in their wake. I remember those scents much more than the ones in my house, probably because there I always smelled them; they were already a part of me. The basement in my grandparents' house had a refrigerator always stocked with colored sodas, and a small bar with a gewgaw of a miniature Niagara Falls which, when on, lit up its wavering sheet of water—it wasn't awfully exotic but different enough to be of prime importance, rarifying a purer love.

The two of them were there until one day my grandfather wasn't and quickly life changed for everyone. A year later my father would move, temporarily, into his childhood bedroom. In a few years my grandmother would go into a home, leaving the house empty, to be commandeered by my father, the oldest of three siblings—a takeover completely providential given that the other two lived out of state while he, by then, resided twenty minutes west with his new wife.

After my grandmother's move, the house carried on a strange abandonment. The years passed, falling calendar pages in an old film. Dust and granulate built up. I believe my father didn't sell the house for so long because he liked the idea of having property. There were also two cars in the garage, one of which, a sporty black-and-yellow Mustang Cobra, would become my first. On a visit, he would park in front of the home on a busy street bisected by a grassy median and walk along the narrow passage to the backyard. He entered via the porch, but often strayed about in the garage, which housed a great quantity of tools, including duplicates of those in his other home, as well as a second tractor with a plow. He'd tune the old radio to talk, with encrusted voices coming through two shoebox-sized speakers, while he dawdled, getting his hands full of grease, adding another fishing rod from a rummage sale to the decaying pile in an eave. He had this same setup—garage, tools, and radio, with the piercing scent of WD-40—about fifteen miles away in his new life. But a certain man likes to switch about and check his toys, monitor his holdings.

Our frayed relationship: all throughout high school I saw him minimally, but we eventually re-established something, mainly through the handing down of the car. In those four forlorn years, I would see my grandparents' garage and the ghostly, mostly occluded house every day. Whenever I left for the day, and because the front was always double-locked we always left through the back, there was the house across the alley, while at night I made out a fleck of the back porch light, a white shining deterrent. All the neighbors knew that no-one lived there, yet it was full of all the furniture and accoutrements that it held when my grandmother had left, making the atmosphere more indomitable, more haunted.

The house would also catch my eye from across that busy street in the clovered fields surrounding a local sanitation hub—land where I played baseball with my father and Clayton for years, as they hit me fly balls with a fungo bat, a shiny piece of wood designed for towering pop-ups by being longer and thinner than the average stick. There I also played with a few boys from high school, a time full of smart-ass repartee that had none of the innocence of father, sons, balls, bat, and gloves. While waiting for a friend to gather the three nicked, muddied, and slimy green balls to send back to the pitcher, I pondered that simple and shrinking off-white house, a relic—the large white shade covering the main window of the living room had yellowed after facing west for many seasons. While Clayton colleged in Ohio, I remained with my mother and tried not to bring up a piece of property she despised.

After graduation, I was deemed responsible. Along with the car, the keys to not only the garage but also the house were entrusted. My father wanted me to check the house once a week and shovel during winter, at least the front sidewalk and porch. I now had access to another realm, but I didn't necessarily enjoy it. Old houses made noises and this one, with its single occupant, had the long-abandoned, mysterious, noisy basement and attic that I avoided because of all the common horror-flick associations. On opening the back porch door, one went down a short hallway before entering the small kitchen. From there, the living room opened out with two couches and an easy chair, along with that same old television and an end-table lamp, both remaining switched on interminably behind closed shades and curtains. In my grandmother's domain, a soft, violet two-seat affair had replaced the article from the seventies—she was short and could lie across it with ease. The larger piece had come from our house across the way. A rattan couch with a brown, yellow, and green floral pattern, it also had two matching sitting chairs now in different parts of the house. My mother never liked this purchase from a rummage sale, and it promptly migrated when my father did. Above this musty piece were old pictures of distant relatives—German and Czech—men and women posed and set in rows as in much early twentieth century portraiture. Aside from the possibility of an ax-murderer hiding somewhere, these glassed-in photos were my main source of anxiety when visiting the old house. The stiff foreboding looks of the people (the gelatin-silver prints of Walker Evans give one a more arty approximation) went to the core of me, while the haphazard poses of people in glossy photos from my era had little power to do so—maybe because those pictures had been made by an official photographer, maybe because people used to be more serious. In such antique photos one gets the uncanny sense that those assembled are looking directly at the viewer, nullifying their egocentricity, as if they had a sense of the eternal and held a spectral view of future generations—even as the ubiquity of the photograph was obliterated around the advent of digital cameras, when people who were too used to being captured clowning around for the image. Those unappeasable and sanguine faces had the weight of tortuous histories that would disappear with their death. Every time I moved to sit on that rattan couch for my new pastime, I avoided the censure of those pusses above, veering toward the slick objects about to abase me. Under the middle cushion of the couch were the pornographic magazines I'd purchased at the gas station from the oddball male clerks, those with missing teeth, jagged facial hair, and pimples galore, the kind of manboys I didn't mind knowing my secrets. If masturbating beneath those photographs was an unconscious attempt to undo their sanctimony, I succeeded only in making a stopgap to wisdom and pain—unfortunate for me, because blows I might have absorbed then would have prevented more powerful ones in the future.

It was a lonely life. I worked full-time as a messenger at a law firm and watched movies every night, a practice I still use as a means of achieving intimacy with other people. I was on my way to a peak weight of three hundred pounds just one year after graduating from high school. I isolated because an overweight, shy man functions better by himself. Who else can cradle him and his fat folds? When those of his preferred sex have no interest in stroking a body so green and rounded, his lifeline is often electronic and illicit, because sports are a public shambles for a body padded with extra flesh. And so, for a time, the only drama of my existence outside work was restricted to ordering burgers and tacos at drive-thrus. My aunt once told a very shy, unassuming, and frightened loner version of myself that no person or persons were going to knock on my door and say, "Hey, are you Rick? Because we've heard you want some friends in your life and, well, here we are." I went to my grandparents' house to escape my own—where the long war with my mother still played out—and to reign in the once bejeweled domain, though never to be seen doing so.

When I finished with a magazine, I promptly cleaned up, turned the TV back on, locked the house, and left. I often thought I'd get caught somehow—even there. So began construction on my watcher-and-listener escutcheon, whose moldings had been set long before. I had my pleasures—I ordered them and attended to them, silently.

In Arles, I could go no farther, and I followed the scent of the bus' evaporating exhaust. Overhead, it seemed the sun had barely begun its transit, though the siesta hour dawned. Back in the centre-ville, the coliseum was too full of people with all-star itches to see vanished history. I believe the gift shop had grown. Mid-week, I visited Malix again. He didn't write much. "A writer?" I wrote: "I think I have to let it breathe."

After some days of revisiting other sights and even the old aqueduct, which I hadn't caught the first time, nostalgia set in for my earlier history here. Only a few years had passed, but I couldn't have still been called a "youth" as I had when I first showed up in Europe. Time had cast its hangdog pall, and my circumspection grew. I had been lucky to know someone on this go-around—the first cast me forging along carefree and wide-eyed, but also determined to take whatever came my way. I camped in many places: Lisbon, Paris, Nîmes, Arles. One afternoon I walked the five kilometers out of town to the campsite, remembering that it had a café/bar. Visiting about two cities a week on my premier trip, I either fell for someone or in with a group in every destination. I knew I could meet other travelers at the campground—the gregarious Germans and Aussies, the Irish and Canadians; the skeptical but perennial Brits; the Italians and French, who traveled in groups and kept to themselves; the odd Eastern European who didn't understand but wanted to know.

When I arrived around three-thirty, the campsite was deserted. Overhead fans and open windows and doors made the space tolerable because, outside, the sun was relentless, stultifying. Most often the site would start filling in after a few hours with new arrivals and those who'd spent the day in the city. I opened my notebook and sipped a Heineken, trying to avoid the bartender's hard face. Rooted in this perpetual position, what could I be other than a writer? Years before it had been much different. I still lived at home; I still couldn't see around my mother. I tried to listen with my eyes. Again I could see myself watching her from across the alley, yet I wasn't in my grandparents' yard. After leaving the family house and then selling it, my mother and I lived in a small two-bedroom apartment. The little over two years there intensified a reckoning, once slated to arrive much sooner. Since it had been put off, a time-sensitive formula had been tampered with, promising meatier ruination.

If you specified a year to me, then as now, I would think of the films associated with that year, meaning those I saw projected on a screen. In that one I had just changed cars. Out went the gas-guzzling Mustang Cobra, and in came the fuel-efficient Corolla. It was my second delayed year in college by the great lake named for the state some one hundred miles across the water. In my last summer in Milwaukee, I came to sit under trees and look out onto the sometimes gray, sometimes green water, yearning, wanting more out of life than a lake that had become ugly in its placidity, its implied inspiration. The lake was my salvation and the only body I could poke, pushing out anger at my moorings and the unfastened sense I had of being in a city I couldn't stand. When the glaciers melted off the plains of North America, the basins they'd carved up were filled in with water that wouldn't stay frozen. The Chippewa called Lake Superior "great," but citizens called them all "great" because they were in or bordering the United States, a country I started to grow more despondent toward.

To go back, it is winter going on spring, though officially it is spring, because some years a rain-infused colder weather remained into May, and sometimes until the third week of June, obliterating the need for spring; that is to say it is May. This year that mass of cold Canadian air is nowhere on its way to being half-spent. I am finishing up my courses, studying for finals, writing long papers in order to make a grade. There is something in that chilly wind tugging at me. I try to ignore with obvious oblivious recoils, but to no effect. I am still in love with my first love, though we broke up a few months before. I am preoccupied, though I can't let the breakup affect my coursework. I put off college for almost two years and am surrounded by people a bit younger—I can't fall behind anymore.

The day of my last final, I drive back from the lakefront into the interior of the city, but I keep going past our house to a once-favored nature spot: Boerner Botanical Gardens. It is situated in Whitnall Park, the largest in the county, with a golf course and a nature center inside its diverse holdings. It's a spread-out series of green spaces, bisected by roads where one shouldn't drive more than twenty. Made by the WPA, the gardens were beautiful, vaguely European, with a long pergola and spreading wisteria and a few koi ponds. It is the best atmosphere I can imagine—cool and gloomy like those canvases and murals of many old masters I've just studied for a semester, an atmosphere in which even summer scenes are stormy and tempestuous like in Giorgione and Tintoretto, chiaroscuro aging the eyes of the viewer before the retina can relay the contents of the paint. The grounds are fairly abandoned, as if in a Caspar David Friedrich without the ruins. A few people around, alike in temperament, but much older. A gray-haired man in a panama hat bends over something trying to grow, while a thumb forces open a stiff flower guidebook with many details on genus, characteristics, and history. A lone woman with flowing hair—maybe a bored housewife considering an affair. I could implant a few details on faces then, but I wouldn't be able to make them into characters, or evoke people I know as strangers. A college friend, just two years older and Indian and in marketing—no, I couldn't. I am not knowing enough about art and I don't have anything to say—though you never know that at the time, or admit it. If you do confess it in your deepest pools, then you aren't an artist but a pleb, a failed sophist, someone who drinks in order to cry, who sadly cackles: Joyce is overrated.

The whole summer is before me. I sit on a bench overlooking a long slope of freshly tended grass, where a sundial unaccountably stands out, though left-justified on the field as if someone planned something else but then decided that the ordering made no sense. After the gardens closed for the winter, trespassing young brigands would slide down the hill, happy to smash into the dial. The sky holds a degree of gray achieved by the force that bends our minds to ecstasy and insanity. I'm half in love with a Europe I've never seen but experienced only in art, mainly though foreign films. The mysterious Paris of Kieślowski's *Bleu*, the neurotic island culture of Swedes in Bergman, the desolation of Antonioni's small Italian towns or his white-rock Spain in *The Passenger*. Somehow this park, in a conservative suburb of Milwaukee, is the closest thing here to Europe, maybe because it has a resemblance to the one in *Blow-Up*—steely sky, wind, and childless women wrapped in the past. I need my solitude, the way a tiger seeks space to enjoy his kill. A scene of estrangement, because of the overly prettified landscape, a setting for wedding photos. I don't belong here; books don't belong here. Would they in the Tuileries? The crux is I'm not thinking differently, but I'm beginning to think.

My mind lights up with images of Vermeer and Caravaggio I found in the college library. I taste my brown-bagged beer and open a book of Serbian poetry my aunt sent me. I page through, re-read a poem or start to look at a new one, then stop and look at the line of leafy trees downhill, planted along a winding trace. To the right, I find a run of birches in a copse, white scuffed bark mixed with trapezoids tinged gray. After writing a screenplay last summer, I have ideas for a new one. It will be more personal, though I'm not exactly sure what that means—certainly not two women in their thirties living in Paris. It will be me, but as a woman, and with the ridiculously suggestive name of Liberty—like our landlord's daughter. She, too, lives at home with her mother; she, too, is influenced by Serbian poetry; she, too, wants to create. All these details will force a chain reaction, but I won't know this for some time, years, and then I will accept how I've used writing to get at the predominant issue of my lifetime—my parents.

In Arles, I had scribbled an effete drawing of a tree I remembered from outside the gardens, on an ordinary stretch of green. During that Milwaukee summer, I'd encamp myself on the downward cut of a hill just outside the crowded garden paths. A large, almost comic-bookish oak, fifteen to twenty feet to my left, shaded me from the afternoon sun. There or in cafés, I wrote that screenplay, while pausing to read from a short but thick pocketbook: *Immortal Poems of the English Language*. Walt, Emily, T.S.—"grass is itself a child, the produced babe of the vegetation"—words steadily losing meaning. Everywhere else but there, in that park, I might have been shown to be lonely and cold, since my present and past conspired to keep me from what I didn't have words for then—my relationship with my mother.

I needed to create, but I'd needed her too. Smug paradox. Whatever my feelings toward her, they were necessary, like earth-shaping fires. She affected my pitch more than anyone else, more than my father, who liked to profess how he'd "made" me—a terminology I was unfamiliar with and so stiffly rejected in favor of the higher myth of the stork dropping babies off. From rattle to remote to breakout, all those hours: my mother. She who introduced me to Cassavetes, who would, a few years later, support me going to an LA film school and incur the debt only for me to drop out after a year. At that time in Arles I began to find myself in her, the catatonic episode paralleled her ping-ponging from overlording to silent treatment. Her *I'll show them* carried the carmine psychopathy of an abrupt shutting-out. Close up, fold over, enfold again—a common drill of protection. She'd practiced this on everyone close to her, even her fast friend, the mother of the boy whose sleepovers I rebuffed. There are so many portraits of domineering and overbearing mothers in world letters that those two adjectives are more or less patented for use with "mother." As ever, but with a difference, my mother rose with dead air weight like a giant parade float—*I am here all around you, but you can't speak to me, you can't hurt me*. Not even a bayonet into that lacquered skin would burst it. And I would try. I already did and would yet, with crueler intent—my tungsten heart able only to be a sham, because who would want such puerile floodlights to keep illuminating all-purpose scorn? I turned the page of the notebook, away from the overgrown oak, my silly tree to write by, and resumed my noodling.

Back in the bar, two young women with pastel backpacks came in and sat nearby. Fair-haired, they spoke in English accents, though this was not true—only one did. The other, shorter and greatly freckled, came from Dublin. But they'd met somewhere along the way and traveled together, as in many backpacking relationships where people often nixed plans because they got on well with someone and hurried to towns they didn't necessarily want to visit just to be with them: for a youth sees people when traveling and the elder sees the place, peopling it with those she used to know.

They were going to have a cool drink before setting up their tents. I could see where this would be going—all I had to do... You can't fall in love with every beautiful woman who walks down the street, so if you die trying you will be celebrated in myth, odes, and social media. I played my first game.

They are six or seven years younger than me. They'd met the week before in Carcassonne, going west to east. Solo travel is rough and two isn't a crowd. The Irishwoman is chattier and aggressive, the taller Brit demure, but what you see isn't what you get. They aren't in lockstep; in fact, they get in each other's way. The Brit is still coming off a breakup and can't stand the thought of men, but the Irishwoman has trouble not imagining kisses and congress with a good fraction of the beautiful ones they see. Though each is well-cloaked, I see other felicities. The Brit tries to make light of compliments, she's been compared and contrasted from an early age, but is more sweet than sour—the bitter juice comes from her friend, along with a birthright of elastic envy.

The game had been going well, yet I remained alone. The Brit had looked my way—only once, if I had to count. But I'd done that already, yes? Tarzan-swinging through the forest, while smiling and talking from the heart, promoting like someone who has privately suffered because that is as attractive as projecting successes and holding money. In large part, I am fetching to the people I've attracted because someone responds to what the world has done for me, not because of how I move through it.

Simpering, I turned from the empty pages to two more just the same. I wanted to get up to talk, but not that day. That day I'd arrived to remember soundly, in color and other detail, the woman at attention over my dreams, and those June weeks in that other year.

When we drove somewhere, she drove, and when agitated she drove poorly, like a teenage boy. It was on one of those days that we ended up at a pizzeria on the East Side, near North Avenue by the river, the more acculturated and diverse neighborhood. The Oriental Theatre was one of two arthouse cinemas in the city with the other one only two miles away. We had seen many films in them over the years. That day's bill was an arthouse rendition with a Hollywood pedigree. To go out to dinner together afterward was our wont. Maybe what troubled me most about our relationship was being seen like this, as two sexless friends crooning around, while young men my age were inducing chicks to recognize their fantasies and give in. After being nearly friendless, I had just built up a small stable, yet a few weeks earlier my first girlfriend had taken an ax to our relationship—she preferred someone ten years older than her. I couldn't quite understand it, but I had to. I never could have believed one could be "replaced." The last person I would talk about this with was the closest one in my world.

As usual, we would say a few things about the film, until the food came—then stuff our mouths. What to say about this one? Good acting, though she never liked Kris Kristofferson; I think it was the mountain-man beard. Kept us in suspense, we didn't know how it would end—then it did. Because this was a pizzeria, we had to wait a little longer for our food and had to fill the space with more than silence, and this usually consisted of my mother's reminding me about certain things to be done around the house or, at the least, in my life: doctors, dentists, an oil change. We would never discuss women and how they figured into my path, though she had met my first girlfriend and liked her very much. I wouldn't wander near that dead topic, for I felt a spinning senselessness rising to find my glad tidings and claim all that was left. For the second time, we ran out of superlatives for the film and she piped out an afterthought, a trifle—on a subject I couldn't have cared less about. But I judged she'd said it too loud and I shushed her, with the brittle excuse that when people looked they wouldn't see a man with his mother, but a caretaker with a woman from a group home, though of course I couldn't countenance the squeal of syllables. The dark interior and low, rose-tinged lights of the pizzeria went well with what happened next. When my mother began on how I should move out if I didn't appreciate her, I could feel the likelihood of vast shock-waves about to strike and I uh-huhed and un-ahuhed my way toward the coming tremor before she abruptly stopped and said if I didn't resolve the problems I had with her, these problems would show up in my relationships with women for the rest of my life.

I had not felt that cold and remote from someone in all of my hours. In retrospect, I could only connect the sensation with the uncouth feeling of having distanced myself from a memoir I'd completed, finding I'd written about myself with a voice that was not only naïve but as dispassionate as HAL in *2001*. The fumes of distant pizzas sickened my gut. It was as if my mother had wanted to openly flaunt the fact of ungainly paraphrasing Shakespeare—"those who have the power to hurt but will not do so"—only to sweep me off my feet, judo-style, by taking delight in her very power. "Cut to the quick" is too weak a commonplace. If shaming can be inventive, she was a da Vinci. Instantly broiled, I tried to shrug it off, noticing she had no suggestion of where to start separating the damage. How could she elicit this, given her involvement, her responsibility? What gave her the right? But she had the right, she had experience.

Finally arrived, the pizza had no taste. The words sank deeper into my stores like super-slow-mo shrapnel on a mission to pierce and then repeatedly gouge my organs. In all our screaming matches, in the time she took a wooden bat to me, nothing had the galvanizing force of that simplistic statement. Days on, I thought, I would read Serbian poetry and Plath—they would tell me all about love, and my mother and her afterimage would pop into nothing. I dismissed her words over and again, but the promise of them returned like a burr still in a sock after washing.

Her statement would blur, glimmer, and then come to frosty stalemate over time. Its eternal recurrence has fallen into abstraction. Its bullying still reeks. The base taunt that it is—*If you don't get this, you won't get that*—sets a shade of blush to my aged cheeks. All the therapists would counsel the same thing she did, but by different import, not by fiat or by destroying my dreams. The statement sent me marching—into the real world. For years it stood by her in her darkened corner, until I watched the women in my life leave one by one and I was left alone on a beach with mother memories... She had left me before I could leave her, but—no, I don't have the courage to simplify in such a piss-poor fashion—fractals persist and a geodesic dome overhead frames channels where the past plays out. I did leave her—repeatedly—and watched myself as I did. I couldn't love her, but, early on, while Clayton chummed around with my father, I admitted I did. Moss has overgrown the rock that memory signifies—and memory is rock, my gaze into it contains something corrosive... but to pull away would be self-harm. Up until her death we kept moving together like members of the same battalion who had to pretend to respect one another but mostly kept out of each other's way. She would look for herself in my fiction and inevitably find something until I learned to create multivalent characters, and I still trotted out her good and bad points combined with problems she never had: infidelity, madness. And then she would refuse to read the fictions—she didn't want that negativity in her life, though she endured my father until he left. Nothing else rinsed through. After I again regained an aloneness that old age bestows, I wouldn't hunt for her image to get me through the night, but I could trouble myself enough to see we would have had a chance with each other and missed out. We could have loved each other better if we weren't so stubborn, if we would have watched less television, if Clayton—

But I'm in a different key. In Arles, it was enough to put off the chase, to reconfigure. No meaningful relationship beyond the signature fuck or a few weeks of such unmooring would come of ingratiating myself, a transient, with other transients. The world of van Gogh and Gauguin, in which men simply went to prostitutes, had been eclipsed or at least hidden and semi-restricted to the upper classes—practices which only continued the dehumanization of women and their partitioning into Madonna or whore. If I couldn't fix my relationship with my mother, I could stop sleeping with women I didn't love. And I didn't care about the deeper implications there. To hell with love.

On returning to Malix, I contemplated writing this out to him, retaining the blunt language, though he knew nothing of my mother or my travails, except those of the pen. Uncharacteristically, at eleven in the morning, he slept. I wanted to wait, but they told me not to bother, he'd been up the whole night—these fits happened a few times a month.

I thought it all ended there. I took the bus back to the train station for the one to Marseille. Near the station I saw the two women from the campsite. They were standing with a map of the city, the glossy top of it slumped over like hot taffy. Crossing the street when I needed to be on their side to reach the station seemed foolish, and just as I almost passed them the Brit looked up at me, strengthening herself like an opponent. She knew I knew she knew. It happens in an instant. Yes, I could point them toward a church they wanted to find. Goodbye.

On the train my legs kept quaking, as if I'd vasovagaled and couldn't control the aftershocks. I tried to write something out but couldn't get it to go anywhere. I needed the farm, to break away from reveries, impressions, perceptions. Or I needed what I would write to have a path, one spanning away from morals and didacticism and into language—not what, but how.

The farm seemed greatly changed, as though everything had been replaced with an exact and truer replica, even the people. All that missed time had already occurred—the world before a birth, so that I would have to ask André or Elise or one of the other workers what happened to the garlic beds, their emptiness, or why was the pile of supplemental fume not where it usually was? And they would tell me, explain an event or a decision relaying it as a shorn and rickety anecdote, a frippery, since everyone had been living the new divergence but me. The fields, though, as I looked at them during the second, third, and fourth days back, began to glow in extremely different lights, even chary. They had engendered food and then been wiped clean, and now the first days of late summer dimpled them; they were no longer mine or accompanying me, they were older, at levels I couldn't imagine. The space of the missing corn haunted. The air too had changed, and beyond, into September, more mistral winds blew, sometimes riling the top layer of the trails so ground up by workers and workshop takers it had reverted to a powdering, cocoa-colored dust rising up behind everyone's heels and peppering our lungs to produce catty coughs.

Yes, I had been gone a short while seeming forever; and there grew the single epiphany in my whole time in Europe, but only half-realized—we judge too much according to the construct of time. It guides our speculations like a bad guarantor—we say we know "he'll need time," or we say "I thought it was enough," but simple read-outs of the data only fasten armor to our bromides; the decisions of the belly, the core, these are unfathomable. Time might be the healer, but only because nothing else is and laughter is only the closest medicine, good for surface wounds. So to "mark time" might be most apt, because time is so fleeting, skeet shot before the launch, the dutiful X on the improvised prison calendar scratched into the bare wall.

I had little to fear in those last two-and-a-half months. I worked almost selflessly—and when those tiring days were done, all I wanted was to sit on a verge and look east at the country, because the sun kept departing sooner, obscured by the uplands behind the farm, with the farthest caravan near its base, shoddy and unkempt and barely used—André said he would give it away for free. Below me, the two horses always within twenty feet of each other. The small pine forest beyond, then spills of knuckled rock before the often dry canyon which the main road hugged. I just wanted to see this land, this space. Be there, side by side.

I thought I would read and write so much, I thought I would need to have my friend in Oakland send me a whole box of books I had stored in his basement. Everything I once cherished had no meaning, at least until I left. Then it returned in fits and starts. Back in Heidelberg, there would be the mild hustle, the space broken into bits, and time into hourly fractures.

On a chilly Friday night, I sat on the prickly, chalky ground of the verge, halfway to my cobwebbed tent, which would be too cold to sleep in. André came over to me with a thermos and two mugs. He loved jasmine tea, and we drank up its relief from the declining temperature. I answered him that I didn't know what I'd do next. He suggested staying on if I wanted, with a very reduced load. I could even come to live with them in town, the house had an extra bedroom. His wife, the teacher, could use me sometimes at the school. No—it wasn't me. What was? When I returned to Germany, I might find the answer.

The wind blew at our backs. I sensed he longed for me to ask him something, because he had fifteen years and three kids on me. I didn't want to, especially given how conscious I was of his supposed expectation. I tried to speak as injudiciously as possible: Someday I'm going to look back on this time. That was all truth, but then I added, Maybe it will have shown me that I wasn't as big or as little as I thought I was. I don't know what he made of it; he had to go home to his family. I thanked him for the wonderful opportunity—seven months in pretty much utter peace.

Over the last weeks I went into town on Saturday only once more. The farmer I usually bought carrots from was not there. A spry woman, probably his daughter, did the selling. Her wide-set eyes were cast hard in response to my spidery stare. She threw her hands into her fleece pockets and then jostled them out, so the fleece bulged over the fanny pack holding her money.

I went to the abbey, but it was cold. Fierce yellow and red and fire-leafed trees mixed with the evergreens. In the bar, the same bartender poured me a beer though my teeth were chattering because I'd walked most of the way from the abbey—hardly anyone drove that road in late October. He seemed to recognize me and poured a cognac as well and put his hand up when I offered money. I foolishly tipped, but I was allowed an error here or there. This farewell drink (two of them) did add up to a vainglorious act, but when it's bestowed, it can be vain in your eyes only. This time I kept my distance from the fogged-up window, holding at the bar, closer to the source. Anyway, I couldn't stay long, the light in the sky evaporated earlier and earlier, and I didn't want to get stuck in the dark. I huddled with the drink and checked the mirror ahead.

Years on, when watching Bresson's *Mouchette,* I was struck by how the main bar in it had a similar layout, and I tried to find where he had shot it—on the off-chance. It didn't check out at all. I must have remembered it all wrong. I hadn't thought of the farm in years. I didn't like talking about my past and those escapades. I wanted time to end like the narrative of an austere foreign film, stopping at an unexpected, almost null point.

Conjugal

I want to remember happy, happy days. And I do, but enfolded with a nightshade of hauntings and screamingly silent dreams. I've run them to myself in many time lapses and ornamental sheens. I've asked Why? but it's the wrong question. I created the person who would not hesitate to surrender the brocade I'd never cease to style however manageable my deserving. The true trouble always comes before what we consecrate as the the real trouble. Age, in that heat, might describe it.

I've made mistakes with Jane, but asking, Why don't you buy some lingerie? is in another dimension.

She has an old gray long-sleeve shirt that has been relegated to a pajama top. She often dons it just after feeding Heather to sleep. There's a decal at the chest, two blue swirls of water like large eyes, with a rectangular waterlogged sign floating just above, and between them, in caps: HEAD OF THE CONNECTICUT REGATTA. Get the joke? Usually a pair of polka-dotted or college-aged sweatpants with the right leg torn in two up to the knee rounds out the ensemble. I am dressed in a white T-shirt with underarms stained calico, a pullover with numerous holes and rips, green sweatpants from the dollar store, and expensive gifted slippers that are coming undone near the pinky toes. We are so dressed at seven each night, the time Heather goes to bed, ready for our evening's entertainment and probable falling asleep on the couch less than two hours after a medley of snacks and alcohol.

No girlfriend or lover of mine ever wore lingerie. I should tell my wife that, though it would only elevate the temperature in our kingdom. I'm sorry I ever brought it up. If a person really changed, that is, if my wife turned into a woman who had an unbridled affection for lingerie, I have great doubts her lover would want to be with her anymore.

We don't talk about the other women in my past, just as we don't discuss the men in hers. Yes, a statement will be made: Bess used to get so goddamn drunk... but we go no further, as if the whole motley crew are consigned to some hell where their right to be discussed has been forfeited in lieu of still floating ghostly in our consciousness. These persons are mostly nameless and unimportant—they've already been inhooped to each of us via the ghastly epigram *When you have sex with someone, you have sex with everyone that person has had sex with*. This inspires no reclamation but gives a tangible sense of metaphysical history—our unique history, the trace we leave, the why behind haughtily pronouncing: Everyone is connected. I'd seen lingerie on another woman—my wife knew this before I put the final querying mark on the origin sentence. Why else would I bring it up? You can rarely go sexual without fiduciary forces flashing at some juncture. Peer pressure, consumerism, the hard sell. There are other energies driving my mistakes, and what they are I know not but they have debased and made my mouth move in reverse—skewering my love when I meant only to take the piss out of me, poor me, who thought to be less angry and hostile by letting bile fly.

Jane's greatest friend, Lucia, confronted me one day—You

have demeaned her, you silly ass. We were drinking, but Jane had left the room. I'd also made the lingerie comment almost a year before, and with our new baby in tow, I'd seen Lucia on at least a fifth of those days. I can't believe she told you that, I said. Lucia writhed as if she had a muzzle on. She couldn't speak—she had an ice cube in her mouth. She slowly crushed it in delight. Oh, she didn't? You told me a few months ago, when I brought that whisky. What? Come on. Rick, I think you might have a drinking problem. Or a memory problem. For over an hour or so I successfully believed I'd never made the lingerie comment at all. Lucia always wanted to see us crumble. My wife had sat muted for almost all of that time, listening to Lucia's own life challenges with a flickering sneer, while I kept imagining astonishing scarlet-hued lingerie fitting her curves. I should never drink, I finally said, though by then I was all alone, sprawled on the couch in distemper, a small hard pillow jutting my head up—a bad posture for my neck's pinched nerve. Eleven o'clock. I thought I would muster a second wind and maybe finally finish *The Magic Mountain*, but I was still in the early middle, not even to the halfway point. Or write a poem, an explication of myself in blank verse—telling my wife about my fumblings so I'd feel better about being who I was. I peered at the walls and drowsed.

Nights like this are rare. We both aren't drinkers. I can say this because I've been with many, more than just Alex. Bedtime is nine. When I get in beside my wife and have a pretty clear idea of her clothing, whether it be the regatta shirt and polka-dot pants, or the red tank top and billowy salmon shorts in the summer, or maybe the umber Yosemite National Park pullover and ripped sweatpants during colder days, there is serenity, like after a great vanquishing.

Just around the corner, through a doorway with no door, in a nook, lies our daughter, still in the first stages of a ten-hour sleep. We all lie in a large semicircle, with sound machines in both rooms and, next to me, a fan on low with a pillowcase draped over to louden it. The noise of Brooklyn is lessened. Though if I'm awake in the middle of the night, thinking of what I'd be like asleep, I can still hear the odd large truck throttling to the higher reaches of the slope. Thunder and fireworks, but no more of the big dogs on the block giving late loud barks. It is in the third setting of the Marpac Shushh white-noise sound machine, a sort of hurricane wind sound, that our relationship has found its best feature. There—on the bed at night, we sleep. We share the space. It's a peaceful sleep. Nothing carbolic I can detect—we've said all we've needed to say for one day, and rest will restore. There can be happiness in sleep. In seven years, I've never gone to the couch. We've always been able to come to a necessary calm. How does one know a relationship is over or on its way there? When one person doesn't want to be around the other.

No, night is pretty peaceful. Our little rooms are peaceful. I smell the linen pressed with too many days of our oils and skin and scalp, the clothing grimed by greater amounts of unwashed time. The pressure leaves off. There is a sweet silence in our hills. This living is eternity.

I never really had trouble getting to sleep, though one year I began to wake up very early in the morning and couldn't get back to rest. I had just moved to a new city, or an old new one. Because of that, and no nap during the day, I began to fall asleep at eight o'clock when paired with friends. I began also to get a bad reputation. The wife of a poet who had me over to their house party was particularly distraught. I could see the point. My first time meeting her. This wasn't a fifty-person shindig—there were just eight of us, all having affiliations with the poetry scene. Everyone sat in a circle in this studio apartment trying not to look in the direction of the unmade bed. Foucault's name passed someone's lips and I seemed to be suspended in the air, though I was on the couch next to a stranger, my head wrenched turtlelike but still resting on his suited shoulder—and I could swear there was a shoulderpad in there somewhere. For the last half-dozen times I saw the couple, I kept trying to explain why it had happened like that. Depression, preceded by a breakup, which led to the sleep thing... She wasn't having it. It proved my own future epigram—people will judge you eternally for the slightest bad first impression.

The winter feels long at this time of year, late February. Almost everyone we know is upset, though we don't experience their anger because we don't see them at all. Either our daughter is sick, or we are sick, or they are sick, or their children are sick, or the friends who don't have children don't seem to understand we can't get together at eight for dinner because we are often asleep around nine. Before starting our film, the two of us sit around wondering who our real friends are. It's as far as we get into philosophizing—will pillow talk ever again take on a propulsive force? When so much is impaling, with sprightliness almost a solecism, one must thrust out.

A female friend of mine from college, Meredith, moved to the city a few years back, and we reacquainted ourselves in the icky phraseology of "It was twenty years ago, but it's just like yesterday," which is a sometimes handy feeling. We have get-togethers, and, babyless, she likes to celebrate our daughter. She often comes alone, not with her husband Ted. Ted doesn't like me. Meredith told me herself. Ted actually doesn't like you, she said, as if she had brought down a heavy piece of pipe onto my kneecap. I suppose this is why we are friends: we both believe bluntness makes the best disinfectant. Of course, she didn't need to tell me, I know basic body language. Ted has never looked into my eyes in the half-dozen or more times I've seen him. I'm not bad-looking. I'm not a model, but I don't have fungus growing under my nose or on my chin. Some men don't like their woman having male friends. It's not that, Meredith said. He's liked all my other male friends. As she is a heterosexual woman who has one platonic non-gay male friend, she probably could have more than one. No, she said, he says there's something about you—he can't put his finger on it. But we've never spoken, I said. I know, it has to do with what you are without words. Without intelligence? He sees it that way.

Ted is a plain-faced, five-foot-ten male from Philadelphia. I should revise that "plain," though he is that with everyone else but me, when a great constipation forms—lips pursed, pulled in, reptilian. But he can't hide his head when he is supposed to be a semi-alert and functioning human being in my company, so there's a dented quality. There's also a vulpine texture to the face, but I misuse the word because I want it to mean vulturelike—foxlike is too pretty. Really, it's a hooked owl face: stiff, but gloomy and constantly plagued, as if he is pretending to be missing all his teeth. His hazel eyes, our daughter's color, were unswerving in staring at the table in the restaurant the four of us went to, or at the ceiling, or in the direction of where the waitress was last seen, though she was clearly not there anymore.

His passion, his source and core, never communicated by him to me, is beer, but it is more apt to call it beer snobbery. He knows all there is to know about this, has fine-grain knowledge of every microbrew in America and runs a website devoted to his joy. Trips are often planned around visiting the growing arrays of stateside microbreweries. In fact, the only time he paid slight attention to me was when I relayed the fact that I had visited a now defunct but well-regarded microbrewery in Bandon, Oregon, in the late nineties. I could tell he was rapt as I told the anecdote of staying in the hostel there, right next to the microbrewery, which I then visited. It was my maiden voyage to the West, and I had brought my own pillow to sleep on in hostels and in my tent. By some misfire, I had brought a pillowcase that I still owned from my childhood; it detailed the *Superfriends* cartoon show and comic characters, with a lineup of all these muscled weirdo nutcases sprawled across it. I had just set up my bed for the night when I popped over to the microbrewery for a taste. An older man soon wandered in, holding my pillow across his chest like a life preserver. Excuse me, where did you get that pillow? The hostel. That's my pillow. Oh, he said, and slowly returned it, with a nod. But by the time I finished my story, Ted's attention was back to the phantom waitress, because no details about the beer or its taste were forthcoming.

Beyond beer, there is another aspect to my and Ted's disconnection: his job and his books. He is a proofreader for a major publishing house and devours many categories of non-fiction even when off-duty. I like literature—poetry included—but he likes books about diets, the economy, or the latest take on the sixties in America. We share a love of words, yet we cannot speak to each other. I don't try anymore, because I have and he simply has nothing to say—torching me into white-hot sadness with his over-the-top antipathy. When another friend and I had our moments, that man would say, Well, at least we can connect over a book or film we love or our shared hatred for someone else, whatever gets us back to our safe zone. Ted flies in a different night. Maybe he wants a child. Even as I watch my own wrestling with a new set of screws, bolts, and nuts meant for someone twice her age, using the yellow nut to ease her teething pain, the Ted saga sears me. Maybe commonality is overrated. And maybe this explains why Meredith is married to Ted. Blunt, severe Meredith with pent-up, insuperable Ted. I will never see the secret soldering point, which could be a bright spot as well. I shouldn't think I understand all that is going on around me anyway. Kierkegaard, in response to a student badgering him about causation, said, Shut up about it already. I reach down and take a red circular slot and press it over the blue screw, then grab a yellow bolt and tell her, Turn it, that's it, while making exaggerated twisting motions. But don't fasten it all the way, just get it started. Then I remember I have to buy a six-pack to self-medicate, and Ted returns. I bought him a cheap T-shirt for his birthday, even though I wasn't invited to the party: *Good People Drink Good Beer*, it read. I thought it might make him smile and sulk. Meredith gave it to him after-hours, when he was tipsy. He immediately found it unfunny. She decided not to tell him it was from me, though he had strong suspicions.

When I get like this, annoyed by people who have had and, I hope, will not have any further trespass on my life, I branch out, beginning with a smug strut, to others in my past who have had more deleterious effects and write about them now that a proper distance, at least five years, has been achieved. I disguise them, often as amusing secondary characters in short stories, the ones I psychically describe—of the main one's corpus I say little, preferring to let what they say and think speak louder. After a few hours of this, when on the half-days I don't watch my daughter, all three of us have dinner together and my wife asks what I did during my part of the day off, I say, The usual. After a pause, she'll say, What are you writing about? It's a tricky question. I'm not really writing about the characters I'm writing about; I'm writing about me and my relationship to the past and present. Really, I'm writing about our everyday life, about her coming home from work and asking me that quicksand question, which, no matter how I answer, unsettles me. I can't say that, though, but I once did, and either she didn't hear me (a very low police helicopter flew over at that moment) or she did but displayed formidable control, because her expression remained calm—she who has no poker face. She probably thought I had said, Nothing, which is often my go-to answer, but she could have been so shocked at what clearly was not a joke on my part that it would take a while, hours, before warming to its import. But I should revise this. I'm writing about our everyday life from the perspective of my past. And I don't expect to be understood.

There's a photograph of us at a wedding, taken by the official photographer. There's nothing too special about it, and, in fact, it's not good, but those who were married sent it to us as a token—one of the few pictures with us in it. A telescopic shot of the audience watching the ceremony. Faces. Those in front are blurred. Those in the middle distance are not. Only two are unobscured. A long-haired blonde in a flowery dress and just above her, my wife, chin jutting out to see and maybe hear better. Both women are teeth-smiling. The dark presence to the right of my wife might have his mouth upturned, but that is blocked. Though with my raised cheeks (their proportions telegraphing extra weight in other parts of the body) and bent, shambling eyes—I could be taking a shit. Still, I like the picture because it captures people when they don't know they are being photographed. The expressions are unique, the real thing—how we truly seem to be when someone sees us from afar, with countenances many of us are ashamed of.

Our daughter has taken to fingering this printed paper photograph, picking over it because she sees the two familiar people there. It's one of those random objects that get filled with a much greater significance because someone affords it such close attention. Pictures help with language, the apprehension of it. "Mama, Dada," she says, in tandem. She doesn't know she is in the picture as well, though the belly isn't visible, growing in her fifth month in utero, cells swirling to build brain, bone, organs, skin.

Because she concentrates on it, so do I. There is nothing like a photograph. The past caught doesn't exist on the screen because screens die down. Books and photographs alone survive. The people and objects inside are frozen and alive. This is my daughter's attempted lesson to me. Screens overawe, like bags of money. They are plastic, soulless. Too much of something. These injunctions aren't enough to keep me from looking.

I sit on our new dark-blue couch, looking after my daughter in the p.m., as I often do. My wife is not happy with the couch, though she chose it. No-one sat on it to test, it came through the internet, all we did was press a few buttons and then it arrived.

I refuse to believe that there is a poorer way of coming to a decision. The couch is a few inches shorter than the old one, and my wife likes to sit close to me, not on top of, but close—yet the partition between the two cushions is now constricting her ability to be based more in the middle. If we both sat in the middles of the twin cushions, it wouldn't work, because a projector is anchored (snug against a recess in the wall) just above the right half of the couch, where we don't sit. The projector gives off heat, but the problem is more the ray of light. Someone sitting there would block it, thus curtailing our most common relaxation in the evening. The couch cannot be moved to the left, because it would start to enter the space of the kitchen table; and if to the right, then the ray of light might be partially blocked by the person sitting on the left cushion. We would both need to move to the right side and thus be at an oblique angle from the screen, too diagonal, and we paid too much money to have a bad seat. The projector could be raised, if we had a mount tall enough—and we do. A cheap rectangular bookcase, a few feet from the projector, would fit in the recess well enough and raise it up. This would free the right cushion to be enjoyed, even by a third person, though no-one visits, and few prefer to be near us with our propensity to bicker, or at least play out our brand of passion-aggression, than to enjoy their own home, solitarily phone-lounging. Yet we don't move the bookcase; it is as if the threat of losing our standard, tense place together on one cushion is enough not to make us one day do it. We would lose much more than our legs' almost always touching if we did—we might lose our edge, which is the basis of the relationship, the grind we unconsciously agree keeps us on our toes, with both thinking the other is lucky to be put up with.

So moving the bookcase isn't actually about making things easier—moving the bookcase would take us out of our cycle. And, finally, we don't move it. It stays and gathers dust with a green upside-down Frisbee precariously balanced atop a wine box full of heavy books, itself precariously balanced on the bookcase, itself a four-foot repository of the large, weighty hardcover cookbooks made heavier by the thick expensive paper inside, with professional photographs of meals we have nowhere near enough energy to prepare. These books were unthinkingly placed on the two top shelves of the bookcase when we unpacked three years ago, with my wife's detritus books: paperbacks like the slim *Poetry After 9/11: An Anthology of New York Poets*, a Norton Critical Edition of *Paradise Lost, Be Thrifty: How to Live Better with Less*, and *Learning to Drive*, 5th Edition, on the lower two. The result of this, the top-heaviness of the bookcase (along with the wine box and the Frisbee and a small baby umbrella we recently bought for Heather—one dollar at a stoop sale—though I don't let her play with it because of its pointy spokes) is another reason neither of us has tackled the chore. Our eighteen-month-old is not strong enough to carry out this task, though plenty willful. Heather has progressed from targeting the cranberry bookcase across the room, with her father's four small square shelves holding his coveted favorite authors' books. From seven to thirteen months she again and again went to nudging down first editions specially ordered from Europe and acquired through deceit from libraries, yet the owner of the books was too lazy to move them to another section of the apartment, rather than keeping them in her sanctioned play area of five by twelve feet. I wished she would grow out of the phase, and, unaccountably, she did. At the onset of her thirteenth month she magically graduated across the room, to the top-heavy bookcase—maybe because the small coffee table, in breaking up easy entry to the bookcase holding lesser-valued books, had been relocated seven feet north, in front of the old red sofa (soon to be new blue) to serve as a leg rest for my wife at the southern end of the left cushion. She likes her feet up when watching a film. I used to have to move the Ikea chair from the dinner table about four feet away, but the wickerwork began to break apart. In the end it had to be trashed, but rather than continue bringing over the sturdy oak-chair replacement, I simply turn the rickety oval coffee table a few inches—by day our daughter's private eating table, until after her bedtime it transforms into a less plush but lower footrest. Obstruction removed, our daughter is free to investigate the bookcase's disjecta, as well as a photo album of her grandmother's wedding in 1976—undoubtedly the main draw, because she couldn't read. The coveted-books bookcase has no picture books, and the covers of the novels and other works of prose are the kinds of covers that don't have pictures of unicorns, bohunks and their demoiselles, or glitzy thriller lettering, just the title and the author—albeit one book of essays has a few reprints of paintings, though they are smallish and in black and white. The photo album is plumbed through daily, but *Paradise Lost* remains untouched. Not even the Cranach cover, a wormy Adam and Eve with fig leaves, is entrancing enough.

But I was speaking of us on the couch, squeezed in, and the matter of our legs touching while we enjoy a movie or film. Years before, I was already well into my "not to be touched too much" phase when I read the English translation of Paul Cézanne's grandson's interview on a PBS special detailing how his grandfather didn't want anyone to touch him and I seized upon this as further ammunition in my fight against touch. A few months later I moved to Eugene, Oregon. Though not well-publicized, this bubble is the capital of hugging not only in our country, but in the entirety of the continent. Hug everyone when going into a party, everyone there. Everyone. Then hug them all when you leave. Every one of them. I hugged constantly for five years. It made me a better angrier man. When I arrived in New York, I carried in the happy knowledge that I would now be living in a place where one is nothing, unseen—you don't stick out, no matter height or tits or hair—and so no-one will hug you. I had no good excuse for the five touch-heavy Eugene years. Brainwashing? Wanting to fit in?—which is close to brainwashing. In typical Eugenian fashion, though standing on Van Brunt Street in Red Hook, I let it go. Most of the women I dated then lived in Brooklyn. You can't touch them too quickly, but then—strung out cold, with not even a piddly methadone-program dose to see me through the day—I wanted to touch them very soon, right away. They destroyed me, and I admired them for it. They weren't ready for me, and wouldn't be until I changed.

My wife came to life on the Upper West Side, but now we are married. She wants a husband who touches her more than periodically and who says that he loves her more than in a monthly "I luv u" text. I have a flip phone and don't respect words when texting, mainly because I don't respect texting. Anyone can do it. Not everyone can write a love sonnet in iambic pentameter. I sometimes text my wife the picture of that sonnet, written during the courting phase—the original is folded up on her nightstand. I send that when I probably have to buy flowers to cover a misdeed, send it as a sort of reminder of my more special quality, however jejune and bastardy—I even put the word "jejune" in the sonnet because without the French prefix, that's close to my wife's name. As for holding each other during the watching of movies or films, I have strict guidelines—if a scary scene is upon us, I will by all means hold my wife's hand, the same for emotional bloodlettings, tragedy. If nothing out of the ordinary is going on, I don't enjoin to hold hands; it is a distraction from the images I prefer to watch unblinkingly, because I like to see every frame of film, even though they've been digitized and aren't frames anymore. Yet I understand the interstices of the physics and metaphysics underlying our couch saga, the struggle to keep love from turning brittle. I understand because after all this time a man is still supposed to take care of a woman, it's Biblical, as regular as eating the bitter herbs dipped in saltwater every year on Passover—as regular as Tax Day.

I have to make allowances. All marriages do. In honor of our thighs being so close, I take to patting my wife's left one, the closer. I'm excited about the pat as a form of affection. I think it's been given a bad name, literally. From the Middle English, it's also a man's and a woman's diminutive—make up your mind! No wonder it has bad connotations, as in when someone pats you before they kill you, evidenced in *The Godfather* and countless other films. "Pat" is close to "tap"—its obverse lettering—and a tap, many people don't know, is the staple of the healing art called tapology. Introduced to me in my Eugene, Oregon years, it is a process wherein the medical professional or licensed "tapologist" taps the patient, who rests before them in a sitting position. They tap at the parts of the body giving the patient fits and also some of the main energy points, many of which overlap with the chakras. I visited one for a mysterious problem, which was just stress, as all mysterious problems are. I had a constricting feeling in my neck, as if my throat closed while a Geist strangled me—the oldest stressor in the book. Added to that, as I stood in public places, I had the sensation that I was about to faint and, as in a bad story getting worse, no-one would help me—I would die. Massive amounts of pot didn't help. I read *Siddhartha* again—no. So I went to Elf, the tapologist. A smiling woman with a limp, she brought me into the darkened extra bedroom of her house and pressed play on a didgeridoo CD. Please, I requested, no didgeridoo. Sounds of a barren strand, Maui edition, seemed fine. Tap, tap, tap, tap. Neck, shoulders, chest, temples. Tap tap, tap tap, tap tap. Everywhere. At one point I asked if the teachers of tapology ever experimented with doing a "pat," but she didn't answer. The surf went on and on, and she kept asking if I felt different, if I felt better, and just by her asking me that every five minutes, I had to admit that I did. I really didn't, but I thought I must, she made me believe so.

These days I particularly enjoy a kind of four-part pat on my wife's left thigh. That is two brief, full-handed pats, but then a pause—hand on flesh or clothing—and a brush, up the thigh, with mild pressure, before I relinquish, raise up and come down once again with a light, fingers-only pat, and then I return my hand to my own thigh or belly. To pat any more than four, and really three times in a row, risks being heaped in with the bad-connotation pats, and I'm keen not to upset the closest person in the world to me. I offer the most exquisitely loving pats—heart-delivered and heart-aimed—better than flowers, because it is my own body, though intercourse is in the netherest zone from my pat-happy consciousness.

So we watch, I pat, she makes a little noise at something funny in the film—then one of us, or both of us, fall asleep well before the film's end and sometimes only twenty minutes into the picture. After awakening some thirty to sixty minutes on and not recognizing the new trouble in the film, I start to undo all the computer cords to the projector. My wife begins a truncated routine in the bathroom, just brushing—no flossing or tweezing or creams. I will not brush my teeth, because I am too tired (I don't want to get too energized by brushing, because when I do it, I do it competitively) and will just go to the bathroom, remove my contacts to prevent pinkeye, and have a small sip of water, to not be taken with a more powerful urge to pee at four a.m. than I usually do.

We flow, one a few minutes behind the other, into the bedroom with a catwalk, though between the two sound machines and toe-tips, our daughter has never woken up. We nestle, briefly, and I try not to pat, keeping that sensation unique, though readily on call. We turn and gather our pillows into our favored pillow placement. Peace descends.

I can't be in present with the rest.

Most people live for trips. We did. The real test of a family is how they do on a trip, and no-one but them is truly interested in the results. Forget hiking trips with tots. California? Too far. Nature in the East is geologically old and puny, we'd sussed it out. Maine is as rugged and craggy as parts of Oregon, though it's a third its size and monochrome. We also took to Maine because it's a forty-minute flight—by the time the thrill of the plane had gone for Heather, we were making our descent. A friend of the family co-owned a house on the Somes Sound. We didn't get a discount. Construction on the summer-only rental was completed in 1926. A small miracle to live there for one week a summer—no TV or internet signal and limited phone service. Because people couldn't so easily escape, things got real.

I've always had fantasies of trips with a lover—how close and loving the time together, the space apart from the grind. A bestowal of sorts, since in all the time leading up to that time we were biding our time, slogging to reach a shoal of partial paradise. It never turned out so grand. Because I couldn't keep up my routine for a few days, my quotient for being an absolute asshole drastically skyrocketed, and usually by day five I was unbearable and flaunting my invisible knives, wanting to annihilate the person who wanted to give me everything except space to write. I couldn't hide things as well back then.

I knew with a toddler on this particular trip, Maine would be about family—and, even more so, family time. I could jot notes or read for an hour or so every day, but all else would be in service of the greater good: watching the baby, cooking, cleaning, buying food, bringing in wood and keeping the fire hot. No-one would care if I was able to read a different twenty-five-page preface to each of Shakespeare's six best plays on our six days there; no-one would be impressed that I gathered the details of everyone present and then mixed and matched to erase any direct likeness of them in people I would soon own by calling them my characters. On the plane, my wife muttered, It won't kill you to be like everyone else for a week. No, but it could kill my soul.

There were five bedrooms. The baby occupied the only one with a single bed. After us, that left three. In the past, we'd come with my wife's family and a childless couple who are friends, but that year my brother and his wife flew up from Indiana, where they'd landed a decade ago so he could teach history at a name-brand college. Also onboard, in lieu of Grandma, who was recovering from hip-replacement surgery, was my wife's uncle Stewart and our other friends Tristan and Tina, who agreed not to smoke as much pot as they usually do, or at least to vape in private, keeping the rumors a little less substantiated.

When we planned out the arrangement months before, there was a great deal of excitement—we honestly couldn't envision this select group of eight persons, with one incapable of a two-word sentence, holding any group animus. Were there any wildcards? My brother and Uncle Stewart could certainly be given to those *getting up on the wrong side of life* days, but Clayton's wife could douse his morose disregard before it reached the coffee pot. If coerced, Jane could neutralize Uncle Stewart's anomie by reminding him of how we still owed him money from an ill-fated investment in a local sorbet franchise that closed the same month it opened five years ago. He had said to forget about it, but we knew better. Tristan and Tina were, of course, reserved, almost complementarily innocuous. We'd been friends for nine years and in that stretch we'd never known them to be anything but stable, sensitive, and kind. They played in a couple's beach volleyball league, though the games took place not on a beach but in a regulation-size sandbox. They tried to get us to join, since we were both over six feet tall—though we didn't commit, until the pregnancy gave us the perfect excuse. They otherwise quietly passed through life, each working in social services, each vaguely interested in what I wrote, though they never mentioned my books after I gave them a signed copy. Most especially, they built a monument to cooking and made use of every last vegetable from their CSA.

Men. My relationships with men were much more interesting because so much was not said. Clayton was four years older than me and there were other problems. He wrote political books, but immediately his long thin finger would wag at me: "Political theory—with a needle's-eye snatch of academic rigor." I'm sure he was also spiteful in the four years he didn't know me. I took no joy in that his first wife left him for another woman. I tried to see around it. I tried to see Raydon, a plump Swede, tamping him down at night into her nest of flesh so at least he wouldn't sleep too tormentedly. He always adored Europe and desired to live there, but his fast-track education and early success prevented it somehow—that's his story. Only one summer spent there and he cut that short to get back to his soon-to-be first wife. He never respected the way I lived there: couchsurfing, the farm, falling for naturally beautiful divorced women with young children: "So, of course, they wanted you around, Rick—easiest game in the book." Then I had the child he never would, and though I'd learned to deflect the odd remarks, he'd revised them and hatched new ones: *How's the composition of the Great American Novel, is the kid helping you?* And: *You're gonna teach him Chinese, yes?*

I thought since Clayton would be fifty in a few months, he might have started to enter a reckoning stage, making peace and finding a kinder self and, for Christ's sake, stop talking about how many miles he biked a day in the little-known squire of Bar Berry Heights by Purdue. While he went out in the canoe with Uncle Stewart, I heard Raydon tell my wife how she had pleaded with him not to bring the bike, because he would just be gone for three hours every day and this trip was about seeing his niece—his only niece, and his only taste of children, aside from the three created by his first wife's family-minded sister. I always gave Clayton presents related to "cycling" (from the start he'd ordered me never to call it "bicycling") or the Augustan period, his favorite in history, going so far as to order books in German, since he could read them, because he'd claimed to have read almost every English-language book about the epoch. His reception of my gifts was often full of truculence. The book was badly written or designed, or I bought him inferior cycling gloves. I employed such maneuvers to a degree with my wife. I would have liked to blame my brother, my father, the German race, but soon enough I would see the glorifying appearance of a freelance payment finally arriving in my bank account and unburdening me of my anger, to be let out in a different fashion in some far future hour. Men get softer with age? It happened to our old man, until he snubbed out as quick as a dying match. It will happen to Clayton; it's happening to me. In response to the presents my brother would give me—a book of poetry by someone he knows I loathe, or a tacky tie—I would nod steadily and try to hug him, but he would half-hug me and pat my back hard, still thinking I had a trace of a disease from the commune I lived at for a summer, a fact punctuated by his having received their quarterly (acid-free paper, staplebound) when I lived in Europe and used his address for mail. The cover displayed ten smiling naked people sitting in a hot spring and waving to the camera—a blurred picture making him sick. And he didn't lie; there were crusted spots of vomit on it when I finally retrieved it. At least we didn't seriously think of killing each other—family first, or last.

After years of the same vacation in the same house, the routine in Maine had become quite simple: make meals, sit on the deck and watch the water of the sound, go down to the dock and watch the water from a closer perspective, go buy more food, go to Acadia National Park one afternoon, take the canoe for a spin, go to the fresh-produce farm, go into the small town and check the discounted books in the public library and check e-mail—then watch the sunset and drink, talk, laugh, relax. I assumed this would be the case again, and it was for the first days.

Uncle Stewart wasn't too much fuss, as long as I drove him to the gas station to get him his *Times*. Heather would be on the porch with everyone, but blockades had to be constructed for each staircase. People quickly caught on that nature was all around—they didn't need to drive anywhere. There were trails from the house to two different small rocky beaches, if thumbing smoothed stone and wading in cold salty water interested, as well as another trail to a large meadow where deer poked about—in an offshoot of Acadia, with more trails leading to larger forests and more impressive meadows. Other than preparing food, no-one had to do anything—which one had to admit was the point. We sat in the various chairs on the porch looking out over the chilly sound (trees had been cut to provide a view), talking of who was in, who not, and our commonalities, but mostly these: food, the history of Maine, and brief synthetic details of our pasts. Tristan and Tina seemed to be concentrated in the kitchen, preparing vittles throughout each day: high-wire appetizers, complex salads, difficult desserts. It almost seemed we had hired them to do this and Uncle Stewart fairly convinced himself ("How much of a discount did they get?) but no—they strove to keep up with their passion and we had provided a healthy amount of food for them to improvise with. I would probably have preferred otherwise, because in their absence I had to endure my brother holding court almost always beside me, as if he was afraid of Uncle Stewart and thought vacation meant a respite from his wife, who had him on nights and weekends and during the summer break when he was most often cycling or in his den, fuming at airplane prices to Rome. Raydon, in turn, often played with our daughter and made as many references to their childlessness as possible. Clayton ignored them.

Outside, wasps disembarked from the eaves and dipped up and down by the food and drinks as if they were strung on a line someone kept plucking. My brother continued describing a colleague he loved to hate—a man my age who sounded exactly like him, though "exactly" might be too strong, since I'd trained myself to listen to only every fourth or fifth sentence he uttered. Before then, I would have liked to hear about such matters from other people. I wasn't a research-oriented writer, and if I found a fact I'd write it that way; I'd lurk and listen to how people talked, which is mostly how they complain and in turn how they live. I've learned more about writing by listening to the vox populi than to any professor. And my brother, whatever else ailed him, was a decorated scholar, often going to conferences worldwide and arguing his case or cases. But he would stay away from his bubble for only so long: he needed to get back to despising his wife in her company.

I sat with my light beer, watching the glinting afternoon waves as an old windjammer with masts the height of a three-story apartment building eased on, heading southerly to the opening, the Atlantic. For many years I'd fantasized a *Long Day's Journey Into Night* type of conversation with a family member or a close friend, it didn't matter which. Yet the circumstances were so hard to correctly align. As my wife napped, Raydon went inside for a snack and Uncle Stewart shortly followed. With my daughter in tow, playing with a toy record player, the same type I'd farted around with when young, I tried to imagine a beginning with Clayton and framed the right opening, like "I think about you sometimes, Clayton," or "When people ask me about you, Clayton, I try to ease their complaints by telling them the story of your making me go with you to that soup kitchen every Thanksgiving and Christmas." He still gabbed about the same colleague, recounting how he couldn't keep up on a bike ride. I waited for a lull, a merciful pause in his rabid feast which continually starved his one remaining guest, but just as there might be one and my breath grew rich at what was in its stew, a new complaint rang out, and then my daughter, attracted by his angst, tried to drink his beer, then my beer, then Uncle Stewart's Manhattan (strange he would leave it behind)—and there it went, my chance at causing initial damage, but in a naturally occurring way, like waves eating at the base of a sandcastle. No big mess, the castle wasn't fully equipped anyway.

Raydon and Uncle Stewart soon returned, eventually followed by my wife, who held another of Tristan and Tina's creations, a lobster bisque with an oily glaze I could plainly call a too-rich sauce. The couple sat to watch with delight while we ate. It was good, we told them so—then we needed to talk about something else. We tried not to let it be politics, but that certainly did dominate, so Tristan and Tina slowly slipped away down to the dock, the perfect place to change the chemicals in one's brain. Uncle Stewart swigged the last of his Manhattan and complained about the unemployment rate, it was too low, no—too high. My wife sat one empty chair away from me and raised her eyebrows, signaling she knew what I had been thinking—even if I've never shared with her my desire to open up to my brother and ask him to take hold of my heart. Raydon seemed to notice this unapprehendable high sign from her position on the floor of the deck, goo-gooing with Heather, but luckily my brother kept trashing a new colleague who didn't fit his bill. He spoke while looking out over the prevailing water, which might have just as well been the blank faces of students unwilling to intercept the import of his drone. The scene almost stayed frozen, but one of us had a choice at that moment to disport and change course. It's the hardest thing in the world to do. I would have been graciously thanked by future generations of history students at Purdue if I had done it and I pulled it off, but I didn't. I couldn't bring *The Long Day's Journey* about. The more Clayton protruded over what should have been a reclamation of calm for us all, regaining the feel of the beginning of time—no cars, no electricity (at least now), nothing except the manner in which we sat on deckchairs, though they weren't necessarily comfortable—the more that old stone of sadness emerged in my stomach. I swallowed. A few hours later, after dinner and sitting in despair on the toilet, I made peace with the stone, and gave it proper breadth—I'd done this then for years and easily remembered my routine.

The importance of the house's floor plan—who would sleep where was the greatest decision of the trip. The main bedrooms were aligned on each side, two to a side, in the corners, with a shared bathroom between them. The baby's room was on the other side of the kitchen, in the house's middle space. Abutting all was the large living room holding the hearth, the dining table, and four old fashionable leather chairs symmetrically positioned, two facing two. We were next to the baby's room, of course, with Tristan and Tina on the other side of us. Uncle Stewart was at the back entrance, by the kitchen, with my brother and Raydon opposite him and kitty-corner from our room—the furthest possible distance in this raised, one-floor house. Being a summer resort it had no insulation, and you could clearly hear a normal cough behind a closed door, but each room was equipped with strong fans and space heaters and, in our daughter's case and ours, the Marpac Shushh sound machine to block out our nighttime socializing in the living room.

Acoustically speaking, we weren't too worried about others' nighttime calisthenics, though sometimes a loud snorer could overcome the loudest white noise the machines had to offer. I assured Clayton that Uncle Stewart would not give him trouble (our father had had sleep apnea) although I wasn't entirely positive—it had been a while since I lied to him and I thought to try my luck. Over the first days I received no complaints, or more of his standard, foreboding looks, whose generation I would need to tease out. From what I gathered, Clayton and Raydon's passions had cooled, and Tristan and Tina would calmly take their before-bed bowl by the window and then pass out, dreaming of their own prime-time cooking show. My wife and I might gather our forces together once or twice, certainly not when people were still up (we went to bed first), but when waking up early and knowing we might have the time to turn the arousal jets on high, and quickly.

All this is to say I was greatly unprepared upon walking into the kitchen on the fourth morning. After our daughter had been babbling for ten minutes just after dawn, I found Raydon closing the door to Uncle Stewart's room. Obviously she wouldn't use the passageway through the bathroom. But why obviously? What is there in me that likes to assume? Was Uncle Stewart an attractive man? Maybe Raydon gave him Swedish lessons? I felt for my brother—even a tinge of protection. Raydon's roving eyes expressed no embarrassment upon passing me, and for that

I admired her. The rest of the day went on as usual, though Uncle Stewart didn't come out of his room in the morning and I drove to buy the paper alone. The woman at the gas station eyed me strangely, as if she missed his mordant presence. Like the garrulous, smug-assed New Yorker he was, he bantered with everyone, knowing how to ask about their family even though he cared only about his needs, while I continued to coldly present my insufficiencies. When I returned, Uncle Stewart sat lordly on the deck, drinking his coffee with a pinkie half-extended. I flashed the paper. What a pal, he said.

I remembered years ago, when I went to Europe for the first time with two college friends: a dark-complexioned man and a grinning woman very close to each other, yet platonic. The woman's sister came along. We were all staying in the same hotel rooms to save money. At one point, in Paris, the man and the woman's sister fucked in the middle of the night. No matter how stealthily, it was obvious. The next day they pretended it never happened. Finally, the first woman, moping and most likely having been harboring some feelings for the man, said to him, You had sex with my sister last night—I think I'm entitled to a little emotion. We were so young. And in Paris. And cooped up. I couldn't blame them.

An hour later I studied my brother sitting on the wooden chair by the corner of the deck, his mouth popping out puffs of air directed at shredding the new work of a colleague on the second settlement during the Augustus reign. I left my lips on my wife's for two extra seconds during our rare second morning kiss—we displayed more affection on trips because so many more people were watching us. No, I hadn't seen Raydon and Uncle Stewart speaking once through the entire first three days.

But I was consumed with Clayton. Would I tell my wife? There was no-one else I could tell, except Tristan and Tina, and I didn't think it mattered to them.

That day we were to drive to a lobster pound for lunch, a place in Bernard, just off the Atlantic. Two cars. Uncle Stewart came with us. As we ordered, the sky turned a deeper gray, and fat drops of rain drove us to eat inside. The smell of dead and soon-to-be-dying seafood in such abundance often aroused feelings of nausea in me. Maybe they were tied into the offal of thousands of dead alewife washing up on Lake Michigan shores in the summer. The silvery carcasses, cooked by full or cloud-capped sun, sent a stench of what I could only call feces and death into my core, inculcating an agnostic dread that resulted in my not having learned to swim and spurring my gag reflex—a sensation equaled only by slippery and slimy bok choy or eggplant in my mouth, or the sight of Richard Simmons babbling on a talk show. On the restaurant's deck I began to catch the steamed death of the remaining crustaceans, a hard-boiled funk very close to that of that contamination of yore. I ate my catfish sandwich in vague horror at the possibility of having to vomit it up. Sickness is trauma, and I began to feel things disintegrating more and more, while my brother seemed to be enjoying himself for the first time. I saw a humbling smile after he made a successful pun on the word "bluefish"—but this was not surprising, I often hallucinated about how those I had most trouble with were at their best when I was at my worst. I wasn't quite there, but I was close. The signs were ever-present: sweating palms, chest pain, constipation, slipped-disc pain, vibrating thighs, seeing double, obsessive thoughts, loss of hearing, chills in rotation with hot flashes, low-grade nausea, being with an original family member, knowing a man taller than me was in the same room (in the corner was a college-age giant as gaunt as a towering reed), and a fear of someone using the phrase "get your groove on." Still, somehow, I could smile. I'd seen it before, taking on someone else's drama, worrying myself into their moat for us to die together, regretfully. No—not then, not with my daughter. I had to be strong and set an example. How else would she sustain the shield she'd need to keep other people's shit off her? I could smile but also flaunt despair, my especial ingot to carry the day. In looking around me, I saw no lobster pound interior. I saw space. I'd been shot putted into the air, blown west, and landed by a Great Lake. Not the one of my birthright. The smaller one with the strange name.

It was better to talk of it as if it hadn't happened to me—that's what I believed for a time. Months later, after our end, working in New Jersey as an aide to a man with MS, I spoke to a guru-type therapist a friend had connected me with. She said quite confidently, All these feelings of loss and despair are not tied to her. It all goes back to your parents. Your salvation will be in examining that time—but I wasn't about to do this again.

Karma—the word is a sham, the action isn't. You meet the people you are supposed to get lessons from—the bitter lessons, those that many think they can do without. In this way, you simultaneously create your own karma and follow the set list that no scroll can afford to paper or ink. Every day can be shadowed by horoscope. Every day we don't know what we have or what we'll get, even if the act of giving is premeditated.

The memories have died well down to less than a trickle every five years or so. Alex was not my wife—I would play out a similar dance with her, though it's easier to remember this ending—but someone important enough for me to have spent years in thrall to. People speak of their great loves, but too often those loves are the ones who no longer occupy them in their lonely hours; it's more those who have been the best allies, not the best roaches. Shameful to trust hindsight, given its smell—we're only as happy as our last meal has been satisfying. Now I sound like the old philosopher who stokes a rage about the world's sufferings every morning but goes on to devour a grand lunch in a four-star restaurant. It could be worse—it could always be worse.

The space of where we came to live, in the city of Buffalo, shadowed our splintering. I don't still feel the band of love or hate, but the confinement of my body in large rooms haunted me before and after my living there—a sizable apartment on the second floor of a hundred-year-old landmarked house, a space we rented for a song. We knew someone—or I did. And he was just leaving. A podiatrist ran a practice on the first floor. The employees of his practice had a private room, a lunchroom upstairs next to us. They were all gone by five and never worked weekends.

In claiming this space, I removed us from a noisy apartment building across the street from where F. Scott Fitzgerald grew up. That piece of history didn't exactly shape my writing into more measured tones; in fact, the time was full of gross experimentation, embracing such modes I usually had no use for, nor would ever again: horror, science fiction, slipstream. I would read those embarrassing works aloud to Alex in a facile attempt to gain minor adulation that I'd immediately dismiss, thinking, but not declaring, You'd like anything I wrote because I wrote it. What she served might have been her squelched naiveté, because she did have strong opinions but wouldn't let them cross over into my reality, whether out of pity or humility. She had a feeling for literature and could recite the odd Shakespearean sonnet for no other reason than she liked how it sounded, not what it said. Putting in her eighty hours a week as a general-practice resident, she had no time to read, but we'd met at the end of her internship in New York. Sharing the written word fueled our blaze at that time.

In other hours away from her, and even in the few we filled, I was mostly alone in our rooms atop the house—for the better part of two Buffalo winters—seasons that began on October first and ended on Memorial Day. One walked up the carpeted stairs of the old re-done building to the flimsy door to our apartment, entering into the hallway where, in proceeding right, the large bedroom came first and then the bathroom, before opening out into a medium-sized living room, with the kitchen just on the other side of that wall—about two hundred square feet of desolation. The floors were a beautiful camel-colored wood. The walls were newly painted and mostly unadorned by two people averse to decorating. Our cobbled together furniture and furnishings, but no TV, left much space, and it would be clear to a knowledgeable thief that twenty-year-olds lived in the apartment, so maybe it wasn't worth it. We easily fitted our shared collection of books into the set-in wall cases, made spaghetti, and acted stupid. The weak-willed forced-air heat pushed us to plastic up the windows in November. Those heating bills frightened, but only because the rent appeared so small in contrast.

For a while I couldn't find work and went to a labor force to be paid minimum wage for landscaping. An office temp agency found me sporadic, slightly better-paid jobs, as I struggled to have somewhere to escape to, since at that time there were few friends. My ten years of incremental writing progress had passed and left me half-mystified. I had begun to draft stories I would be paid for, but I still hadn't read properly, hadn't started to bury something in the writing itself without effort—the pride point of someone comfortable in their art. I kept whispering inside that it was all right. I was reinventing myself—again! Yet the exclamation point's ink seemed to fade and fade, until one wintry day in early autumn all that glistened was the terminal period. And there was no other art to hop to. I left film school when they told me something I didn't like—I took it not as constructive criticism but envy. Hours with the Steenbeck produced a 16mm version of a hell on earth not mine. I told myself my dream had simply floated out of my grasp, though strangely I held the knife with my belly's blood.

Alex's parents, in distant Thousand Oaks, were afraid from the start that I'd begin sponging—and her mother, a real-estate baron who had accustomed her body to a fleet of sundresses in the area's spectacular weather, ran me down in regular phone conversations in which Alex would hold out the receiver to the air so I could hear the tinny squeaks of a woman used to getting her way. It had been a little more than a year, but Alex still waited to see who I was in equity terms, eager to know what I'd give beyond the opportunity for our ritualizing simultaneous orgasm.

The sex-positive months passed through the coldest winter of our lives. By March, delights had become more intermittent. No matter. I'd created the apt conditions for time to write, seeing security in love and rent and few disturbances, but I wasn't ready to take confidence in myself. The high arrogance of my betters and lessers I certainly strongly detested, but any kernel of this had long been farmed out by those mythical and real Midwest ploughshares that made oneself small, a fledgling who portrayed vitality with too much timidity, like the hanger-on actor to whom no-one says: You don't have talent. I had to prove worth in dollars and soon, to make my own, was sent to a bank downtown to count money in the vault. I prided myself on being able to hold a million in cash in one hand. One hundred hundreds made a hundred-thou, and ten of those made one brick, the unit all denominations were accumulated in before being wrapped and shipped to the local Federal Reserve Bank in Cleveland. A close to full-time gig, it lasted six months until one day the temp agency called, just after I left work, to say the bank didn't need me anymore. Some months later the agency again rang to say the bank wanted me back, but I'd passed on to a job with adults with disabilities, my standby position when living in the West.

I'd already started to bend lazily inward upon arrival in Buffalo, waiting out the long hours until Alex returned (and sometimes she got home at ten and eleven at night and had to be back the next morning at six) by picking my nose, watching movies, and attempting to construct delusions of grandeur. The words "reinvention" and "Buffalo" would not coexist. I'd had to begin a life, apart from love, in a dying city, trading in the spunky irreality of Eugene and the know-your-shit of New York—the two places I'd lived since returning from Europe—for the bitter, formulaic guise of a town where inner squalor feared exploding outward, a simulacrum of the heritage I'd had my quotient of in Milwaukee. The small street just off downtown, Allen of Allentown, served as our main source of entertainment. It had a great used-book store, a few at least interesting restaurants, and four distinct bars: the hippie one, the quasi-punk-and-biker one, the highbrow one, and the American-themed one. All over the street lurked the "cool" people, though most were ensconced in their cliques. Alex could sometimes hang out with her fellow residents, but their schedules limited this. I befriended a few of them, listening to their drunken tirades or confessions because I needed something else to hold on to, to make my life real. Or did I not know enough of real life? No wonder I wrote slipstream stories—nothing could be at stake in such an existence, where I pretended to go against the grain, like a transient camping in the public parks every night, scooping out food from the cavernous dumpsters in back of chain supermarkets and then calling the parents for cash when in real trouble. I added further comedy by holding forth that only I could furiously bring ecstasy to this woman I believed to be the only one I'd ever truly loved. A few months after meeting her, I said to my brother, She is the most beautiful woman in the world. He stared at his foot and then started to worry about the Democrats losing the Senate.

Alex had a seriousness that could easily be scrambled by an improvisatory wing-footed California-girl esprit. She typed out "I work hard and play hard" on her half of our shared profile on Couchsurfing—a platform I'd demanded we join. I detested banalities in writing, as I thought she did, but she evinced little trouble in trotting one out, possibly because I'd forced her to do something against her instincts, a scheme to save money on our trip to Europe and the ones to New York. My admiration for her smarts and her doctorness drove my lust, but her "playing hard" took an ax to our flimsy felicity. We were similar—I too clamored for severity but could give myself away to clowning. We both could withdraw as well. My brand was more raw passy-aggressy, while hers (with eight fewer years in the world) was less a simple regurgitation of emotions than an actual, benighted not-being-able-to-access-them brand. This came out slowly, and the first year's honeymoon dovetailed with our major battles about money, time, and living in Buffalo. Eventually her superiors began floating the idea, soon to be reality, that a research year would look nice on her résumé, adding a sixth to the five I thought to be the set term for our Siberian adventure. I wanted answers, though I knew she had to be beholden to her career; I needed to know how much she wanted me in her life, whether I'd been just a convenience to help her get through the bumps of moving to another city, and whether there wasn't any chance she remotely shared her mother's low opinions of my future prospects—an answer I already knew. Money did carry weight. She had a quarter of a million dollars of debt, and I was making peanuts first at the bank and then when taking the bus thirteen miles to Depew to work in a group home. It wasn't about love. Love is easy; security is more important—worth more, as the word promises. The greatest critique of our time, that I'd gladly assent to, was that I'd patterned my life in order to be with her. So what? my college friend Arthur countered. Everyone does that. You love her. Don't let your famlies foul your lives up.

Around the autumn of our second year, a few new persons came into our life. A fiction writer of some repute, Tanner Theale, had just been given a position at SUNY Buffalo. I'd followed his career before then, especially after he won an award for a short story collection. This coincided with the virtual world becoming more and more a battleground around "correct" literary form, with many disputations rising up to be weighed in on and adjudicated by fractious factions. Internet journals started to place more content online, and though the Nook and e-readers had their season in the sun, they rotted as anything browning too long in it will. This was near the dawning era of book trailers and other such gimmicks, with the book business entering a crisis (to my mind) more about mediocre content than about sales challenges. The young guns celebrated the "attack" sentence and consecution of Gordon Lish's teachings, shitting on the current crop of big names while rekindling an interest in Lish's students, as well as Robert Walser and Renata Adler—with Alice Munro considered too conservative and Cormac McCarthy just right. But it was no use. Challenging works were not being published by the merging Big Five and the small presses struggled for respectability. Tanner Theale took no position in this lively but caustic debate and enjoyed his small corner of the U.S. literary world, the cultivation of short stories, first at the College of Wooster and then at Buffalo, to keep close to the family seat in Detroit. If asked for influences, he'd grudgingly name Kafka or Flannery O'Connor. He kept to an even-tempered, passionless tone, no linguistic pyrotechnics, no narrative displacements. Unabashed realism—family disputes, adultery, men who must confront their past, moral ordering. I'd seen one of his stories in a journal I'd found at the bookstore, an old *Missouri Review*. Father and son, the former in delinquency—then a grand "having it out." It made a mark. I found his book in the library.

Tanner was only a few years older, but he'd gone to the Iowa Writers' Workshop right out of college and had been teaching since twenty. He didn't cut a great profile. A prominent nose entrenched in a long oval face, with appraising blue eyes and a short coiffure, the top longer and layered in with a combover reminiscent of the early fifties. He liked to run—he said it made thinking easier. By some coincidence he ended up living only a few blocks from us. He initially acted very mincingly, and I assumed he wasn't used to someone taking such an interest in him, even with the prize—either that or he planned to seduce me. I wanted to pick his brain, and I'd foolishly typed that in my last e-mail before I met him. He said to send him something short to read so he could better gauge my abilities. The verdict: an MFA might do me no good and cost a lot of money. I'd been considerng Syracuse, only a few hours east. He waved this away. You've already published a few things. Keep reading. But really you have another more important choice to make: you can be a comer, a person who gets in other people's faces—and he named a few obvious examples of such compunctionless persons—or you can sit and brood, do the work, make it beautiful, and take your chances on ability alone, a much harder path and one that fewer and fewer people respect. He'd followed that path himself, but he also had the Iowa glitterati behind his dipthonging name. You've been to New York, he said, you know the scene. Only vaguely, I replied. He poured us more San Pellegrino. You've had a lot of life experience. Winnow it down, then extract some feelings from it and make it into a story. The short thing you sent was fine, but start to puff it out. Make something greater than you can imagine.

I didn't like the way he spoke. It wasn't the content, more the word-wrapping from one sentence to another: one sound, a harsh *-t* at the end of that "out," not as abruptly dropped before proceeding to the next sentence (as I would) but melding with the *-m* of "make" and its long *a*. It came off as a prepared speech, something he read from an invisible lectern—a muttering to his "exceptional" students, as he called them year after year—as if he couldn't think on his feet. Maybe he didn't run enough, and I cursed at how he could seem so content without a partner, or a lover, before he mentioned a long-distance thing with someone in Ohio, though it had pretty much stalled. I might not have been exceptional, and I certainly wasn't arrogant enough, but I'd strive to hold up certain truths of my own genesis and self-construction. I looked for things—tells and tip-offs, quietly testing people to find in which direction they bent, that is... full of it or not. Tanner always verged on the former, and so, overall, he could not be trusted. Still, I envied the degree and the prize as I continued having the same argument with myself about graduate school, one clogging me for too many years. I invited him to the few dinner parties we gave, but I kept up my reserve. I could go only so far, but when I finally found out he dated men, I eased a little. And when I later heard he slept with women, I quietly nodded.

One lonely summer day I drove over to Delaware Park's tennis courts in search of someone as unserious about correct tennis form as me and met a Croat called Luka, who uncustomarily hated Novak Djokovic. He was about my age and height, with that shy smile foreigners carry in the U.S. to both fend off and invite kindness, depending on their day's status in an uninviting country. He welcomed me into his life, and soon Alex came along too. I could have a half-dozen or ten-shot rally with him, though unorthodoxically, and we started to share meals, including his hometown specialties like sarma (stuffed cabbage). He preferred to bring people together for large meals at his house as he had done in the old country—cultural mores don't disappear because of geography—and he would help us find the apartment above the doctor and move in. A carpenter, he connected me with a few low-skilled jobs to push me through the lean months. He was generous, loving, and completely depressed—crushed by a woman who still surfaced every few weeks, but he could never forgive her. I tried to get the story without asking for it. The endpoint was that she did something and then he reacted. They were supposed to be married, a family. Now they joined the legion of Buffalo's hopeless singles.

On one of the city's cooling autumn days I dropped by Luka's house and met his first-floor tenant. He was newly moved in. Gerhardt: Hamburg-born but a longtime U.S. resident, owner of a large house in Pensacola. Tall and dishwater-blond, he had mercurial green eyes that served as another portal to expel the complex carbohydrates from his being—he seemed to be eternally goofing off. He'd gone to college in Williamstown through some program for people to escape Germany, though he stopped just short of diploma day. His English was passable, but sometimes a lace went untied. He worked and married or did he impregnate someone and then save? I couldn't get it straight—many of his threads came loose over the next eighteen months, though a few strengthened. He'd come to Buffalo to keep close to his five-year-old son, not the mother who hated him more than the yeast infection from hell. The rent from Florida kept getting deposited into his bank account, one of three of his in America, with a few more in Europe. Hidden well, he said, unconvincingly, before his coffee-stained teeth blanched his bottom lip.

Whenever I saw Luka that fall, Gerhardt either slumped on one of the porch's rickety chairs and smoked, or bent over the enigma of an old Volvo he couldn't outgrow, or loomed inside Luka's apartment, horning in on the man's specially cooked dishes. He came with a sour stench—some indivisible cocktail of sausage, tobacco, and body grime. He didn't like to launder and wore his nice knit shirts into cheesecloth. Moving around like a sloth, he would buttress himself in corners of rooms on the floor where he'd stare at a wall or the ceiling while thinking of the best way to fight a sickness when he had no health insurance; or else he'd fall asleep while talking about one of his few passions, Abbas Kiarostami. I'd become enamored of the director a few years before, so Gerhardt and I had a natural mutual that I refused to play up until almost a year later, after things cooled between me and Luka, between Alex and me—in the weeks after Gerhardt's breakup with Tanner Theale. We'd had something more important in common than Kiarostami, but Kiarostami helped. Men like to talk about ideas and hobbies, women about people and emotions. Alex and I had begun to share very little. I needed an outlet. I didn't care what Gerhardt needed. He probably sensed that and admired me more because of it.

Buffalo in late October. Alex and I had started to make love less often, not for any special reason—so when we did do it, we trumpeted to greater effect before settling into position. In the aftercuddle, I wound my finger through her chestnut hair, pinching at every follicle, something I'd learned from a gorilla special on public television. She didn't offer much, and at first I surmised it had to do with the inevitability of being saddled with the extra research year. I clearly believed she disliked Buffalo as much as I did, but even if so—she was a doctor, this was her life, her entire future. I'd just gotten a story into the *Cincinnati Review*, but that didn't mean a hill of beans when she had to deal with the supreme fuckface chief of staff who seemed to have it in for her after some ER foul-up, coupled with his fragrante-delecto sessions with many residents. If he pulled it out on me, she said, he'd need surgery to return to a seminormal existence. It was also two months since a slobbering call from her mother asking again to annihilate my standing in her life. And Alex drank too much, nearly every night, passing out on the couch before waking up at five-fifteen for the long drive to Millard Fillmore Hospital.

This was Sunday night. We'd spent a peaceful afternoon at the Albright-Knox Art Gallery, probably the best thing the city offered, so I began to lose my anti-Buffalo air. After an Asian-fusion meal on Delaware Street (I paid) we returned for some celebratory sex, and in the transition to a secure cuddling caduceus we somehow hit a tripwire. I knew Alex played with the truth. She lied about the amounts she drank, a behavior setting the table for the drinking—although, with the Hippocratic oath, I wondered how this sorted itself out, especially considering how many of her fellow residents were imbibing as she was. She had gum problems, too, but eschewed the dentist and happily closed the bathroom door and injected Lidocaine when the pain overleaped its usual ramparts. I lied as well, saying that I'd love her no matter her propensity to pass out and I'd never leave her—promises often spoken over the phone on nights she worked on-call, resigned to sixty minutes or less of sleep in narrow, ugly quarters: her weakest time and the hour when she most needed assurance.

What else could her dissembling encompass? I kept plundering through hair until I plucked. Sorry. She usually faced me—it wasn't late enough that she'd be ready to sleep. The neighbor boy, the one outside disturbance in our little pocket of Buffalo, began practicing on his skateboard in the large alleyway between the house and the small apartment building next door. Smack, smuch, roll, splat. Splat! I'm usually not at my best when such things started, and this drove an IV of the confrontational into my system. I asked Alex what was between us. I knew she would not offer a reason until I pulled one out of her. As the clatter went on and she turned away, feigning sleep, I decided not to pull but instead push it out. Can you enlighten me? I said. Kind of feels like you don't want to be here. A few minutes passed, maybe five. If I didn't want to be here, you wouldn't see me. I can't see you. Silence—then I said, Did you come? You know it. Technically, only you do. Aren't you insecure? You think if I didn't, I'd love you any less? You're distant, distantly distant. Is it not allowed? You have me all to yourself—all my free time is devoted to you—I deprive myself of sleep that I need more than anything to make you happy. Good, these are the kinds of tokens that would reassure an insecure person. And you aren't one? No, I'm not. And why aren't you insecure? Because of what we have. Then you've answered your own folly.

I turned and lay on my back. Splat, splat-splat! I needed to stop harping about leaving Buffalo, a city built on so much national disdain. Our love could overcome anything. No matter how saccharine and ponderous that sounded, a part of my core believed it. But I could go only a week before mentioning the dream of one day exiting this shithole again, a killing hand on the throat of our relationship demonstrating my faithlessness in it, accelerating my capacity to deconstruct what I once loved. I would remember how I once loved her. I could never actively admit that yes, I love her now—post-coital favors certainly not counting.

A strand of her hair that stuck to my finger snagged in my mouth after I tried to pick something out of my teeth. That goddamn kid, I said.

Maybe you can get him to move out of Buffalo?

That's good. Remember when I first came here in July and it was so hot and then I took the pint of blueberries and poured them over your body? Why can't—you know.

Why don't we get a cat? We've talked about it enough.

What am I not giving you?

You're giving fine. It's not that. We should just... domesticate.

I'll do most anything to make you happy.

Her petting hand stopped. Maybe that counted toward why I agreed so quickly.

Soon the cat came in, as did his furry graces, and all was well. The peaks and valleys were always there—we could just ignore them better with someone else sharing the space, especially an American cat named after Ingmar Bergman's great cinematographer, Sven.

After the breakup, in the long months of regrets and reprisals, I thought of these types of moments in isolation, as most heartbroken people do. What was my life before that led me into this bog? Living in Oregon and California and finding a trace of devil-may-care in myself, after the influence of the great goddesses others called wood-nymphs and hippie-chicks, I began to sing acapella in the middle of conversations, spurred on by something the other person said, because it perfectly parroted, or nearly did, a line from songs in the US pop and rock charts from 1964 to 1988—and I suppose I did so because I was happy and I had to connote that polestar feeling. When I continued the practice in Brooklyn and Buffalo, more querulous looks followed, especially from "professional" people, meaning those who had to work forty hours a week, as opposed to the slacker class in Eugene, who could often afford to spin about on a part-time salary or a meager nest egg. In love with Alex, I began to break into song a number of times, often without prompting, and often calling on an inane soupy love tune from the seventies, the kind still constantly played on AM radio, something by ABBA or Fleetwood Mac or Heart. One day my internal jukebox turned on 'Love the One You're With' and its icky lyrics. I don't know why it came out at that particular moment, but that time was particularly bad, our final year of trouble, with more distance, more self-loathing, more doubts. Alex stopped sweeping the floor and widened her often teasingly squinty eyes to demand truth—if there was someone else I loved, if I'd just settled for her. Because if I did, if I had—then she could be more at peace in her galumphing with a new man, their union still a secret to me.

A person doesn't change in a year. It's all there and, frankly, it's always been there. Human evolution is a pox—why else have we progressed to simply sitting in our houses, buying things online, and having it all brought to us so we can remain self-stultified? We keep testing to see what more we can get away with, what little we must do to be ignominiously branded "a keeper." She said she never loved anyone the way she did me, but the finish on that faded. Her face was distant, haunted. To be smitten was not enough—she required further pruning, something she didn't know because when you're twenty-seven you hold only nine truths about the world, one for every year of legality. Love isn't as precious—no satisfactions have been paid out. It wasn't that one had to make love in a certain honest yet still bewitching way—and that did occur, as much her doing as mine—but the voices of her contemptuous parents had to be stilled, almost forgotten, so that the terrain within her own speech, mired in unsettled depths, would start to show off the striations of the quiet soul that had to hatch a completely new set of values, in a place parents can never touch.

Our relationship began in a piecemeal fashion in Brooklyn, just as I had decided to abandon the inferno of big city living. We shared a few blissful months until I left her before she could say goodbye to me, with nothing about my departure promising a return. Back to Oregon I went, back to hugging people. Unexpectedly, we gabbled on the phone every week, and in those hours our words had meaning, and some were soul-speaking. After finishing the residency, she went home to Thousand Oaks before beginning in Buffalo, but a good friend of mine just happened to live in Silver Lake, so there I was, pining away. I wanted to take her camping and off her parents' hands, to fly over and up to the Golden Coast, Big Sur, and somehow fit Yosemite in during our allocated six days. She didn't square this with her parents until the night before. She took the Caltrain into LA and came to my friend's apartment, a four-floor walk-up. A hot June afternoon—he had left. The old yellowy-greenish knotty couch from the Salvation Army in the narrow living room. We couldn't resist. After, the wall went back up. Her parents were waiting for her. We went onto the roof at dusk, looking out at Griffith Park in the distance, with puce clouds or duskglow smog above. I suddenly performed the only honor I knew—testifying how I wanted to spend the next week in nature with her, professing feelings as grinningly as a used-car salesman. She chewed gum at the time, and as she moved it back and forth in her mouth, her growing response kept breaking into obliquities I couldn't sort out.

When she had to call her parents, I went to the other end of the roof, avoiding the tarred strips that chessboarded the sinking roof every four feet or so. I sat in a broken plastic chair. Twenty minutes later she placed her palm on my back. It had been decided in my favor—she gave herself to me as silently as sunup. I never asked how or why.

Duplicity—had it always been there? When my brother stopped over in Buffalo for a short conference, the three of us went out to dinner—an inconvenient affair. She had to get up for work, and I went for a late drink with him. In answer to Well, what do you think? he fobbed off some readymades, and after I continually pressed him, he said, I don't know anything about her, aside from what you report. She doesn't give anything away. He paused. Think about that. I instantly dismissed the grouch's shelled-up wisdom, and from a man who had hardly passed a completely happy night with a partner in his life. I examined him across the table at the lobster pound, where he played the flipside of his card, while Raydon stopped paying attention to his automatic gearshift of moods.

I couldn't ever tell him he had correctly foreseen things. I hardly told my remaining family anything about the ending. Too shredded, too enfeebled. I know many people would take the opportunity to get closer to their roots. I didn't. Denial, denial, denial. And at bottom my parents were a vital part of it. I'd decided to give them little of my joy and none of my pain. The silent jury they would remain. Long ago I had cast away, thinking I'd put childish things aside by childishly counting out the measures of distance between my island and theirs. I'd gone astray, but I'd won—remaining bitterly awardless. I hardly ever worked under anyone, often taking jobs where I supervised myself, making my own decisions and living with the conclusions. I felt I carried out the lifestyle in deference to my caca country, clutching to the pioneer spirits, while trying to avoid the stylings of the bilious beats, the ignorance of the hippies, the bastardry of the yuppies, the mindlessness of the jocks—every other clique being impenetrable, but full of the usury known as "depending on others." How could I have survived such imbecilic vendetta-like standards? I met the woman who'd save me without her being aware she would. And, of course, I did use people—lone wolves have the highest rates.

Our estrangement had help. A broken condom. She'd assured me she would take preventative steps. What I didn't know wouldn't hurt me. Around this time, we went to a sad happy hour with Tanner and Gerhardt. They'd met at some dinner party we threw, but the months had not been kind to them. I didn't know which of them to side with. Alex had a possible malpractice suit pending—no room in her limited window for life's little tizzies. We'd mentioned Tanner and Gerhardt over pillow talk, briefly, supposing they were compatible, because why else would they be affixed? Same age, same historical memories, same glint of untruthfulness in the eyes that in collision would only seek prime when it seemed they fished for bottom-feeders. So, glad tidings for their happiness! I never saw them touch each other—Buffalo still retained some conservative mores—and I was sympathetic to their withholding: the enjambed word or phrase, the awkward glance, the cool lusters of randy gambits that dissipated with one wrong word. But they liked to live that way, separately agreeing that to be inextricably woven into the background was to win the table every time.

I'd made love to a man in Manhattan, shortly after moving to the borough of choice just south. Craigslist, in all its semen-stained, vaginal-jelly-filled glory. I went to him in his Upper East Side apartment as one goes to a dentist appointment. Mutual interests. Nothing else in those e-mails to incriminate. He opened the door wanly, as if he pretended to still have something to hide. Rich and Thai, with a tart pressure to his handshake, and all this South to his voice, pipe-organ pumped by the prominent South Asian jowls, while the honeyed skin packed no dark follicles except the groovy wavy statement up top. Kittenish eyes, the kind to make people do things they usually wouldn't. I sat in his living room, nodding at the original Matisse and going sweetly sick from incense he paid too much for, along with all the other unnecessities, after his father had invested in Apple at the right time. Because this is what you do when you move to New York, you live it, you take advantage by leaving yourself naked to another's advantages—the transaction as hardline and raw as the switch-off of moral sense with the hee-haw of a drug haze. We met once every few weeks for some months. It blurred into a fancy-free love, for me. I let him show me off: I drank four-hundred-dollar wine, talked to Julianne Moore, learned to tango, enjoyed opera—more the prologues and arias. I became more of the woman I think I am, but we were both feminine, doling out kisses most plentiful only after forgetting how temporarily secure we were. In other corridors, he fit the profile of a deeply depressed man who would needlessly destroy every relationship, laughing publicly to re-suture the nights he'd featherweightedly run a razor over his wrists, his throat. I'm sure I reminded him of someone—there was a scene at Brooks Brothers that bore close to the sequence in *Vertigo* when Scottie dresses Judy as Madeleine Elster. Yes, he'd seen the film, but he changed the subject. I think he met someone else just as our wheels were coming off. When I received his letter in a miniature envelope, I can only describe the relief I thought I felt as greeny restraint. Before opening it, I fanned my face in its florabundance—the scent of the drowsy incense bringing back those hours and their flutter-by concerns for a man whose every thought was much more expensive than any one of mine. The envelope held a piece of stationery with a rectangular and flowery border supported by recumbent river gods. Inside, misspellings and hardly hidden spite. My youth had prohibited me from doing what needed to be done. When you're young, you don't mind being used, because you know you are contributing to happiness—you give less as you get older, on principle alone. Hoarded memories can always last the lifetime that is a Sunday afternoon.

Tanner's history in and out of AA wasn't hidden. He could stop at one drink once in a while, but he slurred as he herded all four of us into the booth they'd secured at a pseudo-upscale place on Elmwood Street. Late summer—so he'd been unbound by his workaday life for longer than normal, and malice had crept in. He'd had enough of Gerhardt's quaggy network of ministrations and reprimands—moods finally appalling him. While Tanner visited his sister in Colorado, Gerhardt had cat-sat and left the apartment in a shambles, as if a slob torpedo had hit the kitchen, exploding fast-cooking food over the stove, the walls, the cabinets, the fridge. So much for the anal Germans, I'd said. Florida, he said. I'm more from Florida than anyplace else. Well, my old friend Ken had a little imbroglio with Florida, I said. He thought the reason the state had its jutting shape was that so many of the shitty people from the Northeast eventually trickled down to its territory and weighed into the southern land, so it bulged like a crooked erection—but you're from Germany. By this time, I'd obviously chosen a side, because I recognized the quality of the hurt Tanner basted in. I saw him squeezed into the middle of the booth (Gerhardt on the edge, one leg outside and pointed in the direction of the door) as if he'd been backloaded there, bereft of freighting cost, some expired unit no-one wanted: small, sunken, vindictive. I believe his agent had just told him short stories were great but still a dime a dozen. Worsening this, Gerhardt defended the indefensible. No, the kitchen was like that, he said, and described how Tanner kept loads of expired food in the fridge because he was too lazy, and why didn't he hire a cleaning woman? Or man? He could afford it, if he didn't buy so many silly first editions over the internet. Gerhardt himself liked books, admired Philip José Farmer, but the market for antiquated books was over with—they'd never be worth as much as he'd paid for them online. The arguing continued as if we weren't there. Tanner went teary, and since Alex was sitting beside him, she patted his back—he was drunk and she wasn't, the rare reversal.

Things got uglier and uglier, and eventually we began to start seeing ourselves in this reprobate clusterfuck of lonely people in their own special circle of hell—it wasn't lust, maybe wolfdust—though we spoke in surprised tones directly after, covering our shame. What were they doing together? Well, they wouldn't be together anymore. No-one wants to see a dramatization of their hidden features, the intricacies and unforgivables propping up a sinking ship. Whatever we had, at least we carried some worn-down yet visible eros. Later, in the bedroom, we had a difficult time looking at each other until just before the end of our type of love. I didn't fall asleep with her. I left the room quietly, while Sven, who slept by my ass, beyond surprised, followed me in hopes of a snack. My mother had written an e-mail wondering if I'd received the package she sent. I should have received it two days ago. I had, but I hadn't opened it. Something for Alex, something she would ridicule.

I checked in on Tanner in the weeks following, to make sure of something I couldn't name. He denied being unhappy. *Gerhardt's all right—if he could only get his son for lengthier periods of time...* His levity and lack of condemnation perturbed me. I decided he could never be a writer of larger mosaics because of this hugger-mugger attitude. Most successful novelists had passion leaking out of their ears. He showed me the new issue of the *New Orleans Review* that he had a story in—'An Autumn Afternoon.' Not one of my best, he added.

In another chapter, Luka and I stopped playing tennis, because I hit one faulty drop shot too many. We could still drink and watch movies, silently complaining about our lives. He worked with a bunch of assholes, though. I'd met them when he got me a few weeks of demolition work inside an old jazz club being revamped. They were slovenly, potbellied, eternally-aggressive locals who could never outgrow the non-stop teasing and unconscious sarcasm that doomed their relationships and kept resuscitating their hatred of women—"bitches," they preferred. I'd had to endure it for only two weeks, but I saw how they blasted him, the foreigner, with high-powered cannons of bile every few hours, and in offhand moments he confessed a frustration. But he'd soon be getting back to the homeland for almost a month. The way out would refresh as always. Gerhardt had also confounded him. The late rent, his pigpen ways. When the lease ended, that would be the end of him.

The weeks carried on until the largest yearly amount of light that Buffalo would ever see came and went as diffused on a cloudy June day. Incredibly, Gerhardt still had platonic ties to Tanner.

No matter the setting, they would appear together like shuffling tourists or pseudo-philosophers, immersed in an animated conversation. Maybe it shouldn't have surprised me. People in our city were very lonely and frustrated, pining for exceptions from the climate (even in a cold and clammy June) and from the collective weakmindedness. Challenges were few—the best bars in the city were still places where towheads trundled in and tapped a happy guy on the shoulder, inviting him to fight because he looked a little too joyous. Tanner would be going to teach at a few summer writing conferences, and Gerhardt was again given catsitting duties, along with the use of a shabby, fuel-efficient car that he promised to fix the timing belt on.

We glimpsed Gerhardt and his son one Saturday at a street fair. Under threat of rain, we stood inside a quarter-full tent where a folk music foursome played, and we yawningly took notice of the gruff man bouncing his boy on his knee. The child, Sal, made Gerhardt's uncompromising spirit look preposterous. He couldn't be different for once, couldn't decipher the dignity in acting even a little helpless, so that the severest critic would forgive his struggling father-show most misdemeanors. He continued pawing at Sal as if he wanted him to start hitting back. The boy kept trying to get away—maybe to find a woman and elope as a new son and mother. This would have been the same week Alex aborted the child, telling me then it did not exist—before I ever knew it existed, a few weeks after the act. Maybe she'd decided what to do weeks before but committed only later; two or three times she claimed to be going to a dentist for surgery and follow-ups, yet the Lidocaine shots continued. All ill-at-easiness had left her, like that of a consummate actor under the Broadway lights. If I'd looked closer... but I had no cause, even with her role in the matter. If history didn't exist, then humans would have no records of their culpability. Yet we are always surprised when someone close acts out, acts pagan. The eye of the needle is too often the size of our private catalog of human possibilities. And Gerhardt was attractive—if one had a choice to grab a hand or fall down the long craggy face of a mountain and perish. He was the type of person who always showed up; if you went to the store to buy onions, there he would be, more knowledgeable of your iniquities than your therapist was. How does one train for a life like this? To barricade oneself in a tortuous opening to watch the death wriggles of others: he'd call it instructive, though he wouldn't make art out of it, only storing it to further authenticate his bizarre path through the population.

When Sal struggled out of Gerhardt's next hug, I offered to get the boy some cotton candy. That left Alex and Gerhardt alone. In the year after, I imagined those fifteen minutes many times, from untold angles and possibilities, like a sophisticated review system in sports, yet my replays changed ever so slightly with every view and that is why I had to keep taking them out of the file. I often prayed for the possibilities to end, but they never did, until one day I noticed several days had gone by since I had deconstructed those fifteen minutes. I was on the Path train home to Brooklyn from Jersey City, where I looked after the man who had MS. I sat slumped in the hard seat, exhausted from hours of hefting him, as my eyes dipped while staring at a Hispanic man in a Yankee cap before me. Since I despised the Yankees, that raw emotion might have poisoned my flaw. As I verged on sleep, I jumped out of my skin and observed myself from the Hispanic man's point of view, though I changed the cap to a Mets one. The person before me had plenty on his mind but not those fifteen minutes—and with that thought they returned, though overshadowed by the partially formed consciousness it took for me to get out of the seat. I could help advocate for all the time between those two moments, roughly eighteen months, to be obliterated from the slumping man's memory, because then for the first time in years I could experience myself to be one thing and another thing—a wiser but wizening sod—in the same moment. Jung had always spoken of his number two, the name he gave to a more spiritually cognizant and solitary version of himself. The idea of the other immediately arrested me because I had spent a great deal of time alone with myself. Somewhere, in the ten years between California and Eugene and Buffalo, my number two had vanished, projected into the women I slept with. But if this was true, it could only be half-true, enough to loosen my soul so it crept down my pants leg and onto the floor, far enough away to scare me into being much less troubled by my eventual death—any loneliness to include me unawares.

Through the second half of that summer, Gerhardt appeared even more frequently. I don't know if he did finally have a hand in fixing Tanner's timing belt, but I saw him in that car at least a few times a week, often at Wegmans, the main food emporium, stuffing his mouth with bad sushi. Luka slipped from the rest of my picture. Maybe I did have more in common with Gerhardt, maybe we shared a speckled view of things, a certain Caligulan swagger, yet also a Proustian interest in memories, not a just a fondness for Kiarostami. He ingratiated himself and I let him. I was fallen—I did feel Alex and I were headed into deeper disaster. Inverting, I twisted inward—not letting on, especially not to Gerhardt, how we had stopped communicating, except to screw and immediately sleep, though at times I must have given him details or complaints; we hung out a few times a week, either playing tennis (he didn't mind the drop shots) or getting a beer and flipping through our pasts like old parcels we'd never opened. I gradually took hold, because if I didn't, I couldn't remain in Buffalo. It wasn't what I wanted anymore. I didn't like taking a fifty-minute bus ride to work, only to get picked up by a resentful Alex or to be dropped off by her for a night shift and take a sixty-minute bus ride back in the early morning. I'd had it with the same restaurants serving the same shitty pub fare—to hell with Buffalo wings. And what of some other place? Where would I go? The urge for going weighed heavy—how many moves had I made in the past few years? If she could love me... but on whose terms?

Gerhardt, mumble-throated on every other topic, including his son, would give Kiarostami the full treatment. I could hear earnestness radiating when he spoke of him, the man's art—he couldn't be complete scum. Cinema massaged out his knots so he could access tenderness. Kiarostami's gentle images: no violence, though sometimes bleak, and always truthful—you'd have to be strung out or very lowdown to think the end of *Taste of Cherry* anything other than life-affirming. Gerhardt guzzled the beer he drank and offered, What I like... admire... is... he doesn't judge his characters. In *Close-Up*, everything congeals, and people are made happy—isn't that something to aspire to? So, Gerhardt had a conscience. I slowly started to forgive the other shortcomings: the chair-smashing (according to Luka), his public burping and farting, his laziness, his stoner glances, his questionable parenting, his not having to work because of all the money he had somehow been introduced to. I did think I was being fair, because, no—I wouldn't caretake his faults.

Weeks on, with Tanner away, Gerhardt and I went south for a hike. An August morning heated a landscape already overly humid; even the forest had been quickly drained of its nightly chill. We kept to a clipped trail where mosquitos about fifty feet from their private resort of a stream went on the attack. As we tracked through trails still full of last year's leaves, we didn't so much share information as space and time, and this worked in both literal and ghostly ways—birdcall and soilsmell accessed childhood's secrets, kept in our triggered sweat. A placebo of trust came to be, for why else put your lives in proximity for five, six hours? We were each reserved and liked people who weren't chatterboxes, or at least we respected them more—another mark against opposites attracting. While passing over specially cut snowmobile trails and petering-out creeks, we thought about what question to ask each other in those hours of mainly dappled light. As we climbed slight muddy rises, I gasped a little at a nose-piercing humidity I hadn't felt since two years before in Brooklyn. My breath did get short, which would usually happen only in the company of certain cats (our own I'd gotten used to), and brushed me back to the premier experience of shortness, on that bus to my high school down by the lake. Whether out of fear or nervousness, surely both, I'd cowered in my seat then, wishing not to have to attend for another day in my life, with the breathing just another sign persuading me to forge my resentment against all one hundred boys in my class into a spectral, ill-formed shield.

Throughout high school I barely saw my father, though we chatted one-sidedly on the phone from time to time. As for the boys at school, I could only attempt to fit in: become a jock, smoke weed, destroy property, enjoy a porno on a sleepover like everyone else. But the best piece of me didn't want to follow the crowd. During senior year, I began to look for older men to share my nascent thoughts that fitfully tried to describe my undressed feelings. The more I dove deeper into Bergman, the more my world grew opaque, ill at ease, melancholy—soon delineating itself into different-colored hazards that a young adult must choose between. All these acts and flailings compounded a question I could start to dare to ask: where had my father gone? The materials used in his stead generated the revenue to afford the loss, already carrying a grandeur resembling that of the eon-baked stone of Roman ruins. When you become an adult, you realize you actually did have parents—they were there for you, even when they weren't. In most cases your life is not up to them—and slowly, as if you've finally descried a counterfeit notch among the first hundred you earned, you see what power you have over life. Yes, the whole wideness of night is for you—for you. If I told Clayton any of this, he would think me only a bigger fool.

I'd gone through many paternal fill-ins, including those played by women, until I came back to my own father. While I was in Buffalo, he was on the phone nine hundred miles away, mystified by the politicians, impaired by a love of money, but quite honest, even decent. So many people I knew barely had any of the kindness he contained—not the gift-giving sort, but a more twinkling brew, the kind that teased into the air around him: *Yes, I am unto myself, but so is everyone else, and I want to not make anything hard for them—I want their happiness, but I don't need to see it.* Magnanimity, the prick of Aristotle's spindle. It had not always been so. He'd hammered about the world for so many years until the divorce sideswiped him and a depression strangled his gift for selling, a once regaled career taken to shallow waters to eventually die—out of the depths a shark bent on frenzy needs to thrive. A relationship with Clayton was easier for him. The old man could relate to Clayton's career in clear terminology and he admired his economy of presentation; as a father he could apply clearer, amenable brushstrokes to qualify his pride in his dutiful son. So many times during that year I breathed down the other end of the phone, dreading to tell my father, *No, no-one's going to publish anything I've written in the foreseeable future,* when I should have been saying that something between Alex and me had frayed, we were in trouble, love wasn't what I thought it was, maybe I'd been fooled, but I opened up only about the unconscionable hours she worked—how she came home after a twenty-four-hour shift exhausted and had just charred a third kettle by leaving it on after she fell asleep in the hot minutes leading to its boil. And yes, Sven was all right, too. He liked to eat moths.

I had to think of my father on our hike. Gerhardt, with all his European derring-do and faux-Kiarostami stylings, was truly no substitute for the father himself—a top-of-the-shoulder voice shrilly pointed out that I was not of an age when a man pressed on in close conjunction with his father, not once the child lived outside the father's city. Maybe my father walked with me then—not with us. He would have seen through Gerhardt but not said anything. If pressured, he would have aped what Clayton had opined about Alex—for she and Gerhardt were much the same. Clayton took after our father, he'd learned this equipoise years back, while I mainly held that Nietzsche had it all figured out. A disciple of his had stated the central concern with more piquancy: *the speaking subject gives herself away*. It's when you're not speaking that no-one can hurt you. The best seducers have an armory of vocabulary and syntax to flash forward into their desired's heart. Gerhardt waited for what you said, then turned the screw, letting a large invisible drape lift on his show.

The stands of birches and oaks started to disappear, and just beyond a scurf-covered deformation there appeared a large crater—a narrow suspension bridge would connect us to the other side. What could have caused the deformation? Probably the retreating ice that took its course during the Wisconsin glaciation, great larval eons running unchecked by human form. Within sight of this hole, with time jagged from feeling beaten back into the past, I realized that my shortness of breath had ceased for unknown minutes. Incandescently, Gerhardt pressed on, almost in stop-motion visuals, the staple of the old *Paddington* TV show, something we had both watched in our youths. I was acutely aware of putting my first foot (left) on the bridge while the right came off with a bit of earth, my hiking shoe taking turf onto it to soon fall through the narrow openings in its track and burst onto the pulverized ground below with no trace of runoff. Following his clumping steps in front of me, my eyes tilted to the ovoid stain his sweat had left on his blue shirt, and some tarry scent cut my nose, with an iron taste slipping into the stomach. Ricochets of our footwear on the stainless steel measured the time it took us to return to ground. We rose into another deciduous forest and soon pursued a path less weeded, which followed a trickling rill dotted with granite boulders, medicine-ball-size to bedroom-size. Western New York aped southeastern Wisconsin's geology well; only five hundred miles separated what could have been land next door millions of years in the past. A sluice opened and, when I felt for the dent in my head, the day of rocks became a day of diamonds.

One winter when I was maybe five, I walked with my father

and Clayton in one of the hillier parks in Milwaukee County. It was a clear weekday, the city covered by a half-foot of snow fallen between the last two sunrises. We hiked a towering hundred-foot incline, tamping down the already packed path with our boot-prints. Once on top, after Clayton had run ahead, owing to some curiosity I walked to the edge and slipped. I slid headfirst down earth of such steepness that I'd sped to where my face crashed into a boulder while my mind still had me in motion. Though my impressions of the encounter with a rock the size of a VW Bug and the aftermath are vague, I know my father picked me up and rushed me to the service building. The parkies had no towels or cloths to stop the seep of blood from my face, mostly from my forehead, and had to use the backs of sandpaper—one of the few times I saw Clayton scared. I was stitched at the hospital. I healed. Decades on, the dent remains.

Gerhardt and I continued, the rake of a crow's throat signaling something that didn't concern us. Soon, after having weighed the evidence for months, I made a split-second decision to trust Gerhardt and replayed that whole early-winter saga for him, adding and revising details I'd had to mature to christen, drawing out the retelling because long trains of words froze the tears, breaking readymade walls I'd kept long hidden. I often examine my listener in such situations, playing off their reaction the way a stage actor would, judging whether to push or depress my gas pedal, but I couldn't see a face—I told the story to the back of his walking body, so I kept going steadily, footfalls in lockstep with words. Soon the rill extended to a chasm. I remained ecstatic for more than a solid block of time, something I couldn't pretend to do anymore with Alex. I knew he listened; I knew he heard me. He might lie in retrospect about being a little moved, but it would only embarrass him. He wanted the same thing I'd wanted—intimacy, no matter gender. I dismissed any other explication. Later, he leveled his eyes at the dent—what a day.

We came to a new fork and turned left to descend when Gerhardt mumbled something about his once being twenty, free, and driving up and across the continent to learn the nation. I still gloried about my told tale, awaiting more adulation, but hadn't my parents passed on some manners? The plot points of his anecdote were strained, but his voice clarified itself to my ears, and there he was in a fix, outside Rapid City in pitch dark. After his car had gotten stuck in a ditch, he huffed it and hiked to safety and a Lakota took him to his house for the night. It sounded like one of my relatables—one I'd tired of telling—and I had the strange sensation that Gerhardt knew this and continued to tease his brand of harm; he could dust away all the surface details and intuit what swathed me, though I'd later assign him much less power. And I had let him use Kiarostami to see past his falsities. You take from the cinema with an understanding that it will come out later as something better than yourself, since cinema takes from you first, it takes contact, people, the possibilities in love—an Other is created that one might temporarily live in, so the hours might stay strange instead of bitter and so one can stray into magnanimity, not just being a collector of the tokens of fandom, but spreading one's wings a little further, one's Other touching another's Other, despondency given over to intimacy, the child as father of the man because the child finally sees the pleasures in showing the stronger self. Gerhardt didn't want just Alex, but what he gave me in return was fear—I couldn't hold that cold fire.

The day continued, but it never really ended—I had my large

hand in his larger one. We idolized so little of each other, we just wanted something that reminded us of childhood, something far away from the other person who had brought us close together—we'd had enough of Buffalo's tendency to run our psyches into dead-end streets. When I go back over it now, I hear how we never spoke of Sal, except for my puttering mention of the baseball player Sal Bando as the only real-life Sal I'd ever known and had actually met once at a baseball camp. Gerhardt remained mute. Only now do I see how most parents like to hang around with other parents, because they know what the strain is, while single people are like half-formed things, taking too seriously what is explicitly trite. Obviously he wasn't a true parent, and for me to have brought up Sal might have asked for a silent rebuke from him, but we were courting.

I angled for his more obsequious side, radiating toward that intrinsic laziness that tells you this person is not going anywhere, especially in order to feel superior, to pity him. Yes, he needed me to cradle him, and I quietly accepted how he performed to amass attention, the nearest minor Alp to love. Months later, after I returned from a few weeks in New York City to get out of Alex's hair and she promptly left for the Bahamas with a female colleague—our taking separate trips will only make us stronger, we ridiculously thought—Gerhardt and I went to an Almodóvar film and then had a beer. We were in a new bar downtown, or quite old but newer to us. The bartender, in her sixties and with immense tits, had one evil eye, one coy, and a third that could see through people in eerie dioramas—she might have told me not to trust the Gerry beside me. His face had gained something in the days I'd been gone. There wasn't more flesh but more fury beneath—he harried me for not having been able to guess he'd been tupping Alex continually since I left, a fact falling out of its cleft one season later. Couldn't I see past his thin generic-tissue lies and awkwardly set picks while going up and down the court with him? He gazed in my direction, but arched his eyebrows to point above me, in the space where a halo would be—so easy it was to manipulate, he only had to half-blink. He pressed his new cruelty with a sharper turn, when he said, simply, You don't know much about life. Egged on by the slice of Almodóvar's Spain, we'd been talking of other countries—he knew I'd lived in Europe, his land. No, not good enough. He was proving my unworthiness to himself—the verdict had been read, and this was the sentence. One so wanted to yoke the pieces together, especially when they were all there in front of me. Of course, he and Alex hadn't planned a certain way, but with me floundering in New York, unsure of our future together, she'd needed someone to cry to, and with crying comes so much more, all the brittleness reconstituted into the first specks of trust. *You don't know much about life*. The swipe had hurt, as intended. But I really didn't know, and he had kindly pointed this out. It was his Biblical exhortation on the order of *Open your eyes so you may see*.

He wasn't going to make my discovery too easy, but if he kept poking, harder and harder, as his experience had taught him, a blow-up would occur. I never revealed to him that when I did find out for certain—the next year, a few days before the beginning of spring—I immediately called Alex from a friend's apartment on the Lower East Side. The first thing she said was, I will give him up. We weren't together anymore at that point. We hadn't been happy in many seasons. There hadn't even been any possibility we would get back together. Her unexpected utterance explained all the imagined scenes away, with what I had taken to be pain I deserved—I would never know for sure, but this iced some wounds. Tanner later told me, You have to use this. Take detailed notes. But I know you already are.

To return to the hike: when Alex came home, I innocently referred to that day in the forest and how little drama had ensued. She remained in her scrubs to hear me out—an oddity. Then I made her a margarita. She'd be out in fifteen minutes.

Sven sat in the well of the living room window looking at cars coasting down the one-way street, while people walked by in pairs or barking into their phones. We liked to watch him watching—our relaxation. She mentioned having seen Tanner at the hospital. I thought he had been out of town, hence Gerhardt's using his car. Apparently he was aware of our joyride. The hospital she was working at then stood only a mile from our house. Tanner wouldn't have needed the car. How did he seem? Frazzled—he waited on tests. At that second, I began to suspect something—maybe involving everyone, but mostly Alex and Tanner. Not sexual. Something more mysterious. And wild—as if they'd begun to write a play together, but as to a further collaboration on some political design several months in the making.

That evening, while she slept the sleep of one drunk on life's depressiveness, I continued reading Chekhov's stories. A short one told of a son's loss of innocence when watching a pastor (through a ship's porthole) persuade his young wife to prostitute herself to a rich English banker for a good sum. Fleshing it out is his father by his side—who says, Let's get out of here. You needn't see this. You're still just a boy. Three pages. Days on, I read it to Alex when she came home—as a warning, but for what? For needing space from me? She'd passed out just as I came to the end, though Sven looked in my direction, then licked a paw to clean his face. August outside, but the night winds blew cool.

When Alex and I went to the folk festival in Trumansburg for a few days, camping among a crowd that couldn't wait to go haywire, Gerhardt fed Sven and probably stayed on our couch (bed—to smell her), because that was the month he took up residence in the living room of two Argentinian lesbians. To be over near the Finger Lakes, dancing and making love in the tent that held the space of our new-relationship magic some years prior (it still carried in its lining a musk of those heated hours, and we wished it would conjure us back into dispatches of kissing and hissing)—was this our desperate attempt to reignite things, to regain a foothold? No, the tent couldn't help us, but could music be the food of love? It might have seemed so. We danced to Rusted Root and sat reverently listening to Himalayan throat singing, something we'd never experienced either live or recorded, yet nothing could salve us. Later, I watched her leave to buy a drink. She didn't walk so much as if she was avoiding people but as if she herself were soiled. She had some height and usually matched it with long, steady strides, marking a bountiful life inside rather than an outward gloss—a need to be swift, especially out of hospitals; twenty-eight years had taught her that beauty keeps its own pace and is never truculent, otherwise the unwanted get chances to gawk. Returned, she uselessly tried to upsway her broken features. She'd assumed a blue hue into her cool neutral cast. Should I have been happy she took her crying elsewhere? If the blind couldn't see that, they'd hear it in her jumbled speech—here placating, there playacting, always a little spidery, a touch tart. A certain fickle sound gets pinioned in your ears when you fall in love. The melody you go to bed with and wake up to fills the cup you take into the unfriendly world. In being anchored to that love, all one has is a muted bassoon that starkens as it ages. She carried a deep voice, centered in the heath of her wide-ranging intellect—cloven to satisfy Lear's prescription of woman's low tones, an excellent thing I was brazen to call attention to. But no more. Her grave tones were acidly high. And I couldn't even mark the date when the frequency changed. Like Sven, she'd devolved into window musings, before shooting about the house as a human jackal—and she didn't need to drink to reach such an echelon. What she squirted out was like a robot leaking its data in non sequiturs: *I want to make something with onions* or Death of Salesman *really isn't that great* or *I wanted to text you all night long*. The last gave me the most trouble. I'd disabled texting because of the cost, because our plan didn't hold up well and I made eight dollars an hour. I should have given in and re-enabled it, knowing how useful it would be for a doctor, who had hardly any time to send quick information, even if it was "I luv u"—still, she had a work phone. But I'd passed the era to be doing any favors, even for myself—I did my arm-cutting in roundabout ways, fleecing our connection of a vitality or spontaneity needed to speed it out of its valleys. Our lovey-dovey baby talk had virtually drowned as well. Endearments few, except the big one, but without emphasis, without kernel, and less wet. We went in for gruff monosyllables, and at the festival, while Rusted Root sang, though we did some dosey-doeing and neo-tangoing and other things reminiscent of our carefree times, we treaded bilious water. We didn't want to be around each other, but would mostly remain housebound, afraid of escape.

We came home a day early. Gerhardt expressed surprise, but probably inward delight. Nobody cuts a vacation short unless they are having an awful time. We arrived in the early evening to find him napping in our papasan, his mouth lifted slightly to show a too-true resemblance to Snagglepuss. It took him five minutes to awaken, and then he told us of his three days of non-adventure, the most memorable event having been bringing Sal to play with Sven—Sal being able to call the cat only Sen or Ven.

We didn't want him to leave. Then we'd have an interminable Saturday night alone with someone decozened. Instead, we all went to eat at some fattening Buffalo-wings dive and gave him the floor, which he seemed to easily sense, because he spoke more than I'd ever heard him, even during the hours he and I had been alone in the forest. We allowed him every chance to talk, we almost begged him to—a person who has nothing can't say no to such an offer. And in doing so, rallying himself to give life to the information that was so cloistered, but not really guarded, he made truth of that comment, months ago now, about how I didn't know much about life. I handed her over that night, because she could see how I'd taken to his distrait poses, even reveled in his seemingly innocent glares at the neck he would soon kiss. I'd begun to sweat off twice as many calories as I'd taken in.

Autumn before the solstice. The days had a tawny aspect, filled with ever more slanted light. Tanner had time at the start of the semester, so we went for coffee. A new glare appeared on a face not worrying Gerhardt's hard hands into submission. The summer had been productive. A novella—very different for him. The setting, too—Paris. I did that once, I told him. My first screenplay—I'd never even been there. He changed the subject. I relaxed my eyes before they dilated with malice. He could have his right to dominate a conversation, but I wouldn't let myself be passed over entirely. True, I had difficulty seeing deeper into his wounds—if he could only give me something to hold on to. Like Gerhardt, he took a superior position before knocking the joints out of our chance to stand in any parallelogram. Of course, he was more experienced and the more accomplished writer, but he wasn't Tolstoy. I thought to start pumping Gerhardt for something on him—not that I'd ever use it, but to secure some informational bitumen. It would make what was coming with Alex easier.

A week or two later, on the bus home from an overnight shift, I did boggle about these three people and the degree of umbrage and disqualifying behavior rising to the fore because, though near, I couldn't discern. Had I emplaced myself and woven my own artifice with them? It was me, not them. This equation would satisfy for only a few minutes, and then I would light some rationally sweet charges with the borrowed byline *Friends shouldn't let friends become friends*. I had come to Buffalo because Alex's life required her there—I did it for her, I muttered with callow breath. Gerhardt seemed to follow me after being dismissed. He was lonely for male companionship, all companionship. I felt sorry for him. Tanner believed in ushering me to understand the literary world with a few short shocks of advice. We never spoke of the tools of craft in any measurable way, but people could hardly do that outside the classroom. Even Henry James had filled a twenty-page piece with more attention to themes than to matters of language and sound, because few care whether one's words are Latinate or Teutonic words just as long as each sentence let them reach into another's unperplexed head. Tanner could never face up to James; he had a simplistic manner of creation. He accommodated too many overarching strictures in his art—thinking he needed a satisfying plot when what would have helped was emotion, a coloration with textures and lusters coming not from reading, but from living more, living differently. Any project not adhering to formula was abandoned—he always made the text go the way he envisioned instead of letting it guide him where it would, into the infinite territory of the blue. Yet Tanner reversed himself against a man who may or may not have inflicted a blot of pain onto his cowardly soul, for Gerhardt could overcome only the weaker. And soon Alex opened our door to one of his pointed visits. When you think you are doing something for someone else, you are the handicapped seeking what is only heretic admiration, though Freud would have been much more unforgiving toward the dissembler. This is another form of projection, maybe the worst kind. You fill your life with people and their dramas, which are surely part yours, so as not to be out of touch. But if Heraclitus' epigrammatic "all is connected" warms the blood, how can there ever be one-sided fault in a relationship? Perhaps there were no victims or perpetrators in Buffalo. We all pulled for the same team and would come away equally muddied.

In a foul mood, I began to take Alex's car for long drives on my days off. The hospital she worked at then was close enough to walk to, so I'd drive from there out into the provinces surrounding Buffalo: Depew, Amherst, West Seneca, Cheektowaga. The last had a public library with a wider but not bigger selection of foreign film DVDs than the one in Buffalo. It also had a fairly clean octagonal layout, with large, puffy, recombinant seats, an about-face from the downtown library and its cramped, vinegary-smelling quarters, its furniture affixed with boogers and chewing gum from the seventies. I went to wipe away the time spent in our apartment, though I felt bad that Sven would be even more alone. I sat paging through poetry or short stories where morality wasn't so overtly on display, modern *ficciones* that would've astonished Henry James with their etiolations of character, though I sometimes dreamily passed over the covers of the DVDs I'd soon borrow for further refuge. I opened another poetry book—Elizabeth Bishop, 'The Weed': "'I grow,' it said, 'but to divide your heart again.'" Did I also choose not to love? Writing came next—I completed a few pages before the imagined swaying frames in Tarkovsky's snow-suffused films plunged my mind into its slow-motion nightside. I spent a few days drafting a story about Condoleezza Rice, though it would not be published for ten years, when that name only carried a dulled bristling. I copied the tone of the notable satirists of that time because I didn't know how else to write. The sentences came violently quick, filled with a physicality my fiction was usually devoid of. I immediately put it away for some weeks, as many writing manuals suggested, to be revisited in a different mind. But then I forgot about it because the next night, shortly before bed, Alex suggested we end things. Wouldn't that be a good idea? You aren't happy, I'm not happy. And what else? Was there anything besides that? Maybe it wasn't as bad as I thought. We were finished; all that remained was who would admit it first. She won.

I wasn't ready, though, because even as I detested Buffalo, it was where I lived. If I moved out (it had to be me) I couldn't move to a different part; I'd would need to shove off for a new city. I'd have to completely change my life again, which I'd done four times in eleven years. Tiring, emasculating—here was an immolation I'd grown ready to avoid, even if pained. In my early deconstructions, I could see how it wasn't really Alex keeping me stuck. It was me—I could effortlessly turn up my laziness, even easier than effortlessly. The last threads of passion-aggression were leaving since I found myself in feelings I couldn't explain, though they kept expanding like a wave about to crest and blow. I could count on my brother to deride the experience—and he did. It happens to everyone, he said. I've been there. It will be hard for a few months. But then a light goes on. Some people take more than a few months. We're from stray genes, though. Dad seemed to get over things before the first sun went down. And Clayton did offer me money then, which I foolishly accepted. Let's not keep track of this one, he said. I'll write on the check: *Old gambling debt*. A few days later I told him Alex had changed her mind—a blatant lie. She didn't want to go through with it, but now that she'd suggested it, I wouldn't be going back. I wanted to make sure I had every least bit of sympathy he could offer. I wondered if he'd stop the check.

When I told Gerhardt, he gave off the greatest flicker of emotion I ever saw him produce. His nostrils flared and he swallowed something he would've regretted saying. I'd begun to often use the English epithet *mate* as an exclamation point for many remarks I directed at him, thinking I sniffed his desperation for a certain woman, and maybe also his sordid pre-come, after he described his fantasy woman as Sigourney Weaver's 1986 body with Simone de Beauvoir's brain. By this time, he'd found an apartment more than a mile from Tanner and me, so his presence went from semi-daily to daily. Alex had begun her research year, working nine to five, but I doubt they were meeting clandestinely. I only say that now to fit my agreed-upon timeline better, or the timeline I finalized and then finally forgot because I fell in love with the right woman—the juiciest dream of a survivor. My brother was right and wrong, mostly the latter, which he'd probably be fine with because I suffered less. It took a year, all four full seasons, to be free. But then I was free. A year on, I found her—love—and I suddenly liked New York. My brother said, I told you so.

The split happened just after Halloween. Alex planned to go to Thousand Oaks for Thanksgiving a week early and not come back until December. I would return to New York—I had nowhere else to go—and be gone before her arrival. A quietly savage two weeks together, but we remained in the same bed and even had sex every few days, as is any hot-and-cold relationship's wont, ending in an ecstatic despair that soon this would never happen again: but for good reason. We couldn't get on emotionally, and the caustic words of a college girlfriend haunted my hours—I feel like our best moments were in the bedroom, to which I had to offer, That doesn't sound like too bad a deal.

After I dropped Alex at the airport, I came home to Sven, who tried to bite me. I'd teased him too often, as I had done with childhood cats, who became so behaviorally challenged they had to be removed from the home. He must have known big life changes were afoot. If cats can sense the imminence of an earthquake, then a breakup to which they are the closest witness must be as in their noses as fresh fish out of paper, inches from an outstretched paw. I sank to the floor and cried. Soon enough I stopped, and not reluctantly. I had much to get in order. I had to find a job in New York, though I'd be arriving at the absolute worst time. I could surf between one couch and another for three weeks or so, but by New Year's I'd need a sublet or something with a greater commitment. I joined a dating site, because I didn't know how I'd get through being in the city while couples on the streets held forth with wild and ostentatious kissing, especially at holiday time. The two diminutive men on my shoulders told me I was past Alex already, I could move on to others,

I could branch out, especially in the City—and within a few hours I'd set up a date, for the day after I'd arrive by train, along with another later that week. It didn't seem unwholesome. Prickly New York women weren't going out with me because they didn't have anything better to do. And here I felt the voice of Shakespeare's sonnets wash my ears with their panegyrics on not keeping one's beauty to oneself, but showing it to others to create others, to make dollops of humanity that would grow into the inheritors of civilization—ha. When I looked at the situation in this kaleidoscopic way, I couldn't help but be a little happy—and devastated. Alex had decided to put to death what many would argue was hers and hers alone, thus her choice. I didn't see it like that. I could sympathize to a point, but that memory kept getting pushed further and further into angry waters, though parallel with the slight happiness of our physicality, so eventually one would flinch but fall and the other would smile supreme. No surprise to see who triumphed. I met a host of women, many while just socializing, and none of them could make a dent in the dough Alex still had a hand in.

I believed she didn't want back in. But after two weeks, just days before Christmas, she called me in New York, pleading for me to return because, of course, Sven missed me. We talked for hours, crying mainly, sucking up the silence of each other's attention. How is your eye? she said, sometime in hour three. This would have been in reference to that mysterious nerve disorder that had flared up for a week in the early nineties and then subsided, only to reappear on St. Patrick's Day some years later. It kept chronic then, and it annoyed, forever stressing me. The anti-seizure medication the doctor suggested was gabapentin—with a side effect being a possible seizure. I tried everything else—eye yoga, teabags, diet change, self-tapology, shiatsu, qigong, acupuncture, yodel therapy (an experimental soundscape developed by professional Swiss yodelers)—everything. The only working remedy would be to see "through" it somehow, literally beyond the shaking vision, something on the order of an ancient Eastern practice, and so taking many years to get the desired Western results. When she asked, I had to admit that I'd not thought much about it, which must have meant it had improved, though I seemed at the lowest point of my life—a discrepancy to please the existentialist inside.

Immediately after that, I looked about the foreign bedroom I spoke to Alex in, with pictures of seascapes and a poster of *Seascape*, the Edward Albee play, which the bedroom's owner had appeared in Off-Broadway some years before: her greatest credit. The twin seascapes, tilted and abandoned boats in shallow waters, bore a faint resemblance to two glassed prints (in wooden frames) of large eighteenth-century ships in my childhood house (one gray, the other blue)—but of course they would. I had just broken up with someone. They were something my father would have bought at a rummage sale for a dollar total. I didn't know what became of them, but I often stocked them a few degrees away in memory. As I listened to Alex entreating distantly and then distinctly, I realized the boat in one print in this bedroom seemed, though marooned, to bounce up and down, up and down, so maybe my eye problem had been there all the time and now I could thank Alex for returning me to my baseline. Perhaps another worry like this would obviate one of the greater ones, like where I would sleep two days from then, or how a miracle worker could hire me between December 20, the day we spoke, and the two weeks until January 3, when many people would finally be back in their offices.

Later, after I pulled myself off Hannah, the actress, and she clutched the condom with a paper towel, depositing it on her way to the bathroom, I again peered at the lonely seascapes which she'd told me she'd bought at a Salvation Army in Harlem—but now I placed my childhood pictures over them, with my neck prized up by the pillow in a position that forced my eyes upward in their sockets. This was one of the two positions (the other being downward) in which no bouncing took place—straight on being the death of vision. I thought, mistakenly, of the English poetry of that time, Wordsworth's 'Immortality Ode' and certain others I'd read out loud to Alex on the limitless afternoons before her residency, when all we did was nestle, talk, and eat—everything forgiven with love. The paste of Hannah had hardened on my fingers, and when I passed my hand up to straighten my hair, I tasted how an acidic bite of spit had a brutal pitch, pushing people to traduce one scene to react to another. Flow had left my life, and a returning flux marred my days. I'd partaken of this a decade before, as a young man, inured to many of the unbridled qualities we need to grow old to cherish. I was a functioning paralytic, happy to worm my dick into the sprocket holding the spectrums of soul and body as apportioned by my hacksaw lust. I didn't lie to Alex about where I was—I should have. Sometimes lying is prime—the best surgeon for careworn days, because truth, the reaper, is often worse. I knew it would increase the heat, raise the level of toxins. That I could so easily share my latest debauchery, though I still loved her and still fantasized, fooled myself into not seeing the further impurities within my chambers.

She called the next night, a little later this time, though Hannah had gone out with a group of her theater friends. We didn't quite enjoy a facsimile of the four-hour connection of the night before, but it was close. In this version, the cat was not the only one missing me, and information I thought would never get past the teeth of such a neutered person who, in doctor-training, had to learn a unique discretion with patients, with relatives of patients, and with her superiors, startled. Yes, she had proved something, and I told her I would leave the next day—we would spend the holiday together, maybe drive to Toronto or Niagara Falls, the Canadian side, the hotel we once enjoyed. Her silence greatly agreed, but after a minute she broke it, with a slow, guttural *Yes*—not her manner. We were both bonkers, though in different forms. After we spoke further, I bought the bus ticket—and she'd purchased a new translation of Chekhov's stories and wanted to share it with me. Just like old times.

Hannah had soft red hair, a renegade smile, and that theatrical sparkle which circumnavigates questions of trustworthiness. She was my age, had lived in Costa Rica and Berlin, and although her acting roles were becoming rarer, she had just completed succecsful talks to direct a play in Vermont—some generational family drama. Her sarcasm had class and refinement, whereas Alex was too pragmatic to attempt irony, cutting people open in a very different theater. I liked the change. Hannah went with New York, mother-henning in her Harlem apartment handed down by her paternal grandmother, herself a Tony Award winner for set design. Our sex played out blurry, but solid enough, like a storm staying vibrant a few miles downcoast. We had met through a friend of a friend, gluing together by a brother-sisterly chumminess—working autonomously, we could easily be in each other's space without rancor, without dialing for help. Alex and I were too distracted by not seeing each other for so long, living to eke out every last shared moment—maybe this is why people who have intense workloads often get in and out of relationships many times in a long life. Hannah would go on to that, but home-locked for now, we were surprisingly in balance. She knew what I needed—she had the correct diagnosis and a better remedy than someone who depended on me to buy milk and fuck according to her schedule. Also, I felt she'd been with someone like me before—needfully strung out, yet creative, unorthodox, able to get out of the way; I was not a project, but a quarter-good treatment she needed to script-doctor before shepherding it to its next, more pressing appointment. She'd been married early on to some important German playwright who was dyslexic and alcoholic and not a good driver. He ended up in the clink—she said it, and added, No pun intended.

We'd known each other only six days, but had both come. Of all neglected authors, she tomboyishly loved Malcolm Lowry, and could recite the first and last pages of *Under the Volcano*, and did so, as bookends to a bout of cunnilingus meted out before intercourse which stood in for the other 370 pages of the novel. Was she person or performance? She wouldn't unveil the enigma to anyone trying to pin her down and find her blowhole. She fitted herself next to me canned sardines-tight on the chilly damp of the bed's blue sheet. I thought she might be testing a routine, since she made little baby-animal noises of being happy in my presence but not engulfed by it. Really, though, they were reassuring sounds—and I didn't want to do anything, just lie there and maybe think about Alex, because Hannah had settled and what more I had to give made no difference in her frequency. Then she surprised: Ahem, I just thought of my grandfather.

Really?

Yes, yes—incredible. My father's father. He could be a problem.

What kind?

No, he was all right. I think life had torn him apart. When I knew him—there was little need to be angry.

We don't know much about being old, do we?

Meaning?

Am I really going to regret breaking up with this woman when I'm full of other aches and pains?

I love how after you come you get sentimental for the pain that fucking releases you from.

It has to return sometime—and it's not all pain. I can see around the corner. I can see how much more of life there is. I'm well on my way to being a grandfather or at least a foster grandfather.

Luck had brought me to her and the clearing in her calendar, and it made me take Alex's reversal the next day about nine percent better. No voice in it, just text, because being in New York meant I had to add this feature, having already missed out on an apartment tip in my first days. I called her for clarification, or at least to sway her mind. Message. She called an hour later. Isn't this a change of heart? I said. I mean, is this a change of heart? I waited. Silence for five, six, nine minutes, with steady breathing. You're a beautiful person, Rick. Click. With that, the young triumphed over the old. We were of the same generation, but she belonged to technology, though she vociferously denied it—antiquatedly, we had communicated by voice, letter, or postcard only, since I had begun to write our history in my mind, mostly scratching out and revising, the light on top of it all destined to ebb toward certain death.

I lay on Hannah's couch, sweating in the poorly heated place, the angled afternoon light unfocusing to let me see that the latest wall-paint layer across the room hadn't been applied so well. A dizziness jump-started my next, less lonely period of existence. So I had reached an age (the time had struck only some minutes prior) when my greatest desire was to sit or lie on a couch or a comfortable chair and not do anything, or do things that a normal person would assume to be trifles—thinking, reading, scribbling. I hadn't been able to write anything since Alex's first declarations six weeks earlier. Would it ever rise for me? I would have given up anything to be with her, and by saying so, I pursued membership with all the other addictive romantics in the worst blood-brother salute.

When Hannah returned, she worked with me to quell the spinning sensation, though I hadn't moved, my back still crushed and planted. She used some Uta Hagen acting exercise to guide me, similar to what I'd done with the self-helpists in Oregon. I couldn't realize we were at the back end of our time then, but at least I had a handle on how our combination wouldn't be one of the multiple-choice options for our future. Someone had double-parked below us—a delivery truck gave off a ballistic fit. This brought me close to crying. A sampling from her store of Ativan did even more. Stella, I gasp-yelled with a hush. I fell asleep and woke to her cooking a chicken stir-fry. So I would eat chicken again. Why are you doing this for me? Her green eyes dispossessed: I'm not the other-woman woman. Maybe I was just material for her. Actors like to be around people—they feed off the energy, surmounting their sleep quotient in order to keep playing and pretending. Writers love when visitors leave their homes.

Hannah needed a roommate and wanted to fill the opening by the first of the month—an essential to get her through a summer of small payouts for directing the play. I couldn't afford it. I couldn't afford most places. I'd need to take something compromised. No job leads developed. One Monday I bought cleaning products and gave Hannah's apartment a full going-over, knowing she'd be showing it to some prospective people at night. Tanner called to see how I was. I'm making it, I said. He seemed satisfied. He had the feeling he might start a novel—on New Year's Day, probably. I need to muscle it out, though I hate that term. A novel looks better on the resume, a novella is an embarrassment. Buffalo is wearying me. There's a few programs in Utah and Colorado I'm eyeing to switch to. I want to try that time zone.

I subwayed to West 4th. I was all right until I began drinking. All that physical work had felt so good—I missed being tuckered out after being useful—and I pitifully toasted myself, hoping the ghost across the bar might take an interest in my story. If I could have called my father, I would have. He died about a half-year before I met Alex, though died might be understating it. He walked into the Wisconsin woods and shot himself. Perhaps in some way this drew me to seek someone to live with, to build a life, even if childless. His death had mirrored an event early in my life with him. We had gone for a hike without Clayton in a nature preserve on a crisp November day, and going off-trail for a moment we'd seen a body on the ground. He made me wait. An older man had killed himself, the rifle nearby, postioned like the body. We waited with the park employees for the police. The only dead body I would see outside of funerals. I was seven. He'd been used to this. Before Clayton was born, he'd gone to Vietnam as a reporter for a local paper. Worst three weeks of his life. He abandoned reporting to work as a furniture salesman. Nobody could believe he'd had the belly to go there, to take it in and describe it, if not by lyrical impression, then at least by the compressed miniature a respectable newspaper strives to deliver. The only thing he ever said to me about it was that the presence there of all the journalists, mostly TV reporters, only prolonged the war. Waiting with him in the growing cold of that forest, he acted with a ceremony I couldn't decode—the way he spoke to the police, his solemn, precise detailing of what we had found: I heard syntax, not sentences. For some reason, he made me promise not to tell my mother. Not Clayton, either.

At the time of our father's demise, Clayton was embroiled in end-of-semester nuttiness, while I remained stuck at the beginning of writing an abandonable novel. I flew back and drove up to Racine. The woman our father remarried had never been a great friend of ours. Like too many step-parents, she would nix or attempt to delay any significant time he wanted with his kin. He and I hardly saw each other alone—maybe twice in his last decade. I was to take whatever I wanted as a keepsake—after her approval, of course. Our father had put some money away for both of us. When the financial advisors were satisfied, cashier's checks would go to our current addresses. Are you planning to move in the next few months? she asked, over-speculatively. I signed no with a forehead wobble.

Cremation. No funeral. He never wanted to be a bother, and maybe that recapitulated his problem better than any surveillance video. He backed away to leave after once, in his late twenties, swimming so furiously in. He said he was happy with Eunice, whom he'd met at a singles event. Mother had died by then, and though long divorced, he hadn't waited for her passing. To my ears he never compared the two women. He changed after retirement, and after a stroke, as one will. Something he hadn't done that followed him got too close, but it wasn't Eunice. I've asked myself for an answer for years—next to seas, in forests, on mountains... the surrounding birds continually testified to keep watch on what so many before had no choice but to look at. Eunice wasn't going to get anywhere near the questions of why. I would see her just this last time, and she was already eager for me to end the visit. My brother wanted nothing—and he asked me to tell her explicitly that he wanted "nothing." I came for only one item—a painting he'd found at a rummage sale years before, a work by a Flemish artist, a minor one, but possibly from the late seventeenth century. A street scene; maybe the road at the end of town, burnished in chiaroscuro. He'd taken it to a local appraiser I didn't really trust. Eunice, who dismissed its worth, gave it to me only after I promised to show her the new appraiser's comments. It had to go through the high weeds of a New York opinion, though I wasn't after money, more to preserve the one thing my father had shepherded throughout his life and that no-one except him and me took an interest in, until it seemed it might be worth something—maybe I did so to prove him right. I went to a grouch with a pipe in Midtown. A few days later he called. It's from the early twentieth century, maybe the late nineteenth. It's a copy of a minor Dutch painter, though no-one could agree on his true name. It's worth a few thousand for being old. The frame is the best thing about it. I dragged it to Buffalo, where it remained. I'd needed to claim it soon, along with my other belongings—Alex and I had stored them in the basement—though the podiatrist below said I could keep things there a few months.

What would my father have said to me in my state just then? To pull through? To concentrate on all that was good? Gerhardt called. He wanted to know if I'd found a place yet. He'd drive down in a few weeks to see some gallery art, listen to some good music—did I want to hang out? Yes. Why not. But he'd need to get his own room. Could he handle that?

The days wiggled on. The new roommate would have liked to move in a week early, but Hannah said I had the non-tendered lease until the first of the month. Next would be a friend on Avenue A, an Aerobed. She'd be gone for most of the week I'd be there. After that, I hadn't a clue.

Christmas Eve in Harlem with Hannah and a group of her theater friends. After a few rounds, one woman dressed in pea-green, foot to earring, asked if I was as depressed as Hannah made me out to be. No-one chided her for this—a good thing. It opened my eyes to my own frenzy. I could still write sentences, but it didn't feel like I could. I couldn't even read. We went to a film at Lincoln Center on the twenty-fifth, and I slept through eighty-eight of its ninety-three-minutes.

My life has ended. I thought I'd mumbled that in my head afterward, walking to the subway, but no—Hannah had heard it. She must have once been near the nadir I was; otherwise, I'd be out on my ear. Someone helped you once, I said. Doing for you what you're doing for me. She adjusted her amplitudinous Russian hat with her unmittened hands, a sparkle still crisscrossing her eyes. How else does this world survive? she said. The information had no lesson—or I liked to wonder at it. Hannah's path through things was the art of badinage, and she could pull me up short and usher me on with a one-liner, with such a mighty deviation from what the usual claptrap provided. Days like college with no classes: as the winter light fell, we spent many afternoon hours talking and drinking tea, adding some bitter confessions before realigning for the evening and watching a film or a play on film, something I regretted, since the best plays were tragic, incredibly sad, putting the loss of love under the microscope, no matter romantic or platonic. I told her everything about Alex, and soon I filled in the story of my father's suicide, adding details Alex didn't know about, like the letter he'd sent me a month before. The strange things written there: a misbegotten tone, references to incidents I'd mostly forgotten—and my not answering it, too caught up in the struggle to stay in New York and what I'd be willing to do to make my way. Feeling as vulnerable as a newborn, I could say anything. Hannah was the sister I never had, fastened to me, not a succubus or for study purposes—I knew that then. On the sofa, our feet wedged beneath each other's butt to keep warm, waiting for the rattle of the pipes at five to finally announce reprieve from the chilly but shortened, charged hours the week after Christmas.

We revealed everything over those days—and soon, I believe, we were sick of each other, like a song one hears too much. I begged her to let me go off and be by myself because life couldn't continue like this, for either of us. I had to begin to return to who I was, I had to find my own solace in observance and in words. And I walked west in the late hours of icy wind until I came to the girders hoisting the West Side Highway—the Hudson there is wide and fast, its surface glazed, oily, and so uninviting that even the eddies hide. New Year's Eve would begin soon. A text alert told me I'd exceeded the number of messages in my joint plan with Alex. I shook this off and tried to clear my head, but it began throbbing. The wind charged now. I couldn't get warm and began back, under the high overpass near grimy abandoned industrial lots full of small fires within. Outside the NYPD gate, a man had just laid down a sleeping bag for the night and squirreled it into a tubular cardboard box, enfolding that into a moving carton for lamps. I walked over and handed him a few dollars. He thanked me and continued preparations.

The next day, a tawdry day. Another alert. This time, perplexed, I open it. Then I called the company. There had been an error—I should have been receiving these alerts a month ago. We'd exceeded the monthly limit by thousands of text messages. I owed four hundred and fifty dollars. How was this possible? I requested a detailed bill. It was true. Thousands. Hundreds a day to the same number. Funny area code. Florida panhandle. I immediately saw it all from the beginning to the present, one sweep of the desert to another. It curdled inside me. His thick German dick torquing up my ass in an alien search for succor. I would have preferred to have taken that in to my thinning body that now felt young and fat, with the glisten from older, uglier hours—yet I tamped that down. Success had been too easily handed to Gerhardt, some slinky-footed providence—and knowing him for a year, I could say, with extreme bias, he didn't deserve it. I began to quickly form my "I found out" speech, as if I were writing a review in my head and wouldn't jot anything down until I had the first three sentences cold. There would be nothing immoderate about it. I had a few clauses, but then came a corker: *Don't you know? He's just like me*. What would that accomplish? No, no, no. That was encouragement, not censure. Or was it? Might it have been a very accurate pie of parsimony to her fucked face? He had to have been at least like me—a little lazy, a little cunning, ready to forget everything already good in life. I perhaps should have followed Thích Nhất Hạnh's advice—I'd seen him deliver a talk in Plum Village, near Bordeaux, years before—*You can't compare yourself with anyone because everyone is different*. But I was too close to the genesis of the virus attacking me and either/or scenarios would only embolden.

Who to tell first? Hannah wouldn't be back until five. My brother crossed my mind, but I soon dismissed the thought. I even considered Tanner—what did he know and when did he know it? I kept working on the speech, but maybe the new lovers were about to cast off on some holiday getaway? Canada? The falls? She might still be at work, droning about in her thankless research. *How is Gerhardt doing?*—too simplistic, too done. *I thought you should know... I know what you've kept from me*—ugh. There wasn't a good line, and as time went on, a strange reluctance built up—the same as a tendency to keep great news under wraps, delighting that no-one close could figure into my life changes. Alex and Gerhardt naïvely tried to isolate and yet embrace me, one with the wall pulled out and the other coming to visit in order to throw me off—the beautifully mad pitilessness of their recipe.

When I made it through New Year's and slept until ten-thirty on the day I was to move out by noon, I felt I'd gained more than a reprieve, more like I'd quadrupled my investment in something. I recovered some pep and looked up some *Zarathustra* quotes online to ennoble. I didn't pursue anyone—they, with their lies, were pursuing me, especially Gerhardt, who for all his talk of experience was about to fall into a trap. I never thought of it as a true trap until days later when, installed on the Aerobed, listening to the drunken youngins crying out all night on Avenue A through the thin panes of an apartment building with a frowsy doorman, I glibly transformed and then recast my anger from Alex and Gerhardt to the sloppy new generation and back again, forgiving their reprehensibility but only to think more like a thug—yet I'd publicly register as a corncrake rather than as Iago.

Yes, the man was coming to me. This put me at an advantage. I had nothing else going.

Alex couldn't be blamed too much. I knew what it was to be lonely and spinning. Why else had I reached out to Hannah? You live with someone and then they vanish. It's about finding routine, but passion still demands its spillway. Gerhardt thought he had played it perfectly and could even keep up a superfluous connection with me, maybe to gloat to himself. I'd accepted him out of my own deficiency, and Alex did the same. It wasn't correct for him to keep acting the way he did—and to be rewarded for it. No doubt he could work his messy magic on the rubes and the desperate in small-town Buffalo or that lush panhandle where he made his money, where green vines angered for life. He continually spanieled about me, asking more than my mother would. I was lucky I never told him how my father died. His father, a widower, had moved back to the homeland after a US tryout—if that wasn't a lie. They hardly spoke—not surprising. But I began to wish they did, so the elder could reveal some early battlement, plus a late-in-life judgment, a decree to stop his son's sperm from shooting during orgasm.

Hannah seemed to understand where I was going when we met at a café and I said, I'm not doing this to get back at her. It's about him, as you can plainly see. He needs to learn about life.

Won't he know you orchestrated this? She certainly will.

No. Maybe. I don't care. I sniffled. When she apologizes, I won't be trying to get back with her. I don't want to say that it will shame her, but... Anyway, you can use this. It can't go on an official resume, but it will be on the other, the more meaningful one.

Doing damage? To be proud of?

I've laid out the cause. You've said yourself he's a sack of shit.

How do you know he'll be attracted to me?

Because I am. We've talked about this. He told me his type. And you have a glancing resemblance to Alex. But you aren't the other-woman woman—you said so yourself. He's weak. I am, too. You're not.

I didn't like having to convince people. Intially, I first called a guy I used to work under at the University Club when I set up sound for events. Mike had told me tons of stories about his acquaintances, what they did and how he helped dispose of bodies in Red Hook. I wanted him to ask them if they had a "just scaring a bit" option—a broken leg or arm, or both, but not on the same side. I said, He's tall, but not physical, or maybe he is with women. But he shouldn't be any problem. It turned out to be a few thousand out of my price range, but I already had doubts about this. I could easily live with psychological violence, though maybe because I was a writer.

At first I hadn't thought of personally entrapping Gerhardt, then posting the photographs to Alex, but I did four nights before it would happen. Many people claim to be living their most when they are involved in their most risky behavior. The reverse for me. Instead of seeing more, I was seeing less—going blurry and maybe on the way to blind. But I could not stop myself. My primary mission checked out, made sense—Gerhardt had to be stopped. I didn't have to be the one to make it happen, but I was in the best position to make it occur—I used these and other false signposts to continue onward. I felt less, I became more numb. I didn't feel my hunger or my hard-ons, and finally didn't feel like buddy-fucking with Hannah—no, she had a role to play. I stopped looking for a job or another place to live. My friend on

Avenue A, Eleanor, wanted me to move on the next day. I'd gotten ten days instead of seven. I couldn't help clean her small one-bedroom, because she already kept it pretty nice. I borrowed a digital camera with a long zoom from Hannah's friend and practiced photography from thirty feet away into the glass windows of bars and restaurants on Avenue A. I didn't know if Hannah could cajole Gerhardt on the street—it might take more. I aimed in the dank bar called The Library. Then, knowing his cheapness, in the bright neon of a nearby pizza joint, where a man seemed to spar with a woman, breaking her heart with vile shards of his own. I deleted those pictures.

I walked the winter streets, trying to look away from others. There were so many of them. Women and men, mostly young, gabardined in the latest fashions, their hands cozily holding their phones, the headphones sprouting out of them in a droop before plugging into the device's input—I couldn't talk to them, but they wouldn't hear me if I did. At least it wasn't Buffalo. But I had to be careful—if I stayed, I'd run out of having a city to hate and might need another.

Time sped up and slowed down every hour the day before I'd meet Gerhardt for lunch, when my friend reminded me about moving out on Sunday—I lived between those two pillars. Eleanor had become more prissy, but I'd thankfully kept my state of mind from her by going to sleep before she returned late from socializing. I woke at six (I'd be up by five anyway) and went to the modish café up the street for the hours it took her to rise and go to work crunching numbers for some project to benefit the people of Turkmenistan. I did the same on Friday, a day she told me she'd be home, but by nine o'clock the baristas had had enough of my one-coffee-in-three-hours schtick. I didn't know she had left, as she still seemed to be sleeping when I tiptoed in to steer clear. I'd need to go to the Big Library for the day by shooting over to Fifth Avenue and speeding up the thirty-nine blocks in eighteen-degree weather. Subway home for my pains. I made myself a peanut-butter-and-banana sandwich and wrapped it in a Chinese takeout bag. It was funny but perfect how Eleanor and I kept missing each other. I wrote answers to questions she newly posted, because she had apparently left. Yes, I had a place lined up. No, I wasn't getting into photography, only holding the camera for a friend.

Later, Gerhardt called to shore up plans. He wanted to see some galleries, though he didn't name any. Maybe it would be easier than I thought.

We ate at some dingy Mexican place on Avenue A. I didn't want him to see how badly I'd bitten my nails and ripped out the cuticles lining them, and when I used a fork I tried to hide them by inverting and curling my fingers. He licked and whistled while eating, his tongue pushing pintos to squash against his teeth—he'd still let me pay for him. I'd have to ask about Alex—if I didn't, it would be too strange, and he sure as hell wouldn't introduce her to my ears. Did he know it was over between us? He did—no apparent rise in pulse rate. He looked away, but he always looked away, never inviting me in, but drawing me out; and if I drowned, too bad. How's Sal? Not *How does Sal like Alex?* The wife had been newly upset with him for some misunderstanding—probably Sal told her about Alex; what they did, in some fashion. I could have emailed his Medusa; that address was somehow forwarded to me, surely by mistake, with details of some Just Buffalo reading-series event. Wasn't your wife a painter? I dared to ask. His mouth spread open slightly, a shred of white cheddar hanging from a bicuspid. She doesn't paint these days.

The MoMA had a Kiarostami exhibit with films showing every night—wouldn't I come with him? *Through the Olive Trees* was on. No, I had to find a job. On a Friday night? I had to continue constructing my new life. Plus, I had an appointment in a few hours to see about a room in Sunset Park. He scratched his neck and whipped his greasy hair back like a WWF wrestler. It was the most daring thing he'd done, and immediately he knew it was a mistake. Gerhardt envied me more than he could admit—having no creativity marred his having money. Yet I wouldn't let him make amends. Mainly because I felt him too dopey to catch me out. I never luxuriated for any second I spent with him. I was triply conscious of everything I did, was, and would be—three layers of time and that simple one-hour lunch took weeks out of me.

Just before we left, I'd texted Hannah from a restroom smaller than many on planes. The New Museum on Bowery with large windows was his destination.

We walked out into stiff breezes. He folded his arms in his beige windbreaker—underdressed as always. I wouldn't walk with him to the museum. I had some errands before the appointment and had to get temporary checks from my bank in case the room might be the one. After taking the pictures, I'd need to remove the bigger things from Eleanor's apartment. I had a few nights on a couch in Washington Heights, and the nervous couple needed me to deliver things at an off-hour because the management scouted for any hint of illegal Airbnbing. Gerhardt kept silent and walked slowly next to me, though the museum was in the opposite direction. If I didn't know better, I'd figure him for an ultra-depressed person or at least a regretful one, but not on my account. All the while, the silent voices I contained whispered, It's really men you need. He couldn't say anything about Alex, so he said, I wish I could live here. I envy you. All this, and he pointed at a Laundromat before a woman on a video call banged into him and passed with no apology. And that, he said. This is life. I'm sure there's life in Buffalo, I said. And your son. A smile encroached on the mostly disabled hemisphere of his face.

We parted. I went on, cleared my head in seconds, then circled back breathlessly to Bowery. He and Hannah were already talking animatedly. People were watching me hoist the Uzi-heavy camera, but in typical lower-Manhattan fashion no-one intervened. A few minutes later she had her arm around him, and I bore in and took a few shaky pictures. Then better ones before they were obstructed. I didn't see where they'd gone—she wouldn't sleep with him, would she? People at the desk in the print shop behind me were pointing outside. I left, but I had them.

On the subway to Washington Heights, I peeked at the camera's LED until I realized I shouldn't be displaying a camera the size of a large rainbow trout and stuffed it back into my bag.

There is a long line of stations on the 1 line, but I needed to mark time: 23rd Street, but then 28th Street. 34th. There's a reason 28th Street is still open, though no-one knows what it is. The compartment was somewhat crowded, the same as on any other winter weekday at three. I could smell everyone's pockets. The fibers had been stretched out enough that they'd relinquished the stink of storage for summer and even the cooking fumes of apartments where they mostly hung. Leather, cotton, wool, nylon, down, fleece—the coats came from all over, often to crisscross Manhattan, at least a few times a week. The real New York was in the bouquet of couture tying up one's nose. That is energy.

That is the relentlessness. The world is an evil place—some people make money off that, and others die. Were these apparently loosey-goosey thoughts worth indictment? I had doubts, but after eventually getting off the train, I did write down what I could remember. A barbershop quartet of black men had come into the car at Columbus Circle and wended their way from back to front, their vinyl voices diminuendoing, then bursting forward. Buffalo held so little. I couldn't go five minutes without placing the two incongruous environments side by side in order to begin and end in a similar mindfuck with me no closer to the truth—my phantom word for happiness.

I walked toward my temporary couch but then found an open apartment building and went into the guardless lobby. I hadn't spoken to Alex in over three weeks. She should have known what I knew. She answered on the third ring. Everything played out like the fantasy, which would have put us back another year while growing a different shade of resentment—then needing another year to get over that second failure. *If you want me to, I will give him up*. Her quiescence instantly confirmed I had made the correct decision.

No, I said. That's not what I'm looking for, and a young woman with honey-fair hair passed by me, careening to avoid touching within half a foot of me. Honey-fair hair? I grew white-hot because a part of me had returned. Alex continued, Did he tell you? No, it was the phone bill, the texts, the overages. A few hundred bucks I don't have. She continued, It's a hard month for everyone. She died for me then, but I kept living with the dead, funneling new energies into the past to see me through re-acclimating to a city where I didn't care if it slept or not. Those months, and really almost a year, might be interesting from a phenomonological point of view, but now they seemed almost counterfeit—hours one holds just out of reach to warm at private night fires. How much exegesis of rancor, disunion, and second-guessing can benefit the world? How can any of it?—only if disabled and placed as a parable of itself, with as many yards of honey-fair hair as necessary, will it bewitch.

I never allowed Gerhardt to communicate with me, except I did see him years later in that panhandle. I was visiting a writer friend who taught at the local university. The friend and I went to breakfast at some establishment with a very wooded interior, a place where lumberjacks ate. Gerhardt didn't appear much different, a little grayer, a little less smarmy. I'd forgotten that his cash-generating properties were in the same city—a good sign. There was still nothing to say. He honored that past then, and all his exacerbated, berating texts blaming me for their affair faintly flared but summarily choked.

I don't know what happened to their immediate future together, I don't know where they ended up or if they ended. I heard vague details from Tanner, who, on finally hearing from me, said, You have to use this, take detailed notes. It seems you are, I replied. I am because life doesn't hand us things like this too often. This is an unpublished screenplay on the order of *Chinatown*.

Later, I found out. Tanner said Gerhardt had gone to Canada and then had been detained when trying to return. Alex continued to live above the podiatrist for a few years. Then she moved. Gerhardt never saw her. And Tanner never saw her.

Alex and I spoke two times more—about my finally having to claim the bulk of my things, which grew cobwebs in that Buffalo basement. Nothing else. And she'd told me so, before the bad times started. She batted her short eyelashes and said, I could never be just friends with you.

My wife knows the history or, at least, the main points. Hannah directed that play in Vermont—and people responded. She directed more. Eventually she could afford her own apartment in Harlem, two more. She is one of the two truly successful artists I've ever known. We see each other sometimes and laugh about those old hours. She introduced me to the woman I feel is the best American actress of her generation. I'd once dreamed of being close to movie stars and making films with them. If Alex hadn't booted me when she did, Hannah and I would have never met. Do two shallow experiences make a right? I'm only sure the universe doesn't send you a guardian angel more than once in a lifetime.

Later, at night, I did something I'd been trying to do at least once every year up north—play a board game. Resistance ran high, with Raydon afraid she couldn't figure out the rules quickly enough and Clayton silently worrying about having to win and how to be modest with strangers when he did, though his definition of modesty is far from the dictionary's. Tristan and Tina were thumb-wrestling, and Uncle Stewart was rechecking the stocks in the financial section of the *Times*. I looked sullenly at my wife, but at least our daughter was asleep across the way, with the second Shushh sound machine I had just bought—and I secretly purchased two others, just in case our primaries got lost.

There was an old psychological game called Therapy, seemingly from the early eighties, just before the big self-help boom. I opened the moldy box and filed through the cards and their questions with multiple-choice answers. It seemed familiar, thoroughly designed by the East Coast intelligentsia for those same humidifying minds. I simply began to play it, bullying others to participate, on my behalf—I needed a lift after my lunchtime remembrance of a charcoal chapter of life, though I would never ask directly for such aid. Jane immediately sensed this. She'd made me promise to work on my manchild the night before we married. I said that might mean having to go back to the workshop scene in Oregon to move some energy—I'll have to steel myself for all the hugs. She said to forget it, but at least don't make me ask you more than once a day to take out the garbage and compost. I believed I had a fusty tell in those pregnant moments, a slight but noticeable *I Dream of Jeannie* eye blink—an awful tell to fess up to because I thought I'd kept my face stone all those years.

At what age does a female typically discover her sexuality? The other people in the room, who had been laughing or hoping not to have to really listen to anyone, shuttered when they realized someone had commandeered the floor. Clayton kept expressly in largemouth asshole form when he said, What lobster was boiled and made you king? People eventually semi-agreed to play. I tried to pick the juiciest queries while shuffling through the old cards, which often stuck to each other. There were four categories: body, child, youth, adult—the fourth with questions related to marriage, sex, and death. One flashed, and I read it to myself: *Freud said the central event in a man's life was*: a. *His first sexual experience*; b. *His father's death*—I didn't even need c or d. If the answer wasn't what I thought it was, I'd toss the game in the popping fire when no-one else was looking.

When do we think about the most important things in life, unless they come in some innocent fashion? Then there is no end to them. I only momentarily considered reading the card aloud, aching because shocks would pass through the faces of people who knew the taproot—Uncle Stewart's father's death had not been a suicide, and I was pretty sure Tristan's and Tina's were alive. At Clayton's instigation of a foul joke, I leaned over to my wife and showed her the card, adding, At least I know not to ask such a bunker buster as this. Her eyes popped open and rose—she caught the whiff of humbug, the percolating schadenfreude. I didn't stay with one card long, I wanted to get to others, like a child showing his favored toys. Perhaps it was there that I missed it; I mean the opportunity to be supremely intimate—and without touch. Jane knew I had been shaken, but I kept on, and I couldn't decide if my thoughtlessness or my impetuousness affected her more. Opportunity becomes breach, and hopeful, acclimatized love can get discarded. Minuses, even if negligible, kept accruing—how many more would be forgiven? I wondered, even then.

I was afraid. Mostly for Clayton. Somewhat for myself. We'd barely spoken of the death, let alone the method. He had breezed into and out of Wisconsin at the time, on his way to divorce—Raydon not yet stumbling onto any horizon.

I eventually stopped reading cards. People were getting tired—Tristan and Tina said their goodnights. Jane, also. Heather would be up around five-thirty. I threw another half a cedar log on the fire we didn't really need, though without insulation and with a nightly drop into the forties, I right-justified it. Maybe I shouldn't have been in the room, given the *folie à deux*, but I sensed this might be Clayton's and my hour, finally—the crash of discretions begged it. Uncle Stewart and Raydon were good actors: they spoke to each other without a hint, pushing me to think theirs was an arrangement, maybe two parts ritual. Stewart had asked for help with a crossword, and Raydon sat next to him, her sunburnt face at play with something undiscoverable. It's "tête-à-tête," yes, he said. Ha-ha. Clayton fisted a beer and rolled his eyes. I drew up to him, and we spoke of what to do on our last day, though rain might mar most of it. I had the card in my pocket and wondered about presentation, especially with those two as audience. Should I just show him, with the preamble, Have you ever heard of this? Like all megalomaniacs, he would have a bad reaction to being strongarmed. I kept shuttling through scenarios, but I only kept losing sympathy for him. I would just lay it out—the only way to feature the type of truth I respected but rarely practiced, while caretaking the moods of others around me. Then the duo finished the puzzle and said their goodnights, one following the other by two minutes. I'll be in soon, Clayton said.

I offered him another beer. He accepted with only minor distaste: Don't you have to get up early?

No, it's fine, fine. Pause. I thought of Dad tonight.

Yes. Why?

This card.

Yeah? Ugh-huh. Psychobabble.

Maybe. My reflex was to say to him, It really hit home, but I knew uttering something of that nature would be regrettable. I had to remain oblique: I think Freud is right.

I would think you would. Freud and literature go together like a zesty stew. He drank, then drank more, almost all of it at once.

Don't you think his life was... unfinished?

Life isn't a work of art. When it ends, it ends. There wasn't supposed to be any more.

But if he didn't kill himself, he would have lived more.

He couldn't live any more, Rick. If he could have, he would have gone on.

Is that how you so stoically accept it?

Is there a choice? You want me to feel something to prove some inner fictional thesis for your next novel—that's what I see and feel, anyway. I dealt with it in my own way, my own private personal way. You're about to make a silly book out of this, aren't you? Present me as some diabolical asswipe—Jason from *Sound and Fury*.

I never read that.

Shut up. You brought us out here so you could study us.

It sounds like I'm the diabolical asswipe.

He pumped the last of the beer back.

I just want to be close to you, I said.

You just want to be close to me?

Yeah.

I don't like you—you know that.

Had a feeling. Why?

Just shut up.

Keep your voice... the baby. Your niece.

That's why I don't like you. Don't you think I know it's my niece? Ham-handed pokes.

Don't you do the same to me?

So I'm to blame?

There's no blame.

You judge me—I'd call that blame.

I'm trying to understand.

I don't want you to understand, I want you to take care of yourself. He stood. I had my own relationship with the old man, and I had it out with him years, twenty years, before he died. If you have something for him, you know, write a letter.

I have the painting.

What painting? Yes, I know you have the painting, I've been to your apartment. You aren't making sense. "I have the painting." Yeah? I have a job where I get paid and loads of people respect me. But you have the painting. You have a daughter—my niece.

Jesus Christ.

Right. You know, I'd like to pummel you. People like you can't get to me. You think I have no feelings. I have my feelings. Respect that.

He went out to the porch. So much for oblique.

I watched the fire burn while I seemed to be waiting for his return. The day had gone on too long already. There were too many old memories and too many biting words that would make new memories I'd never forget. If I waited for him, it would please him so deeply, he'd just attack me again. If I didn't, he'd be deeply wounded. I went to bed.

I slept late. I didn't know if Raydon came out of Uncle Stewart's. And I didn't ask my wife. At one point I was going to get up—I'd been awake for a half-hour—I heard people clopping around, but I went back to sleep. I woke at eleven, exhausted. I walked into the main room and saw the Somes Sound in a strange light, far transmuted from my usual morning perspective. Everyone sat on the porch, laughing, looking through the half-salted air at the evergreens and the distant, painfully beautiful island still owned by the Rockefellers. When I appeared, everyone in the group had a spectral glare, even my daughter, who busied herself with a medley of blocks—I saw my people with jitters and jerks, my vision a handheld camera. The inevitable "sleepyhead" comments followed, breaking the *Rosemary's Baby* set piece that had formed freely. These people were not my enemies—even Clayton joined in the playful jibes frequented when people bivouac with one another over a short period of time, where everything is heightened, and all idiosyncrasies are under the microscope.

They are one, and I am the other. I would return to this only after the douche of nightsleep, after some marvel recognizable only in retrospect—a daguerreotype epiphany—and one that does not go all the way. I hugged my wife to make me think I could color an end to the estrangement, so I could get back to that calcifying order I often carried as a treatment for existence—separation—even being wary toward my daughter's improvisational delights, as I hoped to disable my own suffering. These episodes would work for me a few more times over her childhood until they wouldn't. No matter—I kissed my child, with a lip rub she isn't crazy about—it's too... something—but she wanted to run free, with her arms loose and fingers wiggling.

A little more ribbing came from the gallery—even, surprisingly, from Raydon. To assuage me in childhood, my mother had told me the kids made fun of my height, weight, glasses, braces, and hair because they cared about me. If they didn't care, they wouldn't say anything. This is a bad way to come to solace, but (with a divagation or two) it is how the world works. I'd etched an imperfect self-portrait in the world early on, and what I made stayed with me, but still we make so little impression. People didn't begin to act too differently toward me when I lost a hundred pounds or when I dyed my hair purple and changed my name to Purple-Flame Head for a half-year. The commoner knows a good story when he hears it, but that doesn't make him your friend. More often, I choose silence, because when you are closed, no-one can get to you. When you participate, get muddy, or run a lap in the race, then you are vulnerable and, implicitly, people trust you—standouts are always happier. Gerhardt and Alex's relationship was my creation, subconsciously willed to make the pain of lost love linger. To lose instead of throwing away is deeply threaded into love's hermetics, strengthening our resentments that I hate to say are retrospective signs of a tarnished love.

My wife asked if I wanted the egg sandwich she'd made me. I started crying. They all thought I was joking, except my daughter. I changed pace. Guilty, I soon put my daughter to sleep, singing "Rock a-bye baby / In (though is it 'on'?) the tree top"—some things never get corrected. People were showering. Tristan and Tina went out to buy things to make a lobster bisque, and Raydon went down to the dock to plunge into the icy water, something she'd gotten used to in Uppsala. Clayton went with her, but soon came back early, just as I took the first sip of my Irish tea on the deck while leafing through an old *London Review of Books*. I showed him a review of a new book on Rome and he seemed curious, though it could have been the night before talking. He asked if Uncle Stewart was out of the shower. I'd heard Jane walking about, so I offered him ours, on the other side of the house. Anything I should know before I go in there? he asked, before bounding off.

I actually have had it out with my brother a number of times, pretty much on every short visit, though that was the last. Our get-togethers were separated from the next by at least four seasons, but grew to two, three, four years. Not much difference in our relation, except the death, which glitters in miniature far away, though pulsing loudly enough to be heard, ambiguous as ever.

I was alone again—my preferred state. All the clouds were gone. It continued to warm up. The wasps were out. One crawled over the lip of my cup, pursuing the dash of milky lukewarm liquid left.

I had thought to tell Raydon my Buffalo story that ended in Washington Heights because Uncle Stewart was old and cold. We would never be alone then or the next day, before all leaving at eleven. I didn't try. It was foolish to think my story would have made a difference—my sense of the actual goings-on will be quietly buried with me. Could Clayton have sanctioned such a tryst? How could he not know she was out of bed for a long portion of the night? Maybe it wasn't my business, though I had always treated life in a way that implied that everyone's business was mine—we being all one charging virus, even when I contested otherwise. But reality is so many things, and so many are not worthy of being conveyed with intensity. Uncle Stewart and Raydon fit into this subset. We only remember the most important moments of life. So many times, people around us act as spins and dodges to remind us of our own confederations against the primary fluxes of living. I told myself the story of Alex and Gerhardt to remind myself why I was married then. Why the long game was the greater game. Why love's broken back was not to be too romanticized, why the crack of morning promises nothing.

There has always been something holding me back, even when I've overleaped and gone far forward from others around me. The concept of fear has no heartbeat in this great force's design.

It's much deeper, primordial, almost in another world—a confrontation some have no imagination for. I could be very successful at forgetting I donned this invisible carapace every day, cold-bloodily hauling it in all weather, so in certain lights by certain eyes, they could see who I am. My blunder (following a great amount of lived time, thirty years more than Raphael, forty more than Keats) was not to have overcome my ego. The self-help technicians would say I didn't allow myself to be big; I constantly undercut my enthusiasm and subtly sabotaged relations, possibly even with my daughter. That may be true. I knew I had a place in this world, yet I could hardly pinpoint it, because it was both not enough and too much.

Nothing I could ever do would answer to the immensity of what's holding me back. To define it as something I can't let go of belittles me and everyone else who has had this tart, bogus statement directed at them. If life were as simple as palliatives like this one, would it be worth living? Most things we don't let go of. We resignedly learn to live side by side when we accept how we can't ignore them anymore, when we forget by keeping up our remembrances. Even if nirvana were to wiggle into my lights, I might continue to be held back just from the scrum of having been in such a position for six decades. And if I had let go of what holds me back, maybe my life wouldn't have changed in any appreciable way. And maybe this is the held-back self talking—making excuses, introducing misdirection to find a rogue way around my differences. I had a feeling the bilge it sloshed about in could assuage my misanthropy, the whole point of its hell.

Maybe the "something" could be proved positive. A static of

the mind, the boundary marker for the soul. It's why I broke my childhood friend's heart by changing my outlook and going home to be alone. And it's why I went to Europe and why I imagined the trials of wanting to share the things that mean the most to me during the day when my wife was at work, only to go clammy at night and switch on a movie.

Heceta Head

The malevolence of the weekend—time for bitter things to rise and corrode my coppery linings, my unfeeling body. It feels good to say these things—well, I think them, and they are unwritten. I've used all my words, and by some luck they did not make a difference.

The middle to southern coast of Oregon has remained as underdeveloped as some barren shores in Bergman's films. The sea spray, its spit, still glitters in a heartless February chill. I visit the same beach a few times a week to take pictures of certain fragile, newly exposed earth, with veiny and wavy foldings and formations in their great cliffs of amber. The sandstone of the highlands has retreated about thirty feet since I first saw them. I don't need to compare results; they're obvious. And who would be interested? But I need something to do, and to be solitary and single—and to get back in my car—is this season's life. I feel not at home, but I've never had a warm sensation in any house. The little shack I rent is on the property of a couple I know from the self-help days. Even I am surprised at how far Social Security goes in this state—the land that avoided the economic boom, though California gladly cashed its coast.

I've given my life to cities, but my important memories are in the country—when nothing more was left, I re-escaped there. The anonymity: who would come looking for someone in these unpopular coast ranges, home to hippies and anti-government acolytes? There is no-one in pursuit, though I faintly wish there were, before reveries cart me away. I had tinkered with going back to the glaciated Midwest of my youth, but I could be too easily found. Even if they're all gone—except my brother, now two states over. I still don't stick out here—khaki trousers, fisherman's hat, a small bag, a scowl on permanent loan to my eyes behind dark shades—though I'm waiting for the moment it might happen. To be quiet is to gain nothing, but even if I preened like a Krishna, no-one would bother me. And after everything, I will still maintain I want to be left alone, when I know I won't survive unless someone takes me into their arms and silently tends to my ruptures.

A helpful voice reminds me to keep centered on what is interesting to others, not blurting out a sentence from Emerson. And not to burrow into the memory of that bench in Paris and certainly not that cross woman standing next to it, indecisive about sitting. But these are never concerns for writers. If it happened in my imagination, it has to be interesting, at least until I throw it away; but maybe I can paste it on the internet, maybe I can fold it away until my eyebeams look at it in matured light. To write is to encyclopedize memory, but everyone has to order their memories, to choose some delicate meat from the hindquarters or shank—parse, reallocate, filigree, ambuscade—and finally desert before a later recombination in a being who has stood long enough to know that you only live once and that all decisions are paid in full to eternity. The woman in Paris is still parkside, walking slowly away from that bench, alighting to search anew, but still desiring what she went there for. Memories are alive—they have pull pins or are bottled with a cork stopper on their belly-buttons, a sprig of cobweb hanging. The load heaves, more weight over years. To be in view of the land looking like the beginning of time is more than purposeful—it's the only landscape porphyry-smooth enough to absorb my angst.

The early days of our disintegration... Sometimes, as our daughter slept, I stood behind my wife, myself in high-heeled boots because she was taller than me—I watched us in our main room's large mirror and fitfully decided that what we were doing had nothing to do with what kept us together and even little to do with affection. "Once the sex goes..." is a truism, but far right of the meaning most take it for. Once the sex goes... then the real relationship begins. The grain of our relationship, the anomalous molecules that got grouted by living together, could turn vibrant no matter the clutching codependence. With the edge came argument and the tug of war inside our moral tales—plays we ran every night, with every one of those an opening night because the signifiers shifted, the leaves changed, the house sank, while personas grew weary or rageful when not getting enough attention. The story had to grow new carbuncles or it would die.

Yet, most of my furor is around men. Father, brother, friends, acquaintances. That's why I had to let a few of them take me and to take me inside them. Women once were everything until I quieted that storm. My closest friend since college days, where we competed in different writing classes, Arthur—where did he go? But it was me—I left. All those invented fictions that sang beyond his years and then—he stopped. Rage is a bastard child to the artistic mire I'd later abandon. Fetid fen, contaminated swamp. The anger of being caught in that gruel. I needed those men's approval—no, I needed them to be struck silent by my prose and awkwardly offer a weak dismissal. Then I would know that the only worthy part of me had gotten to them, and a curious odor, their breath at a crumbling cliffside, would stay with them. The salted sea rising to offer a phantasm of death.

For ritual's sake, in the days of Heather's youth, I would get together with two men almost twenty years older than me for lunch in Manhattan. They were both established in the literary world, though mostly in retirement from it. I suppose they were fatherish figures, though somewhat in repose. At the time, I didn't feel the need to be seen anymore—to be someone well-forgotten is a more poignant farewell, like Hart Crane's watery tomb, his fabulous shadow only the sea keeps. Literary waxings: we spoke of the halls at Knopf narrowing, Pynchon's email address turning out to be surprisingly simple, and the hot-shit young novelist who named his own book the best of the year. Pigeonfeed. They knew I pretended to be tetchy about the gossip, but they couldn't help falling through those tunnels. We speak of commonalities, or we don't speak to people at all.

One of the men had published a few novels not entirely well-received, but not so disregarded. His was a name that people in the know would recall in passing. "Oh, that guy"—given the infamy of his bad fortune to get in a car accident with the twenty-nine-year-old *Times* reviewer who had trounced the last novel of his. He would avoid talking about this, though I'm sure the other, a critic, received regular debriefings. Actually, he did nothing but talk of the past, as if he were dead. Everything before him just a skeleton key to a world where he had yet to suffer his misfortune—this party, this reading, that award, that visit to Cheever. When I'm his age, I told myself, I don't want to keep talking about the past, but surely I already did, trying to keep people from seeing my sewage so they thought me starry. He was so much of what I didn't want and had to have, like a parent: ministrating, but kingly, heartfelt, and thoughtless, a scar for the length of life. I'd never mixed with him one-on-one—the other wouldn't have it, none of us would.

I was lucky to be at these lunches. Some writing acquaintances who thought nothing of me until they discovered whom I lunched with falsely considered me their friend and kissed ass by linking to my work on social media in hopes I'd part with the Pynchon email. What they didn't understand was that I would never have been given such disclosures if the men weren't sure of me, and because I didn't ask for them, I guaranteed their trust. They let me have whatever simulacra of an online life—one they wouldn't engage in—because all their secrets were safe.

Still, there were greater issues. At that time, the novelist's thirty-five-year-old son had just left his ninth drug-treatment program—one of the few personal details I'd been let in on. A smart son, but the addiction had overcome him. He had secured another job for him, as a reader at Penguin. That lasted two weeks. His mother lived in Spain and had ceased to take an interest. At lunch the novelist would lightly pat his thin beard and gaze at the muted television anchored above where we sat, a fit of dropsy threatening to curtail his only surcease from endless correspondence with lawyers and doctors and psychiatrists. These stories are everywhere but hidden and sometimes incongruous with the people who carry them in their gunnysack. The wonder of it is how the degree of the theater's architecture controls the marionette's sophistication onstage. He cowered when talking of the son, who I believe was more devastating for him than the reception of his books. His face tightened until the subject turned. I couldn't look too closely—he had silently asked me not to. Returning the telepathy, I agreed. Back talk of old times, the way it used to be. Vidal and Capote. Cats—the creatures and the play. I added info on my daughter's progress, a dink or dunk here and there, but our path was well-settled. Why was I there? I fed on others' suffering—yes, Clayton—not in the vampirish way, but more as antidote to my own mostly negligible worries. I also wanted to get a better idea of what I'll be in for, if life were to be granted to me that long. They were two of the few living people who understood that words were sacred and words and sounds used in such a way to produce artistic and emotional effects are holy, of the highest order. I went to them because I didn't belong anywhere else.

I can remember walking past a playground after I dropped my daughter off for camp when she was five or six and seeing another, happier father with his. I kept passing the playground every day during that summer to see if finally the racquet-toting father wouldn't be there, but even on a blistering Monday, there he stood—same sunglasses, chewing gum and guiding his daughter to learn a backhand. I went home to be solitary and have my showdown with the page while still reserving a pity-wanting stance for my pains. Why couldn't I contain the model patience and exorbitant happiness of a proudly fit father whose imprecations were soft-edged, yet not of salty tone, rather than full of genuine delight? The bolt of the question smote: the first serious chink in that faux armor of being a writer. I had needed to get back to review the new book on Musil, though my every day was filled with the most metaphysical experience of life: parenthood. And I thought, No, well, you know, I'll eventually have some fun time with her—go on a fishing trip (don't fish) or take her to an amusement park, just father and daughter—and make up for lost time with something talcy, grasping, and as incomplete as a half-hearted hug. I fogged out on these ideas with stacks of books before my eyes. I needed to be there with the books, even more than I felt compelled to make books or make my child happy, an acidly accomplished honor. I could have killed myself right then, carotid-funneling blood soaking the bottoms of volumes soon to be forgotten.

I have no other guise. I am the same person no matter the year. I believed this for a while, until I realized a few years passed when I didn't. Then, before the birth, I began to mostly enjoy the act of sitting. It felt quite natural, with no premeditation, to begin this phase. "Thinking" is perhaps too gross a term for what I really did, and "meditating" too proscribed—I "relaxed" and "reflected." What were the small shared wonderful things one could seize in a relationship, but really couldn't, apart from the coming child? I wasn't ready to answer this just yet. The narrative lines I usually followed were tamped down. We'd just moved into a new apartment on the upper floor of a house that had a yard with a few old trees. I sat on that red Ikea couch, looking north out the window in their direction—a magnolia and a regular oak, both planted almost seventy years before. The magnolia flowered in April, engendering puce flares all over its crown. At that time, Jane's pregnancy had been confirmed. We were riding high and enjoying more of those miniatures around us, the basil and thyme on the outside windowsill, that changing of leaves—or was it that I started to enjoy them? I sat, often with my tea, watching and, sometimes, filing through the past: the travels, the women, the special times with friends when you forget so much except the moment, and my vision would begin to sheepishly wander the walls, past the Pollock-style painting we'd won at an auction, into the white space of where films or movies were projected nightly, but stopping there and panning back in imitation of a shot I had composed in a student film from window to wall, from wall to painting, and from painting to person suddenly seated under window—the last I couldn't duplicate, but I reversed the pan enough to get to the wall I sat against and, in the corner, the painting above the kitchen table, a copy from a nameless Dutch assistant in the 1880s. I wasn't sure why I had put it there, after it had been given pride of place in Buffalo and in all the places Jane and I had lived in Brooklyn before. Then back to the window and the magnolia's glow in the half-light of dinnertime, just before Jane's return from work. The tree's shape, color, and breathing had further demurred and in twenty minutes changed once more, passing quietly into night—to return the next day, where in the morning I'd again encounter its richness in different light, as a billow of silvery smoke puffer-bellied and overarched it a few thousand feet behind from an antique boiler system in a large apartment building up the block. The cold spring night ordered the then-maroon magnolia leaves to curl back a bit like hundreds of small cresting waves, the tree as sea and foliage in the same moment. Time emptied away, and I'd grown one night older along with the tree, a motion I won't worry over after I'll meet it again. The knurls of the leaves tried to straighten themselves for the day promised by sunlight. I flashed to the first child on the way but detoured to a disarming sense of nature cloistered by money, and the squelching of ego drove blood harder into an ulcer waiting to explode. I had grown away from my passions, but the tree grew toward a nitpicky neighbor who dialed the city to round up a posse to destroy it. No wonder I couldn't be a filmmaker; the only form to fit my semblance would be wiggly Brakhage-light or the campy, whiny documentaries with slow "art" shots of landscapes and objects nullifying the words of the people the audience truly cares about.

The days dimmed, but in another year. I would sit, sun-still, then on the new blue couch. I became less interested in the patternings, symbols, extrusions; there was instead the daily rack, with a little wonderment: the friend who got back with his ex for the *n*th time, the latest political scandal, the eye appointment I needed to make, the author's reading I didn't want to go to, a dream of Trieste, my brother's upcoming birthday, and the ease with which my daughter loved picture books. She could engage much more with the mix of pictures and the sounds of our voices, whereas she would be deadened by the screentimes that I rued, given how, next to her, I could look at something I wanted in a different window.

Early autumn and all the green leaves of summer had fallen; the branches bare but not so ruined. Our daughter was out with Grandma buying new shoes, while I engaged the rare and deadly opportunity to be alone with my thoughts. I had moved the blue-black abstraction, dubbed *Cher's Hair* (by the artist), switching it with the Flemish copy of a "great" forgotten painting. Late-afternoon light refracted off the windows of the taller houses down the block, the beginnings of the sun's triangulation. The painting took on a false cast, light bent by non-original windows—the cloud banks reddened, and Amsterdam or Delft or Rotterdam became surreal, on the verge of a tornado.

A parade of sirens down the way, and I fell toward worry—Arthur, lost and living across the country. I told someone who met him once that he seemed to get angrier and angrier, but I later heard the feedback that I was also getting angrier at the world, even with a daughter, and perhaps I had been talking about myself, fearing my own death when I imagined his and blotted out my father's. And if it were true about his troubles, it made sense that we didn't want to see each other—our realities not lining up because so contaminated. Yet that character who laid into me—I wasn't going to take that. I mean, I would for the moment, but even then I quietly decided how I might not have much to do with his shrill tendency to overcompensate, especially when he judged things so harshly he needed an extra seat at the dinner table for his steroidally flexing opinions. We each contain the other to some degree, I suppose that's why it's so easy to hate—and the other thing.

Cold February, cold coast—wind in the ear. But not a childhood winter with arctic cold stinging the nose on an all-white bright day—a blue dusk, a purple night. There's a quality of light on the coast that I'm not too comfortable with. Its diffusion can run thick to thin—a cover dislimning the two-thirds of the year that are cloud-capped. If everything is light, why am I here? I'll take any Antonioni shroud of fog on-screen rather than off. Yet, walking the strand, the surf shooting toward my shoes before disintegrating, I know where to go, who to see (no-one), even how I'm supposed to feel. The ease with which I bring it all back, gathering in armfuls like a harvest. There is rarely a day when I'm not out here breathing memories, while watching some far-off shift of reality—the odd couple on the beach kissing or throwing a Frisbee, their old dog fearlessly paddling in front of the breakers.

I walk over ground I used to nap on when I explored it in my twenties, but I feel nothing for that time, I don't even want the thrill I once experienced, especially when the sea no longer thrills at all—it is a penance. I left a life in New York at the lowest point, but even then, I still knew nothing about the world. There is no leaving the pain behind and making a fresh start—you carry it to the next destination, like toiletries. I had no other place to end. If it had to be a city, I would too soon fill with disgust and find something or someone to thresh any bits of soul out of me. I use the sea, but I can't reciprocate with a shanty, a dirge, much less any written approbation. It has my eyes, the all of me—not much, but no less than all that's left.

The long nights of May and June are in the offing. So many will be happy. Maybe I could live for that and feel those invisible smiles, because I can't be too involved in faces—not even those in paintings. I'm off onto landscapes. There's my book of Brueghel, a book of Courbet, and nothing else—a few scratched DVDs. It should have been worse—I could make do without those things everybody calls essential.

Clouds or stars, there is always sea air, ripe as that canister of pipe tobacco. An owl drops out of the sky every night, and outside, at every dim flicker of my phone in the yard, a rabbit pops back into the forest up the hill. There is nothing to look up anymore, so I point my head to the changeless. It hurts to not seek disturbance—I couldn't even tell when the counterturn began. My imagination wasn't deft enough to preview these slow-burning hours.

The white ruffling of the Pacific—burst shards of quickly manufactured foam. First comes something taking me neither in too deep, nor out far, but breaking out of the diffuse and back to pure white light. Showering the tufted brick across the Brooklyn yards were those waves, and I'm returned to the defamiliarized couch where I looked in vain for signs of winter among those middle distances—through the Brothers Grimm tree and into uncurtained windows, some still holding the lonely unplugged air conditioner. To sit with soundlessness: so rare. Finally, alone—and on a first watch. I sat on something relatively new, with fewer stains. I was concerned, even then, and I used my freedom to ponder the person I had helped to make. We weren't growing apart, or coming apart—no, time had another gun. My daughter shifted out of acceptance into the beginning of a necessary trial. She cast away on this journey with more verve and authority than I would have liked, and with an upward curve in her inveteracy. And whose fault? I had showed her all those cartoons about kids who go on adventures and who are smarter than their parents, though they eventually do listen to them. She jumped the life to come by changing her age to Roman numerals and adding her own twinkling despondency not with me, but more with what I represented—doing away with the niceties, as I had heartily instructed her. So I pitched my resentfulness in a large, smelly tent with bent poles somewhere west of our relationship. And when I could, I took off my socks and went zazen on that couch—sofa—staring through the empty tree across the way to where people I would never meet stood over their kitchen sinks with a never-shifting stare, obviously talking on speaker. They gave me nothing, not even charcoal lusters of melodrama—their life happened on their phones or not at all. I turned to the wall, hungry for the afternoon glow down the hall in the west-facing bedroom, but no—I had to keep looking in the living room, trailing over her old art posted for years on our wall, as if we lived in a shared college-town shithole. Look at it. Look at all she had made, who once couldn't flip onto her stomach. Family portraits, a day at the zoo, our house, her favorite place being the playground—not watching a video next to Daddy, we wouldn't let that stand. Bright neons, vibrant combinations, the lacquering of lines my wife drew for her. An acid spittle glazed my teeth and I rotated away, back to the hemorrhaged light—fucking cloud cover into Staten Island.

If memory is a kind of thinking, and, if after a certain age, it replaces thinking...

I woke earlier than usual and drove to the water, louder for the surrounding darkness. I had taken 101 south, but too far as I hit the fifteen miles-per-hour serpentine and decelerated, passing the death scent of a skunk's last moments before a Y turn and crackling onto the white-stone drive-off with one vehicle, an old VW bus with fogged windows.

Down through a forest both reedy and daunting, though having little change in the forty years of familiarity. I turned a headlamp on, I turned it off—this needing to prove myself never goes away. I walked in the dark dawn before getting tangled with an exposed tree root, and on the fall my shin bounced off a small boulder. A hell of a bruise I will never show off. Minutes later the theater of rhododendrons opened to seascape—a beach even narrower than six days ago, with the North Pacific gyre pushing south a cold current after peeling along Alaska—graying water yearning to be verdigris.

Arthur came back to me. The closest anyone had come. So far from his birthday, I still began the imponderable there in the empurpled dusk, when we were so young—and thin. He was who I wanted to be, but also already a friend—what humbug casuistry had I hatched? Younger, but smarter; as daring, less afraid—not mordant, easy to talk to. So what if you become friends with who you want to be? Keep your friends close, but keep your examples closer. From the earliest hours of consciousness, I never took in a friendship that wasn't based on utility. Fraternity, egality, and utility—it's really all the same. I can afford to be wrong, but I'll never know otherwise, nor care.

We had stomped across the beach on a few occasions, separated by twenty-five years—and now another fourteen. The beige bands of sand weren't changed, though a shade lighter. On bare feet, we were atop winter damp, as being inside cloaca, bound for greater enigma.

The sea was hungry for figs. Down the strand and around the occlusion of land is the Heceta Head lighthouse, with steel cables the size of pulsing fire hoses pulling it inland, close to rock, to never careen into the diffident Pacific. Our unripened eyes fixed on it, and then a sudden burst, running to waves—him always winning. Our days were writing and reading, then dreaming—impastoed full of a larceny one hopes will be tossed away in one's early thirties; or will all nights end in a tapering away into mindlessness before sleep gentles the conscience? Kippered by our shared solitude, we found focus over old poems, giving ungainly readings of translated verse: *I know that my grief will not stop the green.* Of our own we were intoning our lines as if written by someone else, as the book instructs: *Who has not sat, afraid, before his heart's curtain?* With curtailed gestures and wry romanticisms for us to fall in love over and over—this be our verse. But we could choose stoner calisthenics and also bore a few competitive hives on our bodies until a histamine lowered them and our spirits watched in a greater devilment over sand, sun, and learned hallucinations—that, our poems were like that.

I remembered differently, like a tide pool suddenly filling, because I recalled it the week before and nothing like this even touched my mind. Was he alone, cruising overhead like those no-nonsense angels? A silent seek-and-find? The dead return in profound ways, braiding with the everyday so a grave gray dust rises foggily—and I can utter this only since I am living, walking, and caring about wet and dry. Closer to him is the painful memory, and, for a last time, I'm ready to unkiss his cheek.

The need to be apart abated briefly in my twenties and found me just when I thought I had claimed my writing voice, ultimately a failure of both pitch and attitude. When I went east after Eugene, Arthur pushed further into the Bay Area, glorying about the indelicacies of that too expensive city, finding love in those microclimates of cuddles and pulchritude. Happy to have the right jacket—his grousing face upturned at all the pretty people who would take him in and prize his junk. There were these stories, but fewer and fewer were directed to me after I must have shown an unexpected chill—temporarily embargoing such frivolity, since we were supposed to be creating or maybe learning how to mature. He'd stopped writing. I thought I didn't think but I sat in judgment. And I harbored it, fannypacked it tight, long after we'd fallen out. Nothing for months—and then out of the gloom, his messages: *I never had a woman like this... and she's stopped her life to regale me... it can't go on, right?* Then weeks of photos of the new face. Too intimate, I thought, though they never crossed the line—but it wasn't on their account. He'd relay, *Your eyes only, And she knows—she knows her husband could kill me.*

How did he become this type of person? From Rilke to cutthroat in five years—but was that a stretch?

Our thirties and forties were cordoned by those devices and signals until our intimacy became regulated by people we'd scoffed at. Moss had overgrown our longings, and we weren't too bothered by the hypocrisy. We followed such a miasmal path, barking but not biting, though wounded. Dragging something we did not admit nor could not avoid, though freely feeding off everybody who felt good. Yes, we'd branched out to our true destiny without each other, but I thought we all had to make nice with such an inevitability. People change—plants and dogs die. If he was upset (and I knew he was) he would tell me. I assumed he felt the same way.

Then a situation overlapping with my past shame and chronic anxiety hit with metamorphic force. It was on one of those fruitless days in Brooklyn before the separation. I found myself writing something lachrymose, work that just six weeks earlier an inner brat had labeled astonishing—about Alex Just as my daughter started grade school, I continued to think about Alex, to hope she had made her way happily. And as the hours went by in those humid April days, my passion for words I produced, sounds and meanings, melted away. I had fifty years logged, and within such a history, both banal and thrilling, I thought I could carry myself to a finer resolution that I assumed time would soon demand. I needed to turn back and not necessarily rectify, but reinstate, attest—use a stabilizing force to take the place of what I had lost, someone who knew me when I didn't believe in myself, since some of that same silt now mixed in the man who grew carefree at the wrong threshold. By not concentrating on sentences, I could relax again—I could go back to pure seeing, or something close. Best to celebrate with my old buddy, though I didn't know what he'd been up to for ten years.

After my wife gave me the go-ahead, I explained to my daughter about the trip. The why and the who and for how long. She stirred and broke from my reassuring hug, shrugging, then darkened in a corner with her dolls. I looked at a text message from someone I didn't like and slowly walked into the bedroom to catch the winter sundowning on the nearby church's bell tower, standing above the roofline like a castle rampart. This melded with pictures of my father watching a Wisconsin sunset with a light beer in a cupholder—no chip on his shoulder. I often compared scenes to complexify them and make me happy, because I'd been in both places once—it had been drilled into me by all those high-school English papers: compare and contrast characters and stories. I didn't compare the actual environments so much as the flagrant feelings of the experiences themselves. In Brooklyn, I held a greater intimacy with myself, where a more fearless outlook helped in mediating a certain truth I knew, rather than the truth I wanted with my father. I hoped he might come out with a morsel I would immediately approve of—like something about his father or possibly even *I always felt more for you than I did for Clayton* or *You have to let Clayton do what he does—when I had a chance to make a difference, I chose not to.* And he did say these things over the years—or now, thirtysome years after his death, I've marked up my history enough that I remember such offerings. Could he have said, *I'm going to kill myself, but I love you?* I might have been alone then, but I needed the unexpectedness of company.

During the entire uneventful drive to the blue hills of North Carolina, where Arthur house-sat all winter (one week left until the owners came back), a stream of unsuitable ideas assailed. I fought them, these large Q&A loops stacked with conditions and preconditions for happiness and survival—who was I to be going into it so messy? If this is what shot forth with no creativity for balance, I'd have to find another hobby.

Just by smelling him for about thirty seconds, after I walked into the grandly decorated house, I knew nothing would get accomplished—we'd re-enter the ruts we'd dug for ourselves long before and, if we could, we might end up playing video games instead of getting high and pretending we were crying about some perceived slight like drunk fratboys. Something had happened on the trail of those years, and he appeared about as easy to talk to as a wild goat. I wanted to bring out submerged feelings, and he still kept trying to interest me in the latest hot-shit TV show. As we sat facing the bug-infested forest during our first hour, he took his scraggy hair and made an off-kilter cinch: half pony, half pig. His eyes were ground down as if a jeweler had removed them and gone to work, then plastered them back in. He complained about having to thin their forest in November. What did he do in all the other time? Bought stocks online. He'd made five thousand, then lost it all. At that moment, he was up one hundred. There was this woman a few towns over—he just waved his hand. He asked about Jane, but then immediately changed the subject to his idea for an ice-cream parlor on an Indian reservation.

I fell asleep easily enough in that foreign house scented by too-fruity potpourri, but I woke up just before dawn, crushed—tire marks on my pajamas, I truly saw them there, his car. My balls were still heavy, and I shifted them and their master, ostentatiously hefting as if I metered an apothecary scale, because I hadn't ejaculated in, I didn't know... months, and still, no desire flared—grim preview of the following decade.

I fought myself for hours on that alien bed while drinking blasé tap water certified by the county. If I could confront Clayton, why not Arthur? But confront him with what? *You haven't turned out the way I thought you would, but I really don't know what you wanted to be.* Had I already grown too old? After two days I'd had enough, and when I told him, over omelettes I made, he feigned surprise and then blurted out a few token complaints with a little too much English on the suffix in "reactionary." Not his normal, but he'd left an opening for me and, just as quickly, knew he had invited castigation, even lorded it over abandonment. His father had left at twelve: And I heard a sad song in the air, he told me during youth, but when pain grinned, he didn't want arms for a hug—he wanted palliation without love and I gave him: Ah, my friend, you do not know, you do not know... and then, I shivered to think I eternally played out this scene with him—four, five times, a whole week of this dreadful diurnal theater gluing our history into something for the discard bin. If he could only hear my thoughts... but that danced as the easiest, newest excuse for feeling I could grasp. He then huddled over the half-omelette like a convict. I had missed his closing of his opening—it had fled, back into his stomach, where it could freely wound at every meal.

Around us the hilly spring-bloom burst, fractured, and blurred—a bad imitation of a good Cézanne. He wasn't reading, he confessed, he'd forgotten how to fall in love—these were coming out at shorter intervals, and I disguised my anger as surprise, when it wanted to be mewling glee. I'm headed toward angina, he said—I didn't know how or why. They all came in a headlong rush as I readied to leave, though we still sat, an old magazine between us, until all the joy we had shared and remembered began to plummet—I was older, I should have known—and he, who once didn't believe in long goodbyes...

A burning to piss brought me out of the room. I pretended to be talking on the phone to my wife, but I pretended for myself. Where is he going to go now? There's a woman in West Texas, whose daughter is in trouble with the law... He's going to drive into town like Orpheus descending and he will fuck her and they will go down, down, down—and in two months it will be over again—for the fourth time, fortieth. And I went into the front yard and kicked a few tulips and thought how my generation might have been the last holding any dregs of human decency, proof I was as full of shit as the rest of them. All those people in the book industry who seemingly treated me with strange silence or ungratefulness were just trying to protect themselves. I had to go back to Arthur and make the case for something warm to counter, to make us all right for the next time, but I was too unhappy, too unsure. I choose to act more the child. I needed something from him, but I wouldn't ask, because I didn't believe in myself; I felt my family was about to break apart, my fault—I couldn't trust him with that and hear some foul-mouthed reproach with a sprig of cliché. If he threw out the familiar watchwords *Translation—give me the pussy*, I would have killed him. There are too many people who think they have found their meaning in life by rescuing others, but neither of us could claim such medallions. We asked for love but offered droll dispassion.

After I had packed up and started to mutter tidings near the car, he dickered with a Weedwhacker. Well, you know where I'm off to after this, he said. I nodded. Something wanted to step out of it, this doom, an ingredient for those shared readymades to carry us later, even at the last second. His murky eyes violated themselves, right rising, left lowering—but that was all. Our time of crisis, though we talked ourselves into corners. If one of us were a woman—yes. You don't learn nurturing from men and you don't do it with them.

I drove back in an awful, itchy state. No music. What family? How to get through the upcoming summer of drowsy, resentful days, even the next weeks? Only when driving into the dusty, grimy Legoland of crippled concrete and rusting metal that is the madness of the turnpike and sundry spurs, corridors, and potholes in New Jersey did I finally trace a picture of Arthur in a sort of daguerreotype, an action shot of him lingering on a dark road, fearing for his future. Plunging his heap of rust off some cliff. For weeks I expected to get the mysterious, nettling call, probably from the West Texas woman I'd once heard pleading with him on a quick check-in. Amid the scornful sizzle on a late June morning in the city, when wafts of urine and dogshit reach the third-floor windows, I realized I'd already removed him from my life—even faster than one-click. When the body part doesn't hurt anymore, you don't pay attention, but this cutting off was more dastardly. I couldn't confuse his problems with mine—and that he had barely asked after my family... but he did, glancingly—I just pretended he didn't. Anger drives one to start disagreeing with oneself and all past happiness is shame-bombed. Yet, then, gone—Arthur out. Twenty seconds, thirty—and I prismatically agreed with what had been internally decided weeks before.

The months piled on. And when my wife asked about him, for the latest, I shrugged it off with slight lies—he could be living the same life, but wouldn't I wrestle any hypocrisy beginning to warp something smooth-functioning about my living? There were limitations. You put the people who hurt you into a special shoebox—they sit on the shelf forgotten, and they gather dust. I had my special place in Arthur's life, no matter that he didn't have a shelf to store me on. That same week we fully agreed to begin the road to divorce. Isn't it all a matter of voltage? Preserve, preserve; provide, provide—for you don't know when...

That summer I carried over the outage at Arthur's to the shriveling hours with Jane. I fought them both on twin fronts—Arthur in memory, Jane in the everyday steam of Brooklyn that urged me to lash out. *It's the city,* I contended in calls and emails with those who for one last time made to soothe. Hannah would call me out—and it would take a year to forgive her moxie. Yes, Jane and Arthur loved me, they forgave my ever-widening tours of darkling plains which delivered bile in each interaction. The brownout cut me down and I sat silent, exploring the cobwebbed attic of memory with moonlight less than a quarter of that permitted to earth. On its floor I became more level—I didn't let their love in, I worked to salvage the part of my soul that feared good cheer. A child shows his toy and a man hides his. My toy was not so desirable—but I had been telling myself that until the day before I sank deeper on the beach. You don't have to lose love to give up. If only I had a weaker memory—a spray of sand hit my lips.

Ten years streamed by. Arthur called on a random, agitated afternoon. My impulse was to say, What happened? What's wrong? His voice had degenerated, or an unwieldy cord haunted his throat and his curdling words came as if from tape delay—before they reached the listener, he seemed to half-hope they might break apart like space junk. The sentences continually faded—there was someone next to him and maybe they could help. A young woman described the condition. Maybe he was too young to have such a clampdown, but it did happen, and it was happening. I yelled for her to put him back on, but chaos followed, it sounded like a visiting doctor had discovered contraband in the room—three voices moaning. I called who I could call. They hadn't seen him in years. And a week later the same woman rang (she identified the place as a hospice in Albuquerque) to tell me of the death after a brief coma. It was on her own time—they weren't allowed to call anyone, but to live with herself, she had disobeyed.

It might have ended there. I had deleted my author website, but Arthur's sister found my email through the Wayback Machine. We'd met a few times in Oregon. I couldn't remember much, and she gave hardly any local details, and had only one question: What had happened that we never reconciled?

I stopped walking south as soon as I entered the shadow of the shadow of the great rock. Ascending it would lead to Heceta Head and that lighthouse—witchy name, witchy place. Hobbit trails—Heceta Head: does the land reflect our pop-culture stewardship? The thing about memories—you get to have more of the good ones, it's a choice: I thought this and immediately dismissed it. Stood there counting the rolls of foam and, beyond, one ore blue, the next green. And bringing my hand to my head, a vanishing—my shadow disintegrated, dowsed by foamy whites.

I want him back, and the next voice the same as the first, but more guttural and unconscionably self-satisfied, *If I had made my choices—*

To the north a woman and her dog, who seemed to reverse course just before my mind told me to look. Their behinds to me as they walked back, the white pooch peeking a few times.

...

Late summer it was, on the same beach—and she didn't even look, though she may have nodded, while I pointed down at the book in my lap. The full afternoon sun made the glare purple. But I was... where? In Chekhov... *He's told nothing. Yet I'm happy.* After many minutes dwelling in the cloaked consciousness of a twenty-year-old, I made out her nudity while she torqued through a sun-drenched yoga session on a sand-sprayed mat. Fluid movement, the wigglesome veins lining her neck—the full breasts poised by youth's invisible bra. Up and down—a sprung rhythm to her routine. The bloomed tree of pubes. Her trust quelled my arousal. Perhaps she sensed my uninterest in sex—and the book. Today this wouldn't happen—but I'm lying to make something else apparent. The old man is a figure of folly—more mercy for a very old man, but my age makes me just the type to bring the sword down on. If I were a young woman, I wouldn't do it in front of someone like my fusty old male incarnation, either. And I briefly slipped and saw my young unmortgaged self from that woman's point of view—a little sad, a little bookish, some funk you feel sorry for. This revisiting wouldn't last, I cheered, yet the window-lock I thought I could un-depress didn't work. The reviewing couldn't be reversed, and I instantly began to live with the void, not the whole. I continued to walk back to the trailhead through the mushy sand and soon dizzied, swiveled, and aimed at the horizon, where a long freighter moved southerly soundlessly; and I tried not to think how, yes, there was already a taste of what dreariness I would come to—nothing can beguile or stir that didn't first exist in our being, secretly waiting.

But this wasn't knowing oneself, this was constructing oneself—work that should have been done in one's twenties. The foul beguilement continued to haunt as I trudged up the rooted, wintered turf, passing the small groups or lone visitors who start to accumulate on a Saturday morning, though I kept Dostoyevskian and lock-limbed, only to attract more attention—so then childhood fears began to rage, awakened from slumber.

I took my inhaler from the small medical bag in the glove compartment. My ex-wife surely wouldn't pick up a call from me, and I thought of others, but they were all gone, except the only person who said I inspired him, a young writer from Idaho. He still wrote, but now taught locally, just to be close to the Snake River. I'd have to confirm something for myself. The remarks of an old friend usually suckerpunched and made you think you'd lived a lie, but in my self-sufficiency I could easily do so myself.

I drove the car awkwardly, seeing my hands on the wheel as thinner, younger, and pointed at the ends, not stubby. I had been under the impression that people can and do change—but I began to swim crosscurrent. More gassy bubbles of feeling percolated, and I luckily made it to the driveway, before another raw segment of beliefs crashed down in a landslide. Inside, there was nothing, just an old warm beer no-one wanted to drink. Having sat on that beach, innocently learning a new trade—and I had to be responsible for the scent I gave off even though no-one could smell it?

The strange day became stranger when I fell asleep before ten in the morning, sleep being a response to trauma, a stance I choose when I can't see the world anymore—a cat's death, a breakup, the leaving. More resolved memories would become unresolved in the next, breathless hours. They came at high speeds or not at all, since I had no control, and they chose the rapidity of a knife-stab in the gut rather than the brain. Should I have read more Horace or Dante? Who I had read never signaled how aging could be as vividly unreal as drugs or how a piss taken in old age can come out as arsenic. I'd often gone by the motto that I didn't have a problem with being wrong, but this was before I remembered all the mistakes I once anointed with an audacious Rilkean pathology of being unique things in themselves. And for years the epigrams of Heraclitus had fooled me into pesky unilateral thinking, kids fishing saying to Homer: "What we have caught and what we have killed we have left behind, but what has escaped us we bring with us." I was a broken man, ambling out from the back porch to search for the imaginary garret where I might start a semi-stable time-wasting activity.

An icy mist had fallen while I dozed, and the manmade grass carried a violence of watered green. Outside, my hand hovered through it, and I turned downhill, where 101 had gone too quiet for a Saturday. I waited. Time surely couldn't stay out of joint too long, but it did, and I remembered sex with someone barefoot and libidinous—a painter, all lemons and onions. A woman I would never have had the heart to hold for long. But that was prologue, it was sex—first eerily in turn and then boldly provoking our worst sides—stamped by her menses and my fetid seed. *Or are you afraid*—one of us said this, or it was written in a Jamesian look gone pixilated in digitized consciousness, as we stood on a cracked sidewalk in deepest Bushwick, a newly ignited winter scene just outside some gallery opening. It wasn't the sex—but it was. And it was never the orgasm, or the absence of one, but something she did with her arm or using the word "ersatz" that made my balls weighty with joy. I let myself be dominated and it felt better than good, because I tasted what I'd been missing, not just beside but also in how we saw the earth and composed arcane elegies no-one we cared about had ever understood before—little briefs on the patterning about a landscape or the man in the corner of the party we both noticed. Our huddle—we named it a coven of two. Yes, in twelve days, we were already demarcating our history; a bad sign, but I let it pass—I wasn't ready to complete the transaction yielding loneliness. I'd kept myself clenched in the fist I'd become since maybe thirty-five—when you've built a convincing case for the world to leave you alone, the exhausted dopamine enriches, blood holds in fertile oxides. Lucy invented more and more of our terms, hence her overmastering. This surprised, since she was the successful artist—she had much more at stake, people demanded her time and she'd *fuck you* them and deliver hours to me in a brown paper bag of seismic effect. The show was in three weeks, but she was spending whole afternoons making authentic Thai, Japanese, and Italian dinners, while I put more things in storage and sat in my cage on a box of hardbacks, drinking cold tea from a broken thermos and hallucinating a new life for us together, but much too soon and with a visiting daughter a childless woman would rather not meet.

It happened so swiftly—it was amazing how I didn't have to do anything, like having a rich friend pay for your life over a course of weeks. It wasn't the sex—and then it really wasn't. She made confessions to me every night, trusting I wouldn't respect the patrician gossip, the end-over-end family dramas—a father a higher-up at the Guggenheim, and remember Jeanne Moreau? Well, he and she... My confessions were paltry, but she listened—she might have been thinking about how to get out of her contract with this Chelsea gallery as her eyes ballooned to fill the holes I revealed—even the daddy-daughter malfunction. Aged forty, but fifty-five in off-hours, with the uncanny ability to swing her larger breast into my mouth when I seemingly needed to suckle. In no time it was routine, and the shrewd winter days revealed us as conscripted; we sought whatever healthy blood bubbled in the ruins of others—one of us gave crack to our ego so the other could be destroyed more fully.

Interstitial flashes of Hannah—and then the show that was in three weeks suddenly dawned, and there I stood face-to-face with the fly-by-night jet set. In the car back to Brooklyn Heights, she said it: This isn't the life you want—a flagrant phrase, an adult's rejoinder to a child's naivety. I wanted to challenge her own adherence to it, but wisely shrank back to the new asphalt I had to track upon. I thought she might counter with: But they're good people, they gave money to—I couldn't hear such swill. Born under the clangor of a mother on the verge, I mistook the power of women or I too easily ceded mine to them in a very un-Roman tribute (or did I read that somewhere and appropriate it?) while still blinking for mother-mercy. Melville made little out of the love between man and woman, and that answered why I couldn't write like him. But Faulkner—women aplenty. Me? I kept waiting for a mirror to say, If I say I love you, you'll check to see if that's in a book. I breathed in her hair when my nostrils ejected the stench of the car service's air freshener. Was there another way we could? I asked. No, she said—You could be hidden, but not never seen. My daughter's pinked face reciting state capitals loomed in retrograde.

Two months later, I reversed myself and asked back in. Wisely, she did not count my pretensions ever again. This last dying fall from love—nothing really doesn't come from nothing. Wind, the long nights, late spring—klaxon from the road.

Needling rain drove me in, and I bumbled into a box in the closet. I thanked myself for keeping a few photographs, though not of my daughter—there are degrees of pain. The white whale had been poked, and she wasn't going to let the least bit of vexation roll past. Any thought of her still gets accompanied by the haunting keyboard ring-a-dings that tell me it's 1982—the real prime time of my life-situation, because it was then that I first feared the longing that puckers to the skin, a beginning to the bleeding. The child of me attempted to join with the faraway image of her—but I sickened and attempted a scissor step. Only I—the archaic torso I've become—can change my life, and I boiled water for the expensive tea I hated.

Something must have clipped me in my sleep. Frenzy after frenzy followed, and I continued to draw out my carbuncle tongue in awe as I sat near the window, waiting for the common American house spider, my friend, to help me pass fifteen of the day's harder minutes.

To think, for years, I'd barely mentioned it. My daughter's misbehavings were just like mine: every time I looked at her, I saw me—maddening—and this pressed play on the past, providing me with a double dose and in Dolby surround sound, putting myself before myself. But I did tell, didn't I? I told a friend when we were drunk, and he laughed and said, Funny. At age three, four, and five, my anger built, and by seven I began to foam.

I held apart from my daughter in shame, wishing she could choose the other path—be like her mother, be like Dora the Explorer! And her mother had pointed at me: See the world, goddamn you. Go finish your book at your friend's house this summer. I couldn't do that and miss a month of her life, but I did and the novel came to nothing—weak-willed and heartless like its creator. I should have known my fate when my successful writer friends didn't want to talk writing anymore and urged me to drink or fall in love anew—or, they hoped, both. I returned a day after her eighth birthday because of a bad storm on the road from Arthur's, and though she said I was forgiven, I couldn't forgive myself, abducting any strong feelings as a pox on the mess the writing life entailed—or was it the life of avoidance under a different name?

And my number two said, Great, now that you aren't going to be a writer, you can be a father—but that second self wasn't the innermost self, that still raw potent afterbirth ruling my life—easily regurgitating anything not meant for its belly. Throughout many weeks and many months, I believed it was simply a choice—drop the pretentiousness, since I'd dropped the pen, and become the happy dad I seemed to encounter everywhere, but the bitterness made of blight was too tasty. When you're fifty you don't treat sorrow like sheets to be changed—dashed dreams will always dominate the brain pan with dark weather. And when I really wanted to feel sorry for myself, I'd tell a soundless tale of how I lost all the most important things in my life within weeks of each other. One day a therapist intuited this and justly asked what I got out of such a callous recounting. I looked at the picture behind her—a Turner seascape—and moved a muscle I didn't know I had and laughed at how I got to be the victim.

I couldn't leave such fool's gold and even gussied up the equipage by landing on the Oregon coast. *Oh, he lives by the sea. An ancient mariner who doesn't know how to swim.* Again I approached my loss, but let off just before she turned her majestic face. Oh, I'm old and cold and afraid.

I sat trying to cry, but I only knocked upon an essential ambiguity. A voice whispered, Don't take the past as what happened, treat it like your plaything. On the ground, at my feet, were places for my shavings to fall, but no rose in that steel dust. Some moment, some lived experience that had never happened because there wasn't enough thunder in the sky. I kept revolving my thumbs until I could achieve the desired amount of welter in the picture, a pure timbre in the sound instrument. This moldy crate of besieged fancy I dragged into fatherhood, determined to reject the Kodak moments for those of my choosing.

After a few hours of sitting by the window, another wave of sleepiness seized me, and I went into the bedroom. I opened a book of poems and found the favorite I hadn't read in a while—so she dies at the end, is that what happens? More and more, the early memories came. When I was younger, in my forties, even,

I remarked how older people almost constantly spoke of the past—and it happened to me, elemental in my undoing.

The summer after my father left the house, a strange man came into our reality. The roof and the gables needed repairs, certain rooms required painting, and the rotting front porch needed tending to. Clayton had gone to live in Michigan (his collegiate career about to start) and I kept searching for what might make me passionate in the weeks before becoming a sophomore. I learned the adult business of compartmentalization—and I saw my father once a week and on weekends. But summer had a devouring maw all its own. I dreaded it. A sweat formed under my arms, and raw rashes stained the days. The smell of baby powder made me weep. The hired help was a painter, a paper-hanger, a carpenter—and something else. An outcast really, the same as me: Doug stood with a slump and sat with a slouch, but he was mostly bending. With a Beatles mop haircut, a mouth missing important teeth, and one eye glazed over in a jaundiced jelly, he stammered and recited eerie jokes he thought would calm people's nerves about his disjointed presence, though only unsettling them more. He was somebody's nephew or half-nephew they had to keep finding things for, because there had been drugs and arrests, but now he'd been good for a few years—he even intermittently saw a woman who didn't realize he had fully prepped for a life of disturbing the peace. He didn't talk about women with me, measuring some sense of boundary, but mentioned Castañeda, and Suzuki on Zen. Thirty-three years had given him the radar to recognize other lost souls and reach out to them with an uncannily adept Midwestern-dude chumminess—

a mystique not to be discounted—and he'd say, Hold my old holding hand, without voicing it and without our touching. That was the Midwest—the uniquely placed gesture, the right length of scrim on the window, the right beer in the fridge, the mower left in the middle of the lawn as monument: no words, but things themselves, standing for ululation; it's what those on either coast could never understand about it—not what is said, but how it's not said. And though I broadcast coldness that first week, he broke through my plasticity masquerading as rock.

Just upstairs, right above the baseboards was a place now solely my mother's room: a repository of toil and impossible scents in fluted and ribbed-glass dispensers atop a mirror tray; clothes laid out on the room's only chair (orphaned from its dining-room set, since we were now down two persons from last year), a Georgia O'Keeffe—the state's pride, no matter the mesas and skulls—and an end table purchased in a little Chicago antique store, brought back blanket-wrapped in the trunk. Downstairs—and though subterranean, it was more of a reef—Doug put up stakes. The basement had a store of abandoned tools—a treasure chest for a Midwestern man—and cool spaces where he could return to cut wood.

There was little to do on those unrelenting humid summer days. Reading did not yet take on the shine it would regularly polish on my person, so I would glower, fantasize, and watch films. Doug became not so much disturbance as radiance—I didn't know he had secrets, though he had them garbled as folderol. It became most natural to share space with him. He had charmed my mother—given the ages, there was no sexual jeopardy.

As I pushed the recall button, inhaling varnish and paint thinner, I began to sense a version of myself stand away and turn his back from me. This new person was weighted with a judiciary air and face fallen and hollowed into Doug's front. Would he grow up into Doug, or a Doug? The gross weight of age, those full-throated decades, nesting in the prohibitive picture of my history that I only carried in a side pocket of my wallet.

My head had slipped off my hand in Oregon, and I imagined walking over to a couple of outsize scrolls housed in a compartment of an altar. And deep inside the younger one, I found how indeed I was remembering not my childhood so much as the man I'd become, a younger version, if that man had lived to become my age, which more and more it appeared to do.

I resisted, as I had effortlessly resisted in youth. I couldn't wait for eventide.

After some years, I prayed that my daughter would not be like me at all, given my poisonous intrigue with the nightside of psychology—covert tirades against people I didn't know, people who could never know me, and bilious envies and jealousies all having to do with writers and attention. I had had lunch too often with the novelist and critic, and was still mindlessly adopting their attitudes even after being shown the folly of being too bookish, or rather too hungry for adulation while not driving down far enough into the strata, encountering newly dripping objects for public show-and-tell. Of course, I wanted her to be better than me—and to have a better role model. I wanted to be thought of as a guardian, someone to obey, but probably someone who should retire at five o'clock to the guest cottage so that the real parents could take over. I would not show love but concealed-carry mercy. If you are around someone for some length of time, they aren't only watching you, they are becoming you, there's an inevitable IV from your behavior to theirs. This disavowal of my duty arrived only a few months after my other foolish wish. And then I spent the next twelve years trying to strengthen the foundation of falsity I built on. There were so many mistakes in just over a year's time. To put down the pen, but to still retreat from parenthood—alienating myself from my wife. And before I moved out, I remembered myself, nearly spry, though with all the bagginess of the past, prowling around some loft in Manhattan—when I and everyone I liked wanted to be in Manhattan—before clustering next to a woman whom I thought to spend my next days with, but who would not have me, as she was used to money, shopping, island trips, and tapas. I talked to her guy friend, telling him, though I pointed my breath at her, how I truly didn't have any regrets, everything I'd done was supposed to happen, and she gurgled her wine at my West Coast spin-doctor routine. She might not have fully dismissed me until those unctuous words and then she bloodlessly dimmed any interest and reduced my throat, scented rooibos, to a pesky port one endures in a café—she drank lattes.

With the age-old reversal inherent in desire, that woman and I would have been totally unhappy and might have lasted a month—a rancid maggot-filled compote of stinking piss. The object of desire always has its own private echelon that will not admit those other certain pillars of life—family, work, friends, morality. My cravings had only suspended my regrets in the theater's fly loft, where a couple of underemployed pseudo-artists lazily held the brittle ropes, before I let go, indifferently, on a vacant Tuesday in my fifty-eighth year. By then I'd moved out—living in a garage in Beacon, being sent pictures of Heather as she grew up under another man's wing: a big daddy who helped produce the sister they always wanted. I filed through earlier history shortly after, to remember my father sitting with his afternoon old-fashioned, say, in recognition of sun and his son and alerting me to how, in the sixties, when the culture broke and the bustle began, he always thought he was keeping apart from the crowd and its lovin' spoonful energy by holding onto his job and keeping clean and respectful. But no, he had fooled himself—he'd gone along with everything as he offered no opinion, letting the wave take him to the shore or the rocks, he wasn't too concerned.

...all those men from youth, even Clayton—now strangely invisible—who lived to watch the hair or tilted up from the calves to the thighs, expanding and synthesizing into the twin pockets of an ass: those men who used to make fun of everyone's body and face and almost everything else, especially the feelings I might parade; and then once or twice, after the scorching sarcasm, the ungainly deflection that it wasn't their fault, they were saddled with it—they'd lost their illusions. Where were they now, these craven legions? And could I call one to profess how I'd come to the same end, that it made little difference that I once had one up on them and seen through the charade? I'd taken a much greater fall with my prideful failure, but they'd interrupt me and say, Stop feeling sorry for yourself, take something for the pain—pain for pain; in the end, they knew how to inspire. But I would always have my loft moment—and I searched for that woman. Phantoms—a picture of her married and happy and kissing her son, born blind.

I visited people on my drive across the country, staying at middling but not louche bed-and-breakfasts and having much more intimate conversations with those strangers at the dining table than with the old friends I'd see. They didn't approve of what I'd done and didn't believe how it hurt, the caryatids of regret I hauled. Their partners often changed the subject of the conversation: When are you off to Oregon? And on that awful, endless three-thousand-mile trip, timed to overlap with the blaze of autumn in late October and early November, I finally teetered and thought, on the outskirts of Missoula, in the shade of a gas station's lone tree, that I must be mad—I couldn't start over again. I called young Henry in Boise—and he had had success as a critic, but now taught, his free arm winged around a novel he couldn't finish, and at an insurmountable distance from the publishing world. I had burned out on my age group—I couldn't trust them to not reject me—and went on to the second-next generation for their lack of knives in responding to my ill-formed sentences, hoping the pity inaccessible in the elder set might make a small storehouse in people who still took love for granted. First, I had to deceive—I already reached Oregon (Yachats—it's beautiful!) because I'd be passing Boise or within distance of it, and then I began to talk down to him, but immediately apologized. I started to treat him like a priest, while I rattled off my feelings as I examined the cracked travel mug stenciled SUNSHINE that I drank from while driving. We talked of literary history and characters' motivations and novels that had stood the test of time because of the style in which the content was delivered—not storytelling but words and arrangements of words, though we pass most things in novels as we pass things on a train, and yet the razor-edged reversibility of writing and reading—we read not to see the world, but to see our lives, we both agreed, and I felt bettered even though we spoke of a passion that ultimately broke me. And after ten more minutes of that, I did not want to thumb through my life and problems anymore, I wanted to stay on Joyce, and then on Henry's lovelorn moments, which were much more important to suss out since he could still change, and an hour later, he tried to stop things, saying: This was supposed to be about you—don't I look the asshole. I kept quiet when I should have immediately reasoned, but my eyes were burning, his caring had been too much—his co-feeling finally brought me out of myself and I vanquished it by pretending the connection had blinkered, and I said, Hello? Hello? Never would I outgrow the caretaking. White nights—then again my portion.

It was two or maybe three in the afternoon, but thickening clouds made the light dim. I didn't think a Saturday could have such hallowed force. They all said—a new set of they; my neighbors, ostensibly—how it would change me living with these yearlong shrouds of light, easily grating to so many millions. The coast ranges and their thinning and clear-cut forests: a cleft of history you rise to, before dropping to meet the ocean—Here are your waters. My neighbors—I thought of examining them closely, but soon abandoned such scrimshaw plans, sometimes feigning to keep current in the face of them. They wouldn't become friends. You don't make friends after a certain age; you see the same people at the café or store and noddingly talk of matters having nothing to do with your heart. Five years. So they know I'm serious, but too serious—give him a wide berth. They know enough of my past that they don't want to know any more—

if someone has car trouble, I'm the second-last person to be called; the last doesn't have a car. They know I don't work with my hands and the pen has been put down.

Once, the daughter of a man I'd gone on a few hikes with until he threw out his back brought a copy of my lone novel into my vision. She'd bought it online. Five bucks, she said. Almost twenty-five years ago, she said. When is the next one? I smiled and signed. Helen is her name. She works at the veterinary clinic. She is kind and her clear eyes don't know frustration. I had a falling-out with her father over some remark about remarriage—so Helen could get on with her life, "like in Ozu," I wanted to add—and he swatted at me as strong as he could with his chronic injuries. I told her to give him my best. She nodded with a certain ceremony. He didn't visit me, and I wouldn't visit him. There had already been too many mistakes, too much language I wasn't careful enough with. If I could have written it down before I said it—but who would accept that? I knew exactly what first impressions I presented to these people: broken, but stoic; embittered, distant, judgmental; calculating for his own benefit; cement-hearted New Yorker who wants to play pretend, no matter his previous half-decade in their state. Some novelist wrote how when a man got to a certain age the world suddenly became more beautiful because one started to reconcile with one's own death, the last years allowing a last passionate look and "all that had been withheld would finally be given." My methodless mornings: when I see it's almost eleven-thirty and the day feels within moments of drawing to a close. As with all fictional braiding, some strands were true, but those false ones jabbed like steel cacti needles—maybe there is late softening, but I try to cover it up with a rising sympathy I will renounce. So, finally, art can't save and it's too late for action.

I've spent many hours of my days considering how to reinsert myself into my daughter's life, but I couldn't even fantasize a way in. And, to answer that same novelist, things that are withheld will not be finally given—weren't they withheld for a reason? Such is fate—a word I began to define as the sum total contents of an antique store (often visited in my youth) holding "small florid ancientries, ornaments, pendants, lockets, brooches, buckles, pretexts for dim brilliants, bloodless rubies, pearls either too large or too opaque for value"—a confluence of objects from another time all gathered together, with dust wiped off, to form a haphazard house of mirrors. These merrymaking and somber objects weigh us down and bury us all the way to the finish line, and though we might have been comforted, no-one remembers their magical days alone with their things on their deathbed—they want only peopled memories.

If I knew it was the last day... And it could have been. Nothing would be made easier. And if you do know... It was thirty-two, thirty-three years since he ended it. And maybe he had a good reason or, better, an excuse. You get sick, you're in pain, every day the same brittle ending.

I've already written a letter to my daughter. My ex-wife will give it to her in five years. It's an attempt at explanation, though I don't know if it goes far enough. I could send another, but I fear I am no closer to a clearer, more satisfactory type of entreaty.

I sat there for maybe forty minutes since I first thought, I'll begin to track myself just sitting here thinking and then I might be able to see the last traces I make as I lessen, or maybe I will see the overbearingness making morose this whole rather small domicile. The cheap plastic clock has borne the ticks—how excruciating one minute while it plods on into the twenties and thirties, the interminable forties—a whole goddamn minute, as if a hospital needle has been in my vein for hours, taking out what will be put back in without my permission. I was afraid to go outside, though it had been only a few hours. I listened. I heard the lighthouse call a ship. The sky had browned—would there be some five o'clock light before the disc vanished in a bank on the horizon?

Yes, if I could share this. There hasn't been a visitor—an invitation. And I used to ask—Invite himself, my enemies might say. It was so simple. I'm coming to San Francisco next Friday—*Great! We got a floor, put the couch pillows on it because you're too tall. We'll cook some food, go to some parties—we know you go through women like I go through underwear so it will be interesting to see what you have in store for us—you know I live with my girlfriend, it's a loft—should we buy some gear for your visit?* Such fun, such fun—completely easy. *Hey, we're going to have a poker game at North Beach. It's the middle of Wednesday but no-one has a job, or they work at night or on weekends.* Those were the best days because nobody wanted anything from each other, though "required" is the better term. So little to take seriously! And it ended by degrees—a long sunset. But I wanted it to end—laziness couldn't sustain it. Maybe love, but nobody knew anything about love then. And yet there is no return. They're all gone, and how many times could I go up to the goofy young on the sidewalk or on an on-ramp and hand them a twenty? What kind of bet is that? And what do they feel?

They haven't gotten truly mad at such a—I know my customers. And the few that do press: *I'm, oh, this is for all the times someone helped me. And I didn't ask, but I did need.* They gave me a break, or a gift, and they didn't think twice. *Don't you give things to people so you can feel better about yourself? No, well, someday maybe.*

And so I sit alone in restaurants on national holidays—grim hours. Fiddling with a phone, but more often lowering my pulse by reading some book review, wishing I could be standing in front of a kiosk in Paris, 1966, and reading to abase myself after maneuvering around the melancholy in an attitude out of a Giacometti. My mother and I used to watch old couples in restaurants who sat in silence, years before phones—no hope, seemingly looking at everyone except the persons they were with. Why were all the chairs in Paris pointed at the street? We grew up in torture chambers—booths. The large Greek restaurants with grease for the whole family. People dressed like they had just come from a portrait session. Maybe there's nothing wrong with our country other than how our eating is non-ritualistic. And I would sit across from her and begin to sweat because what could I say, it had all been said—and I was happy, wasn't I? Then what could I make up? I missed my father—but that wasn't a lie. She set and sent me on my path more than anyone, but isn't that true of all writers? And failed writers? They teach you how to feel, a father teaches practicality, and you keep the plates spinning until you go dumb and sounds fade. But to feel—and how to pretend there is no feeling... these are the machinations made manifest by a life more informed distaffwise. I tried with Clayton, but I finally hardened, and when he tried to reach out, he came away with fingers bloody from my coral. He feigned surprise—and I quietly hope his soul will get another go-round, be born poorer.

She treated me differently from Clayton—and told me so: Clayton belongs to your father, but you are mine. The two of us in the dayroom (when people could still find meaning in the term). Dad at work. I watched Clayton disappear behind a door down the hall. But what happened then, whether secrets or open conspiracies, is missing. All of the beginnings are people walking away—my life began when my parents separated in the cool gloom of late spring. Four became two, and the procession of lonely dinners began. But no, am I remembering those dinners or the ones with my ex-wife, even before the birth? The sepia tint is the same—one-on-one and what to say? Any news? How was your day? I countered with little because I was planning the next chapter, the next turn, when I shouldn't have been writing that type of fiction in the first place. I listened, but all the while declaimed that my gut spoke the truth, and when one disobeys so much, they are let go. No blow-up about it—one starts to get ignored. Then parades true pain, though it's too late—and that is what the mind can never get over, that there was a time when the alternate path existed, shining with joy, but the will absconded with the necessary elements. I returned to what I had been trained to be: docile, unbespoken, passionless—a zoo animal not shitting in view. Off to a corner I went to graze, in my own mock museum setting, and though all my toys and other natural interests of youth were gone, I rearguardedly acted as if I still had them, distended from their weight like a sow's teat in danger of mastitis. People can see those invisible things on you, in your spirit, without one blade of word offered—an antagonizing aura that gets only worse as the collared being asks for something.

Even acknowledgment—to hell with love—comes in a scalding geyser.

And I could never go back home like in some hamstrung Hollywood movie and see the past looking even more desperate, the corner store a real-estate office for condos in neighborhoods that shouldn't have condos. The smell of Milwaukee from the hops off the Marquette interchange to the scent of lawns constantly mowed: this endures in memory like the tang of certain lovers—and I took this history into Oregon and California to disembowel it, but no; and then New York, Buffalo, and back to Broadway to wash out any old bacteria, seeing if it might mold over into fungi for easier removal, the impossible dream. Nice surprise—the unease returned, even during my stravagating over land I measured in two separate decades, while an ancient voice steered me away from land's edge. This is the return I get when I'm walking the agate-lined Pacific theater in moonlight, not the lovers, not the endless days of twenty-five with health taken for granted, when you believe the visions of Rilke are possible. No, I am marooned in Milwaukee with teenage doldrums, inverting the truism "Wherever you go there you are" into the worst nightmare—the eternal recurrence of auld lang syne, not the high holy days of being cut loose on a foreign street, shivering, and not knowing where you'll sleep, as the brain builds synapses and concourses. Europe made me, it took the particleboard banding my consciousness and reinforced it with art, ego, fantasy, falsity, jealousy, while New York touched off a pigment to force me into a crude and snarling stance, while still certifying my own privacy—so I gained an outer dishabille to wear when defending territories becoming more and more rarefied and unshareable. I malfunctioned and later called an older friend who would broker no sympathy and staunchly told me, Don't hide—dogs hide.

After Doug had been toiling at our house for three weeks, I grew more lax in my ministrations to a growing quiver of proclivities. Just before his lunch break one day, I walked down the basement stairs and stood before him in a blonde wig, my gawky body sheathed by a glittering green strapless dress, with balled socks making breasts in my too-big bra. Only because he didn't laugh instantly did I know I was safe. I've forever wanted a photograph of my face at that moment—to examine the eyes, whatever their splendor. He looked at them—he looked at them more than he looked at the clothes or at my inwardly-turned horripilated arms, those of a virgin. But I somehow kept my face owlish, feigning teenage imperiousness with a foolhardy flint. I'd ransacked a bag my mother meant for a Goodwill pickup, but the bra had been given to me from a boy in school—he'd taken it from his older sister to revenge himself and wanted me to hold it until he asked for it back. That was in the spring—they moved in early summer, but I'd been using it for a while. I certainly wanted to be around women not my mother, but I didn't know how to make that happen, what to press. In this way I could feel the buttons and fabric, while elucidating much more that I probably couldn't have thought unless I traded identities temporarily. More sensual than sexual were those summer frolickings, but mostly they concerned control.

He kept quiet, sandwich in hand, and watched as I moved forward for my dress rehearsal. If I could have described it then, it would have been with improbable words, considering my age, but there is nothing like the thermobaric power of a gaze. You don't know what you're doing and then you do a little more of it. He took another bite and, as in responding to television, watched to see what else I had to offer. I was too afraid to use my voice, because I was sure someone else's would rise and maybe never go away. I walked in socks around the basement and pirouetted for him, but I would not smile. If we did anything, it was going to smell like peanut butter, but it already smelled like peanut butter. Before long, he led me upstairs and we went into my bedroom.

The measure of a man... Unwittingly, I had been doing this with Doug. What occurred had nothing to do with experimentation or finding oneself or discovering something about myself, it was all trust, unlike that kittenish man in Manhattan who was all about accomplishment. I had no attraction to Doug's attired or unattired body—he resembled and even spoke like Bill Murray in *Caddyshack*—only for the inner energy that didn't judge or attempt redress but welcomed: the possibility of collaboration. He wasn't necessarily an inspired individual, and drugs and religious obsession and paranoia would curtail his life, because nothing became him like the leaving it while driving in a van filled with stolen Catholic relics and going off an interstate on-ramp to plunge and crash, breaking all the statuary and all his bones so they mingled when cleaned by the road crew.

It was a lonely summer all around, since people knew about his struggles and he began to separate more often, silently whimpering home each night to a destitute West Allis apartment. There he watched action movies when he should have been readying to work with teenagers. Like so few adults, he had a way to connect with them—not sex: I was sure our interlude a one-off, and he admitted as much. But I can see him in his apartment, doing the things you do when you live alone, like farting and leaving dirty cereal bowls all over, while lingering by that teasing phone, both salvation and enemy. The hall light is on, obliquely yellowing the small living room, where he is half-asleep watching the Brewers toil out west in Anaheim. It's late, but he puts off having to go to the bedroom, though he won't start going to the bars again—too many enemies, and sex has no fulfillment, or too much; orgasm opens up to a vast stretch of desert he can't escape. He also has this well-paying paper-factory job that he can't screw with—he's burned so much money in small-time schemes, creditors are on the hunt. He wakes up during the bottom of the seventh, with the Brewers down by three, but he doesn't want to watch the Angels bat. Perhaps he should pull out the old Castañeda, but he clicks through the late-night shows and catches Michelle Pfeiffer being interviewed by the schmuck. Some strange waves pour over him, and he begins to see through the charade—not Pfeiffer's, but his own and the show's. It is camera placement, it is the effrontery of the host, his barrage of silly questions—how else can a person react to such obsequiousness but stare? Pfeiffer is a livewire, not a waxen talking robot, but she still is forced to create a persona of commodity, in rapport with the viewing audience, which is to say "consumer"—to sell the idea of herself as a person who lives the life we all desire. But this coy-kittenish side is a put-on, it's in the contract for the pipeline between the network and people like Doug, who are the overworked and underpaid and who come to television as a salve to their many unfulfilled notions about existence and morality. His life, no matter how much he feels apart, is tied to such quotidian motions, everything in its place, this is what keeps him awake and not Pfeiffer—he stopped looking at her minutes before and maybe many, because there is another guest on. This momentum leads to a new charge for some distant ridge he would love to get atop. Start with the biggie—leaving Milwaukee for Chicago, Minneapolis, hell, New York... Arizona. He imagines a different time, a different smell—not the Percodanned envy, hops, and sour stench of Brew Town, but the desert: deceptively uniform, extreme, but hospitable to those who live calculatingly, with a high white sun-summer haze and the chill blue mornings of winter. He has read that play: *We should be working with our hands*—he said this to his missing brother and burned inside that there wasn't anyone to go with him and explore, more to help him get through the first difficult days. But then, a loosening, a pulsation, and the next day he calls places in Flagstaff to see if they are hiring and asks an uncle for a loan to attempt the move, the change—the gruff man surprisingly assents. Doug gives notice at the factory and is two weeks from making the crossway trip in the April following the summer I knew him—all because of Pfeiffer's particular putting-on of airs, or was it that graceful head with the spaced-out lizard eyes set back to temper the souls of men enamored of a certain combination of petite, sanguine, and throaty, stamped with an ineffable name? And then—a wall. He thinks it's coming from the stomach, but it's up top; the voices of the past trying to curtail him; real jealous people ripping his plan, though they don't even call him a friend—they were put on the earth to take things out on the people closest. They never mattered until now. Sad, sad days. He will be missed and miss out and a chain reaction begins—his uncle will continually remind him about that loan and call his mother and, eventually, though she will be forbidden to say anything, she'll badger and harp—he could fuck his life up on his own, but to start fucking with his family's money? He starts drinking to still the voices, but they turn only more viperish and uncouth—daring him to even start driving west. Still, he plans for someone to come and push him, to make him wake up early, sit in a parked car, turn the key, and leave town. The days wind down until the end of the month, and the landlord wants to know when he'll be out so the new tenant can move in. And there it is! Someone has saved him—he has to go. Though he waits until the thirtieth, he loads the car in a strange state—all the hand-me-down furniture from his family is left behind, but he has the important things, his tools, the skill saw, deodorant. Every trip with a newly filled box and his arms slung with shirts and pants gets slower, so that his feet are almost stuck to taffy—something more and more fairytale-esque about what he's doing. Yet incredibly he is in the car and driving 94 West to Chicago—so he's going that route—in the slow lane. Other cars accelerate past, their owners juicing to get to the big city for the day. Past Kenosha and then the border comes up, and he exits on some county-line road just as the morning sun is obscured, pulling to the shoulder in an already decided state of mind. He tries to fool himself: Well, maybe he'll go—he can still do it—there is no law. But the calibration inside is already set to the city of his birth. He'll need to call on the only friend who'll still offer up his couch to him—and then all the haggling that even one night's bad sleep will come with. He crosses the viaduct and starts the return trip, but who was he kidding? He never took the uncle's money. He would have ruined himself, but maybe it would have been worth it.

I believe some people carry themselves and another around at the same time, and Doug was one of these—Doug and the Anti-Doug, but this Anti-Doug, unlike the Anti-Socrates, was the one who should have shown up more, tanning himself under western skies instead of locally at Bradford Beach. Not that he'd needed to be in Arizona, just somewhere... where the Anti-Doug could have shone.

I doubt the Anti-Rick could have. Did I try? I did try, I did love. A motion in the wind, but wind growls every day. Hadn't I lived, and lived almost all I could—no regrets or not many—in a production that I kept mostly secret? But when you live all you can and make too many mistakes, few want to be around your corpse: at least after I'd visited the shore a hundred or two-hundred times, I could begin to say this. Of course, I'd take grief over nothing, and so I sit and build hackneyed temples to false foreboding, the platelet count dropping. What are these days but autumnal friezes full of valediction, forbidding, and mourning? I saw my late espousèd saint... and I do dream of seeing my daughter who has been made dead to me by me. If I could find a way around the other man. If I am the wrong man and he is the right man, there is still recourse to escape the dereliction. Meeting it with a sad song won't cinch any strain of forgiveness—nothing will be seen, not even the former ways, those snatches of irreality when Jane and I were happy, just at the beginning, near enough to the new-relationship energy when no-one searched for any underlying sense. No thought, nor countenance—only the action of the stream, leading to the lake of love. From heaven to hell seems a quick journey, but time plunders our sense of time, and age teaches about those underlying suppositions, substandards, the formulas in the rotten core.

I nested on masculine ova. Arthur, Henry, Doug, her new father. Is this so strange? If to free oneself of fate carries the whip-snap of being fateless yet fated, there is no separation from the me and the Anti-Me, they strengthen the days—twin rivers flowing crosscurrent and contrariwise to create the supreme channel, the innermost self earmarked to love and to do damage.

Why on this day? Location—forever I would try to dial down and escape the stew the Rasputin parts of me pushed towards. The dimmer had gone down even more, but a streak of light beckoned, and I threw an energy bar and a thermos of tea, a grandiose last meal, into the car and drove back to where I had started.

The eye is the first circle—and it felt like my gobbly old vitreous finally began its detaching transit when I pulled onto the white stones of the turnoff. Four or five times my shoes scraped the asphalt I crossed over as if it rose to warn. But I would get to the beach, that light. The ground gave, and the sandy descent began. I'd forgotten the bar, but I had the tea, and I raced, returning to the trained days of knowing where that fifty-year-old rhododendron root stuck out to avoid another bruised and blotted shin. Down I went into the fragrance of Sitka spruce while the rhododendron leaves glowed milky green in the pre-dusk. Soon sand was spritzed into my loafers, and the path narrowed into that still humming buttress before beach and its gloomy light.

A few people north and south. Instinct took me toward Heceta Head, and a few steps later I sank down and opened the tea. Tidewrack kept getting swallowed up as the cries of friends daring the waves sputtered in and out. I pitched an ill-tuned echolocation between me and the slumping mass of forest grown over ocean rock. Two women and one man—or was it the other way around? The haze of the sunset remained mitigable. You could get ten seconds of glory, so you'd better pay attention.

The tepid ginseng made little difference. I had to get to the end of the beach, but alone, no other shades around. Many times over the years in this geography I had tried to forecast, to measure out what remained. I should have known that when I began to act improvisational, for the first time in decades, my worrying about the demarcation line would be shredded—and then what I lived for could flower into new meaning. But I broke away. I could not write down what I had no words for anyway.

The dusk winds started, and I snapped my hood into place.

About ten years before, Gwen, a friend of my wife's, told me Jane would be remarrying. Gwen had ceased being friendly to me but thought I should have this new information. I admit I wasn't in the right frame of mind to receive it. I had just begun the final volume of Proust—the enterprise of reading it I had instilled in my mind as a "practice." For two years, while I did freelance proofreading for a pittance, I read and then re-read each volume before engorging the vast supplementary materials with copious notes, crazily thinking the world needed another book on how reading Proust is good for your life, though not for me—signed, A White Man. The decrease in seeing my daughter over that period took on a powerful astigmatism, added to how she hardly mentioned anything in her life when we met—and I didn't ask. We talked about the latest TV show she had an obsession with or the kids in her ballet class: what they felt, their troubles. When I counted up, I'd seen her six times in the prior year. Ah—but it was the new man (and Proust)—there were two, *le deux*. If a man have not order within him, he cannot spread order without him, so my disorder could stretch eleven miles from Harlem to Park Slope, but did it do even that? I didn't abide in my wife anymore—my genes were my only influence. There is no known sequence to explain why ten years should tintype someone's soul with the stain of another's, a form one day they will roundly reject and go to lengths both private and unconscious to erase the bitter—and the lovely—from memory; the world never recovers from what is done. But without our peroration, she would have never met Michael—and Heather would not have the sister she desired. Peaks and valleys, peaks and valleys.

He looks a little like you, Gwen said—then paused, because the subtle hesitation would be plenty of room for my imagination to shower me with possibilities to follow the implied "but." I did not remind Gwen she had once lightly trailed four fingernails over my at-rest hand in a movie theater, but I was more attentive at that time before I aged into "a man who likes his afternoon Negroni." Which is to say, I now counted as an elder consumer with a certain discretion tiresome to all people, even my close friends. I had only one question for her, but an uncharacteristic calm kept me from asking—Is he an American?

Michael was—and from Los Angeles—which somehow made it a tenth of a decimal point easier. He was fifty-two and quite beautiful, with a penumbra over his "bald by choice" head. They thought they might adopt, given my wife's age, but she had frozen her eggs—and she was pregnant already, they were married already, too; Gwen liked to play with tense.

I met him weeks later when he picked up my daughter—our daughter. When he appeared, she made to hug him wildly, but he dissuaded her with a few pat-pats—taking the knife in deeper, though later I confirmed his innocence in this. Excepting the no hair, he did look like me, but a superficial, younger me. I now accepted banishment as a great boon for my former love and progeny; anyone who feels they can do better probably will, if only for the fact that they are wiser. Documentary filmmaker (video maker?) and an award from Sundance. In the middle of a large project for PBS about adoption. Three years later it finally premiered to wide acclaim. More awards, more interest in his future. Could I have imagined reviling him if he wasn't nice, respectful, left-leaning, and vegetarian? Had I had such a bio, or was it a chimera? Same height, but I looked up to him on that confounding patch of mud in the Long Meadow, which the parkies never fully resolved to fix. Though my palms became slicks, I stuck to smiles for show. I thought the real fall had begun much earlier, but no, here is where it started, my arms waving, my weight enhancing the plummet. You can do what you love and love the ones you're with—there is no secret there. And you can even do what you dislike and love them—and then there are people like me. During the next nights I dreamed of monologues I delivered to Michael: I will be going away in a few weeks and I'll be gone for a long while, extremely long. It's something I have to do because I feel I will end things if I stay in this city—

I don't want that for Heather. And I realize my only other choice is confounding, worse than that of a frightened bunny. I have to go away. I need space to reconcile what has gone wrong—and maybe I can make a fresh start or at least an attempt at one, but I'm positive that I must leave, or I will, quietly as possible, take my life. I ask you to please take care of them—and your coming addition—as best you can. My heart tells me you will. Please let me put my trust in you, though I can't promise the same in return. I will go to the sea and hope to hold on.

What was delivered instead, after my car had already made it into the corn of Iowa, was something much more innocent, even banal, by which I invited my ex to come to the cliff, daring her to overstep it to see if her heart had room—it did have five minutes left.

Can you promise me you're not going to do it?

I can promise that if I get too close, I'll go to the hospital—I'll fight it off.

I heard breathing.

She'll never forgive you, you know. Either way.

She could understand one day there was no choice.

She won't believe that, she knows what the quality of weakness—

Michael will tell her.

What?

He'll tell her—he knows, somehow.

You need to go to that hospital now.

I have often imagined someone interrogating me: *Why couldn't luxuriating in the humanities have ironed out your rough patches? What about all those screeds detailing how reading makes one a more empathic person?* What about them? The failure to succeed in art has made you grow cold, gelid, and impotent. All three of them—mother, lover, and daughter—marry in an instant... which became the instant on the windy beach, reverberations from the rock I walked toward, even with the last people still loping about: the young smiling woman raising her arms in joy and the man pulling his pants to fold his wood along his thigh. I didn't walk around them because the new cries I heard proclaimed my innocence—I couldn't harm any creature anymore.

My bare feet dug deep and shoveled up sand. The tide kept pushing closer, and soon I walked into water. I turned and they were on their way back to the beachhead.

The skylight upshifted away from tungsten—a radiance spread—but below my eyes, informing the sea where I'd returned, some glass underwater there. A formation I'd longed for.

There would be time—I could get to the jigsawed rock. And I peered at the horizon, where another tanker moved too swiftly based on the rates I'd witnessed over the years.

I couldn't change anything in my letter. I couldn't change facts, either. My abeyance to the sense of violation—and it was violation not abdication—would change the superstructure of the torment.

There were no fables—I had run out of metaphors years before. My daughter would either take the explanation of Michael's or remain loyal to the hardheartedness of her mother, if only for a season when she might reassess. And I brushed off the spiders to send her the tidings I had selfishly kept locked, because they were always there. It may not mean much to you, but I do love you. And I won't wish I had been a better father—won't that only reduce me further? If I could have known what was best, but I didn't. Maybe I'll come to something, to some buried pottery I'll meet with a shout—and it is too late, no matter if it was correct. I can't return and ask to be let into your life again. It's this iron time—no forgiveness, all hate, and harder hate, with a vicious spine-tingle from scorched bile. No, the visionary company of love... here is something to trace—broken hierarchies, those ruins still supporting our breath, our love of life or life of lust.

I neared the browning slope, forcing sight down to the strict waves where no trees grow. Thunderclaps slammed the volcanic rock. No man could swim around the bend to the sea stacks of Devil's Elbow.

I gazed again at the wearied rock, scouring it to recast the inflections of all those salt-strewn words we carry in the twisting bag bruising our back. It didn't relinquish words, but images—while napping in a chair on a mild afternoon, my father's face, drooped and semi-stiff, and the mirror-image: myself, flash-frozen, the jowls pulling the aged cheek fat closer to the lower jaw and the eyelids creeping and opening, just like him, who, when awakened, would always be pointed to me or would quickly revolve, robot-like to my face. I'm in that chair and, nearby, Heather is holding her sister or being held by Michael. How could she not be there to see me? I had made the decision when she was five, but I didn't begin to face it until I came to the rock.

I knelt in the water, and a wave brushed me to safety. The pain's coordinates drifted, recoiling in stones, not slabs. I could have made an expression like a film actor—and I imagined the absolute lie of a shrug to the small angel who tries to remind or to press the delicate question. And she told me, *Old man, have you forgotten so much that you don't remember anything you ever knew or felt about love?*

The clatter of a semi downshifting raced through the trees. The rock turned to a particular gray. Rock from a past that had never been present. They were all in this rock, this stone—I began to make out shadows.

Acknowledgements

I would like to thank the editors from these publications for publishing excerpts in a slightly different form: *Berfois*, *Ligeia Magazine*, *The Rupture*, and *Lapsus Lima*. A portion was also in the anthology *13 by 11: Short Stories of Life in Diverse Places*. I'm very grateful to Daniel Davis Wood and Garielle Lutz for their support and hard work. Thank you to family and friends who have helped me through the years.

About the Author

Greg Gerke is an essayist and writer of fiction, based in New York. His work has appeared in *3:AM Magazine*, the *Los Angeles Review of Books*, *Tin House*, *The Kenyon Review*, and elsewhere, and he edits the online literary journal *Socrates on the Beach*. His story collection, *Especially the Bad Things*, and a collection of essays, *See What I See*, are also available from Splice.

SPLICE

ThisIsSplice.co.uk

Milton Keynes UK
Ingram Content Group UK Ltd.
UKHW012308040624
443649UK00005B/292